CRITICAL ACCL

"Bernadette Dyer is a folk singer of the Caribbean and a weaver of fantastic, moral and spellbinding tales. Her words induct and seduce, instruct and soothe. Elementary in style, but philosophical in subject, she be Miss Lou at song and Aesop at the story telling. To open her books is to be enlightened, and one closes them knowing one has been refreshed and improved."

- **George Elliott Clarke, internationally renowned poet, Parliamentary Poet Laureate of Canada**

"...a wonderful collection of stories that have common universal themes in a multicultural context. The themes of love, identity, tradition versus modern beliefs are woven well in stories... with unpredictable endings."

- **Karen Lemmons, Goodreads book reviewer**

"...a beautiful piece of literary art. Richly written, Dyer takes the reader on an historical trip through World war I and the Holocaust. She eases the reader from one cultural experience to the next with ease and grace. With each page the reader is captivated ... If you are in to quality, no nonsense fiction...Bernadette Gabay Dyer is your writer."

- **T. Rhythm Knight, Apoo Bookclub**

"Bernadette Gabay Dyer ...brings a unique voice influenced by the Caribbean experience and sStorytelling tradition to the Canadian Diaspora in ways that unite cultures and foster insight and understanding."

- **Nicole Lyn, Actress & Celebrity**

"The sometimes whimsical, sometimes mystical. sometimes nostalgic, always poignant collection of short stories is definitely more than "fair". Bernadette Dyer skillfully navigates the immigrant experience, which is the common thread that weaves its way through this great collection. Its colourful characters grab hold of your heart, and leave you wanting more. ...Ms. Dyer's voice is obviously steeped in memory, passion, and a rich and diverse family history. which act as jumping off points for her vivid imaginings, which shares with us in brilliant detail. A definitive MUST read for short story lovers."

- **Cheryl Philips, author, book reviewer**

"Bernadette Gabay Dyer has made her indelible mark on Canadian letters with her novels, stories and poems as well as a storyteller. ..Her literary work reveals her commitment to exposing world rooted in her unforgettable Caribbean heritage. She is truly a writer dedicated to continuous exploration of new narrative strategies and new themes that harness the power of seeing the world through different and caring eyes. Regardless of genre, she is, above all, a masterful storyteller."

- **Olive Senior, Award-Winning Author, of fiction, non-fiction, poetry, children's books.**

Segovia Stories

Segovia Stories

Bernadette Gabay Dyer

mosaic PRESS

Library and Archives Canada Cataloguing in Publication

Title: Segovia stories / Bernadette Gabay Dyer.

Names: Dyer, Bernadette, author.

Description: Short stories.

Identifiers: Canadiana (print) 20210393491 |
Canadiana (ebook) 20210393505 |

ISBN 9781771616201 (softcover) | ISBN 9781771616218 (PDF) |
ISBN 9781771616225 (EPUB) | ISBN 9781771616232 (Kindle)

Classification: LCC PS8557.Y47 S44 2021 | DDC C813/.54—dc23

Published by Mosaic Press, Oakville, Ontario, Canada, 2022.

MOSAIC PRESS, Publishers
www.Mosaic-Press.com

Printed and bound in Canada

ONTARIO ARTS COUNCIL
CONSEIL DES ARTS DE L'ONTARIO
an Ontario government agency
un organisme du gouvernement de l'Ontario

Funded by the Government of Canada
Financé par le gouvernement du Canada

Canada

ONTARIO
CREATES

MOSAIC PRESS
1252 Speers Road, Units 1 & 2, Oakville, Ontario, L6L 5N9
(905) 825-2130 • info@mosaic-press.com • www.mosaic-press.com

These stories are dedicated to four inspirational women:
Rita Cox, Afua Cooper, Olive Senior & Itah Sadu

ACKNOWLEDGEMENTS

Thank you to the Late Horace Goddard, who believed in my work.

Thank you to author/editor Cyril Dabydeen.

Thank you to Krysta D. Ball and Bill Jermyn who helped in putting my manuscript together.

Thanks to Nancy Kay Clark and the High Park Library's writing group, for listening to early drafts of some of these stories.

Thanks to R. Greame Cameron and Ursula Pflug.

LIST OF STORIES

SEGOVIA STORIES

Carlos Fernandez Segovia has dreams. His dreams flow like the rushing waters of a never-ending waterfall through his fertile mind and become nebulous and arresting tales. It is more than fitting that when I first encountered him he was in the fiction section of the library where I work, surrounded by some of the world's finest literature. I was immediately drawn to him, for although he was an adult, he reminded me of a lost boy with that slight crease in his forehead and his hands stuck stubbornly into his pockets. He was attractively dressed in Italian casual wear, but when he spoke I realized he was Latin American. He asked me for assistance in finding Shakespeare's plays, and at close scrutiny I couldn't help but be arrested by his handsome profile, even as I steered him into the drama section where I felt a secret satisfaction as his broad hands caressed each book lovingly. He must have been twenty-nine or thirty, and his pony tailed hair was as dark as his eyes. I could see an appreciative smile on his sensuous lips as I pointed out each title to him.

The hush in that room must have held enchantment. Perhaps that is why he didn't see me as the boring middle-aged helpful black female librarian that I am, but as a sympathetic ear, for he proceeded to engage me in conversation and spoke passionately about wanting to write plays as potent and tragic as Shakespeare's. He said he was searching out competent actors to play demanding roles in a film he was producing. The leading lady would be black, and coincidentally would be a librarian who had suffered a broken heart. She would spend her days whiling away time in the contemplation of her ideal man. This man, he said, would naturally be Hispanic and full of dreams, as well as passionate about wanting to write a North American screenplay about unrequited love. Ultimately this screenplay would result in the fictional character attending Toronto's annual film festival as a contributing filmmaker. Carlos Fernandez Segovia said the filmmaker should be played by none other than Antonio Banderas, the actor, or a reasonable look-alike. It was by no stretch of the imagination that I observed that Carlos Fernandez Segovia would have been perfect for the part.

From that very first meeting I had the feeling that Carlos Fernandez Segovia accepted me for what I was, warts and all. He invited me out for coffee and beer, none of which materialized since he either couldn't make it at the last minute or else he became too passionate when we got together in his flat and never made it out. But there were quiet times, too, and those are the moments I relish, for his dreams would come spilling out like little fish that cascade over dangerous rocks in a swift river.

"I must tell you about Milagros," he once said. "She's my older cousin. We grew up together in Ecuador. I was five when she was sixteen, and she was the most beautiful, delicate creature I had ever seen. Her hair was as dark as the interior of a forest, and her eyes as blue as the Pacific. And such skin—smooth as glass and radiant! But I, little Carlos, was just a scrawny boy, all knees, tall for my age, nothing exciting to speak of. I still can't understand why Milagros could never take her eyes off me. I would often catch her staring, and her expression reminded me of the way one would stare at a delicious cake. Then one day she took me aside.

"'Do you like kisses?' she asked.

"'No!' I said stubbornly as Milagros held me in an aquamarine gaze.

"'Well, I'll kiss you, anyway.' She kissed me full on the lips and held me fast until I found myself enjoying the feeling of being smothered by her. It felt to me as though my very eyes had gone blurry, and the rest of me had turned to cotton balls.

"'One more little kiss, Milagros,' I pleaded when she pulled away.

"'No, Carlito,' she said sulkily. 'That's enough until you are older.'

"Even though I was so young I couldn't help but realize that Milagros was using me as a sort of target practice, since she was already the love interest of all the best-looking boys in our city. She was totally unmoved by the attention her beauty stirred, and then she attracted handsome Jose Garcia, the young captain of our local soccer team. At seventeen Jose was well built and smouldered with sensuality—the perfect match for Milagros.

"One day he asked her out, and in her excitement she spent hours getting ready for the date. She found the perfect dress and the best hairstyle and makeup that made her already perfect eyes sparkle. She was nothing short of a vision. However, when Jose arrived to pick her up, he was fresh from a soccer game— sweaty, frowzy, and mud-stained. He obviously had no idea how much importance Milagros had placed on the occasion. Therefore, it was I, young Carlos Fernandez Segovia who reprimanded him on his oversight and put him to shame. Since then Milagros has had no use for macho men. In fact, she ended up marrying a cultured stockbroker from London, England, where she now resides as an aristocrat."

Carlos Fernandez Segovia says it was Milagros who first turned him on to kisses, and that she was also the one who made him realize that women of all ages can be beautiful. I, a librarian who loves tales, was so totally fascinated by the story of Milagros that I imagined her as a young Elizabeth Taylor and found myself astonished by the beauty of the Segovia family.

Months later Milagros's story still haunted me. When I saw Carlos Fernandez Segovia again, I asked if he was still in touch with her and if she had ever contacted him. Carlos Fernandez Segovia looked at me blankly like an innocent child. "Who's Milagros?" he asked. And in that significant moment it dawned on me that Carlos Fernandez Segovia's stories are legends. Some he remembers, others he forgets, and they are not all necessarily based on fact.

Once, I invited Carlos Fernandez Segovia to breakfast at my place. We lounged around in chairs, drank tall glasses of orange juice, and ate fried eggs, dumplings, and cod fritters. He told me he enjoyed my cooking, then leaned back in his chair, utterly relaxed.

"This reminds me of the breakfasts we used to have in my country when I was growing up," he said. "Those were the best, and I remember my mother liked to have houseguests. One summer we had visitors from Montreal, a woman who was Mama's old friend from school and her beautiful daughter, Carmela, as well as their boxer dog, Pepito. The senora was very prim and proper. I imagine our mothers thought Carmela and I would behave like brother and sister. But we had other ideas. We couldn't take our hands off each other. The moment we were alone, supposedly taking the dog for walks, we would use the opportunity to explore each other fully. I was fourteen and very much in love, although Carmela was almost eighteen. But summers don't last forever and Carmela would soon return to Canada. She told me her mother was so religious and proper that she would never accept our relationship, so we should keep everything undercover, so to speak.

"One hot afternoon Carmela and I were so eager for each other that halfway from home we realized we had forgotten to bring the dog. Reluctantly we returned to the little guest cottage behind my house and were about to call Pepito when I noticed a strange silence in the compound. No one was home in the big house where I lived, so I thought perhaps that Mama had gone shopping. But suddenly our ears were filled with the sounds of groans. Carmela and I approached the guest cottage with caution and, peering through a half-drawn curtain, we saw Carmela's mother and Pepito in a compromising position. You can well imagine how startled she was to see us. After that Carmela and I lost the attraction for each other, and I suppose she still lives in Montreal and that she and her mother have both forgotten me."

Carlos Fernandez Segovia told me he has another cousin, also called Carlos, who was starting a clothing firm in Canada and that they would be travelling together to Montreal to make contacts and perhaps rent a factory. When he left a few days later, it occurred to me that now that he was an adult, he might well resume his relationship with Carmela. On his return to Toronto he telephoned to say he had indeed seen Carmela. She was more beautiful than ever, but unfortunately was married to a wonderful French Canadian and had four young children and a happy but boring life. I wondered if Carlos Fernandez Segovia and Carmela had taken the family dog for a walk or, if like Milagros, Carmela had ever existed.

The next time I heard from Carlos Fernandez Segovia he telephoned to say he was helping out a friend who had overdosed on drugs and was hospitalized. He wanted tea and sympathy, and I was happy to oblige. Carlos Fernandez Segovia proceeded to show me photographs of actors he had chosen for his film. "Filming begins in March," he said. Sure enough, the leading actress was black. I felt a prick of jealousy, for the actress was beautiful. Carlos Fernandez Segovia must have sensed my emotion, because he said, "Surely you didn't think you were my first Jamaican. My father is a physician in Ecuador and we used to entertain diplomats. I couldn't take my hands off the daughter of the Jamaican ambassador. I can't remember if her name was Carmela. It was so long ago."

Carlos Fernandez Segovia often spoke of his immediate family: his father, who is now a cancer specialist; his European drop-dead gorgeous blond mother; and his two brothers, Simon and Hernan. Photographs on the walls of his flat are proof of their existence. They are placed directly beside the photographs of the actors, but it is interesting to note that filming on his movie has still not begun.

"My brother, Hernan, is not like me," Carlos Fernandez Segovia said, pointing at the photograph. He is quite blond, as you can see." I noted that his brother looked suspiciously like Brad Pitt. "He is very handsome and wants to be a graphic artist. And although he is only twenty-one, he once had a fiancee. The girl's name is Bianca. Hernan studies day and night, but he makes short films and videos as a hobby. He has a little studio in our home. His equipment is very expensive, so he set up a surveillance camera in the studio without telling anyone, not even Bianca. She used to sneak into our home when he was away and wait in his studio for his return. But she began to feel neglected and wrote Hernan a threatening note, saying she would kill herself if she couldn't see more of him. Needless to say, Hernan was upset, especially when she continued to make it clear she didn't want to live without him and constantly spoke of suicide. Our family was surprised when Hernan gave her her walking papers. We couldn't believe he was so cold, for Bianca was so devoted. But Hernan later revealed that on replaying his surveillance tapes he had caught Bianca on film in the arms of our gardener on all the occasions when she was supposedly waiting for him."

Carlos Fernandez Segovia told me that one of his best friends back home in Ecuador was an older man of about sixtyeight who had been a real ladykiller in his youth. This man had recently died of AIDS, which caused Carlos Fernandez Segovia to speak somewhat regretfully about an occasion when he and friends had visited a gay bar in Toronto and he was kissed on the lips by one of the male dancers. I reassured him that AIDS wasn't spread by kisses, and he confided that that kiss was the best he had ever had. What of Milagros? I wondered.

It was only on rare occasions that friends of mine even met Carlos Fernandez Segovia, for he was almost always unavailable. However, I did get him to meet my publisher friend, Martha Cox, at a dinner at my place. He regaled her with stories of his trip to the gay bar and told her a tale about a young friend, Harry Perron, who he had met at acting class. According to him, Harry was set up by a woman in the Dominican Republic who claimed he was the father of her unborn child. She tried to bilk him out of thousands of dollars, being totally unaware that Harry was gay. Carlos Fernandez Segovia said that Harry told fabulous stories and was the one who had recently told him about a Canadian man who several years ago went skiing in the B.C. interior, got lost during an avalanche, and was presumed dead. Years later this same man's son, Ethan, went skiing in the same region and, by coincidence, was also caught in an avalanche. While lost he came upon a wall of ice, and in it he encountered a face staring at him. The visage mirrored his own, and he realized that it was his father's face trapped in ice for all those years. He and his father, in that precise moment, looked about the same age. The young man collapsed from shock but was later rescued. Although he searched, he never again could find the face in the wall of ice.

"I should write a screenplay about it," Carlos Fernandez Segovia said. "It would have such plot, such drama and suspense, even more than anything by Shakespeare. I must ask Harry for all the details."

Martha Cox said that Carlos Fernandez Segovia was a little too slick for her, but with his looks she could forgive him anything. The only thing, though, she said, was that his stories were far too realistic. No one would buy them.

"I want to write a screenplay about a family from your country," Carlos Fernandez Segovia told me excitedly once. "Perhaps you could help me with naming people and locations. I would also like to write about a poor man from Peru who wins the lottery, and I'll let him also write a screenplay about a young filmmaker who goes to Hungary to a film festival. These two stories are very tempting. Maybe I'll call one of the Jamaicans, Sheila, since that is your name, and I'll let her meet a young Hispanic man called Julio. I love the plot but don't know what to do with Julio. Should I kill him? That would make an interesting plot. Maybe he could be a bad man, or perhaps a man like me. Help me. I value your advice."

The last time I saw Carlos Fernandez Segovia we were in a bar on College Street, the trendy part, and he told me he was late arriving because a friend of his, an older man of sixty-eight, had been drinking in a sixth-floor apartment and had accidentally toppled over the balcony. I wondered if this was the same older man who had previously died in Ecuador from AIDS.

I never did help Carlos Fernandez Segovia with his stories, because the next time I went to visit him he wasn't home. His neighbours told me he had been admitted to a mental institution in Toronto. They said he was either not allowed visitors or he himself had requested not to see anyone. Yet, though unable to visit him, I often imagine him in the institution surrounded by other patients and even doctors, that strange otherness about him as he takes centre stage and mesmerizes them with tales as he once did me. For surely Carlos Fernandez Segovia's dreams still flow like a never-ending waterfall.

FRAMING

We are the early risers, my granddaughter, who is three years old, and me. At first light, we are both reckless with the desire to face the day, and not waste a moment.

I hear her slippers slapping with slow heart stopping rhythms that fills me with trepidation. She might stumble, unmindful of hidden dangers on smooth wooden stairs. But I restrain myself from rushing to take her hand, and see her safely across morning's dim halls and kitchen floor, as silently we sneak down the back stairs, and out to the garden.

How fragrant and fresh the air is there, and how raucous the early morning bird song. Flowers coming into bloom stand in attendance, as I watch my grandchild surrounded by the beauty there. I cannot stop myself from visually tracing her steps, as she flies on short legs to the distant back fence to examine loose soil and the plants there that struggle to survive where a short garden hose cannot reach.

She brings back blossoming weeds, tattered brown leaves, and dry twigs that snap in her pudgy fingers. And I find not far from where I stand in the filtered light, a dead sparrow. It perhaps had fallen from one of the tall trees standing guard on the left side of the garden. The bird's head was turned to one side, and its beak was tightly closed. Its sweet song had ended. My granddaughter stared in trembling wonder, wanting to lightly touch the stiff gray brown feathers, and wanted in her innocence to coax the bird's revival.

Together we planted its remains inside a circled rockery of blooms. But my granddaughter wanted to remove the newly laid earth to once again see the bird whose heart had long flown out of our reach. I divert her attention by furrowing the soil, and scattered flax seeds, that in time would burst above the soil, to become stalwart seedlings. I watched in silence as granddaughter sought out Black-eyed Susan blooms, and tightly squeezed one or two between her thumb and fingers. I smiled as I watched the yellow halo of the blooms in the rising sun reflect gold on her skin.

When she hides herself amongst drifts of pink cone flowers, she is invisible, as I pretend that I cannot find her. With trowel in hand she digs small holes among Columbines and the Hosta, and I can hardly dare to move or breath, lest the moment might shatter and fragment, before its memory is framed.

THE NIGHT WATCHER

It was early in the 1970's that I immigrated to Toronto from Jamaica, and as a new comer, I was surprised to find that there were so many immigrants looking for work. I had foolishly thought that work would have been easy to come by, as long as one was well educated. But even with my BA from the University of the West Indies, I was to find that there was fierce competition for the few positions advertised in the local newspapers. Back home, I Jennifer Bramwell, from the well known Bramwell family, would easily have been considered for employment since my father had been a manager of a department store. However, after his passing, I felt extremely alone and abandoned, since my wayward mother had long since left us and gone to live in England. I was twenty four years old, when I decided to start over again, and left the island.

Once in Toronto, I went to several job interviews ranging from Short Order Cook to Machine Operator, I hardly had qualifications for any of those positions, and it was no wonder that I was advised to get Canadian experience before continuing on my job search. I began to feel absolutely wretched and desperate as I watched my small savings dwindle.

Then one gray morning after having attended an interview for a Catalogue fashion model, things began to change. I knew that I would not be considered for the modeling position, since I was of average height and weight and could not by any stretch of the imagination be mistaken for 'statuesque and slender' as the advertisement had demanded, but somehow I began to feel more positive since I felt that I was at least making an effort. With such thoughts in my mind, I boarded a TTC streetcar to make the long journey home.

I hadn't sat down long before a stout well-dressed young black woman headed towards me. Her hair, unlike mine, was quite kinky, and her lips were painted bright red. She hesitated for a moment, before sitting down right beside me.

"Hello." She said hesitantly, "Did you get the job? I'm asking because I just saw you at that interview place. Light-skin people like you always stand a better chance of getting work. Darling I tried out for that job too, but I could tell that they was just wasting my time, asking a whole bunch of rubbish questions until they said that I didn't suit."

"No I didn't get the job either." I replied.

"You serious!" She said looking perplexed, as she challenged me with her direct gaze, "With your straight hair and all that, I would think…." But she didn't continue.

"This is Canada," I said, keeping my voice level, "Employers here are entitled to hire whosoever is more suitable and qualified for positions."

"Where you from girl? Do you really believe that crap?"

"I'm Jamaican."

"Me too; but I don't swallow that stuff. I felt like telling them about them parts. But anyway I just held my tongue, and by the way, my name is Yvonne."

" I'm Jennifer."

"Well Jennifer, you going far on this car?"

"Yes."

"Well I'll be getting off soon. I have to go buy baby formula"

"I guess you'll be going to the Mall."

"Yes the Galleria Mall sells it cheap, and since I going get off soon, I'll give you my phone number. I bet that you bound to find work before me. So call me and let me know. I can assure you though, I need the money, since I have a young baby, and my husband don't have much of a job, just a little handyman work now and again. Back home we would have friends and family to help out, but darling, not here. By the way you not married, are you? I didn't notice a ring"

"No, I'm single, but trust me, I need money too to cover rent and living expenses."

We didn't say much else after that, and after a quick scribble, Yvonne shoved a piece of paper with her number on it into my hand, then she stood up, waved, and left the streetcar. I wondered if I would ever see her again, I really could have used a friend. So far, I had only made one friend in the city. She was a Canadian girl named Kati, who was a little younger than me in her early twenties. We lived in the same apartment building, though she shared her apartment with her boy friend Joe. I had often seen them on the elevator, and eventually we had begun to converse. They both had honey blond straggly hair, and blue eyes. They could easily have passed for brother and sister, especially since they dressed alike in threadbare bell-bottom jeans, and ill fitting denim shirts. They were always wearing strings of colourful beads, and it was no wonder that I often overheard the Superintendent referring to them as 'that hippie couple.'

I soon learned that Kati had come to Toronto from Vancouver, after her mother married for the fourth time. I was quite curious as to how such a shabby looking couple could afforded to live in the apartment, and I suspected that they were somehow involved in dope dealing, but later found out that they was financed by Joe's father who was a construction worker.

A month or so after meeting Yvonne on the streetcar, I came across her phone number in my purse, and on a whim, I decided to call her. She greeted me like a long lost friend.

"Hello darling," she said with a chuckle, "guess what, you call at the right time, I just got a job on Bathurst Street in a shoe store."

"Really! Good for you. Glad to hear that you found something."

"How about you, did you find something too?"

"No not yet, but I'm still trying."

"Well you know what, I and my husband is going to have a party this Saturday to celebrate, and I want you to come. You can bring a friend if you so choose. Our place easy to get to, it is almost at the end of the Dufferin line above an Action Pharmacy. It has three bedrooms, though one of them is as small as a closet."

It was a quick decision on my part, but being lonely, I decided to accept her invitation, and since Kati was my only friend, I told her about it in passing. But I was taken aback by her excited reaction. "I'd love to come with you", she breathed, "My mother was once married to a Trinidadian, and boy the meals he used to cook were fabulous, these Jamaicans might be good cooks too. Its too bad my Mum divorced that guy; they used to smoke up with us once in a while."

"Your mother smoked pot!"

"Yup, neat, eh? And she is at least sixty; anyway, those friends of yours are bound to have good food at their party. Wait until I tell Joe about it."

I hadn't really intended to invite them to the party, but now I had to follow through, and I wondered what Yvonne would think of them, and I had a bad feeling

On the night of the party Kati and Joe met me downstairs in the lobby. Something about their glazed eyes led me to believe they were already stoned, and I couldn't help but wince at their shabby jeans, not to mention Paul's waist length tangled hair, that looked worse than ever. I tried to tell myself that perhaps the Jamaicans at the party would not be well groomed or dressed to the nines as they usually were at the parties back home. I even somehow hoped that Kati and Joe would take a cue from me, since I was appropriately dressed in a formal looking short velvet black dress, with a single stand of pearls at my throat. But neither of them seemed to have noticed the difference in our attire.

When we arrived at the party, Yvonne and her husband greeted us at the door; her eyes were wide with surprise as I introduced Kati and Joe. She might have thought they were street urchins. But she didn't say a word.

'Come in, come in," her husband called out politely, "The music start already, and some people dancing. The food is out on the table, help yourself to rice and peas, jerk chicken, curry goat, and potato salad. Which ever is your pleasure."

Kati and Joe stumbled into the room, and settled themselves on the bare floor in a corner of the living room, oblivious to the well-dressed guests around them. I was too embarrassed to join them on the floor, so I found myself a seat on the sofa surrounded by laughing strangers and blaring Reggae music. It wasn't long before Kati and Joe got up and helped themselves from the food table, only to retreat several times back to the floor. I watched in horror as they washed down bottles of beer, and proceeded to share a joint as casually as though it were a cigarette. The other guests were stunned and grimaced uncomfortably. What a relief it was when Kati and Joe suddenly came over and told me that they were leaving. I was reluctant to join them, so I remained in my seat, though I had misgivings about traveling alone at that late hour.

A few young men, seeing that I was unattached, asked me to dance, and wondered if I would like to go home with them, but I mumbled something inaudible in reply. But it was thanks to Yvonne's husband whose name was Alfonso that I was rescued.

"Jennifer is staying here tonight," he said, "It is too late for a young lady to travel home alone, or to go off with people she don't even know."

"That's a good idea," Yvonne said, bringing over a tray of cocktail patties, "She can sleep in that small room on the left, there's a cot made up in there."

The music continued to pump until after 2:00 am. Then finally the party began to wind down, and I overheard some guests laughing and wondering out loud what had become of the weird hippie couple who had been there earlier. I was embarrassed, but too tired to really care. Then as the last of the guests departed, Alfonso excused himself, and said goodnight, and Yvonne showed me the tiny guest room where I would be sleeping. "Have a good sleep." she said, "I'm turning in to join Alfonso."

"It was a nice party," I said softly, "thanks for inviting me. I'm not tired yet, so I could do the dishes."

"Well you don't have to," Yvonne replied, sleepily, "but that would be really nice of you, since I have to get up early in the morning to pick the baby up from the sitter. But don't stay up too long darling; some of the dishes can stay till tomorrow."

Yvonne left me in the living room, and the house was swallowed up in silence. I quietly made my way to the kitchen, and immediately began to fill the sink with soapy water, as I collected the dishes and cutlery that were scattered throughout the apartment. I knew that I would have to wash more than one load, and I started on the smaller pieces. The soothing clink of the cutlery and dishes broke the silent monotony around me.

I had almost finished the second batch of dishes, when I heard the sound of footsteps coming towards the kitchen. My first thought was that either Alfonso or Yvonne had awoken. Then the footsteps approached, I furtively glanced down at the half empty sink, and called out apologetically. "Hope I didn't disturb you, I'm almost finished here."

But when I looked up, I was surprised to see a tall young handsome man wearing a pin striped suit, standing at the kitchen door. He was as dark as ebony, with unusual gray eyes, and his cheekbones prominent above his welcoming smile. :"Let me give you a hand." He said, as he reached for a dish-towel. "I'm Raphael."

"I'm Jennifer" I replied, and silently we worked together side by side washing and drying. Every now and again, I found myself sneaking glances at his attractive profile, his mop of dark curly hair, his full lips, and lush black lashes.

As soon as we finished, Raphael steered me into the living room.

"You must be tired," he smiled, "I'll play a record on the stereo it will relax you."

I hoped that he would not play a Reggae song, and was pleasantly surprised that the song he chose was soft dreamlike and classical. "That's a favorite of mine." He said, as he leaned over the stereo, "Do you like it?"

"Yes, very much." I replied, and I he came to sit next to me on the sofa.

We sat in silence, and the haunting melody seemed to embrace my very being, until exhaustion crept over me like a cloud of incense. "This is nice." he whispered, and I noticed that the glow from the streetlamp outside on that moonlit night, had painted us both silver. "Its beautiful," I sighed, and I could not take my eyes off of Raphael. What a beautiful man, I thought.

His fingers gently brushed against mine, light as a feather, "That song is called The Night Watcher, I hope you will remember it, though its time for you to go to sleep" he whispered.

I still don't remember falling asleep on the couch, but that was where I woke up in the morning. Raphael was nowhere in sight, though a soft pillow was tucked under my head Yvonne and Alfonso were still asleep, as I quickly found my purse and slipped out of the apartment. I did not call Yvonne that day; I was still too recently embarrassed by the remembered presence of Kati and Joe at their gathering. Yvonne did not call me either, and it was not until a few months later that I finally had the courage to make that call. Curiosity had got the better of me; and besides I somehow felt that I had lost a friend.

Yvonne was happy to hear from me, there was no mention of the party. I was taken by surprise when she told me that she and her little family had decided to move back to Jamaica, My first thought was that perhaps Canada had somehow not lived up to their expectations, and I felt some regret,

"I've got a job." I said brightly, hoping to change the subject, "I'm filing documents for an Insurance company."

"Do you like it?" she inquired sounding genuinely interested.

"Its alright," I lied, knowing full well how bored I was with the work, especially since I was so much more capable of doing something more interesting. But even as I spoke, something nagged at me, and finally I let it out.

"How's Raphael?" I said, keeping my voice level.

"Who?" She replied.

"Raphael, the tall handsome gray-eyed guy that was at your party, he was wearing a pin-striped suit."

I heard when Yvonne gasped, and for a moment or two it almost seemed as though she had stopped breathing. "You couldn't have met Raphael." She said finally, "He wasn't at our party, and another thing darling, Alfonso's cousin Raphael, who by the way loved pinstriped suits, died unexpectedly in Jamaica the very night of our party. And that is the very reason why we going home. We've decided that it would be best for us to be with the rest of our family."

SOUP MORNING

I used to carry my memories like precious jewels. I would savour them and clutch them fast, but I am not young anymore. Approaching old age, I sit in my window-seat staring out at the house directly across the street from me at 108 Greenpark Avenue. The house has offered me an oasis, a respite from the tedium of living one day after another of monotony in a boarding house where I have begun to gather dust like the china and figurines I have so carefully stashed away all these years.

In this my one room, my world is closed against voices from the past and from the rest of society. Here I move like a sloth from pillar to post, establishing rituals to mark the passage of my days. I brew tea, I pour, I drink, I lay my cup down. I slide my swollen feet into well worn slippers to take my established place in front of the window. It is where I have spent the last thirty years watching snows, watching wind, watching sunlight paint colours on leaves. Thirty years of Springs and daffodils, irises and the clover that races like lightning through the many flowerbeds that dot the street below. My fingers have ached from holding my place against the cold wet windowsills, and my eyes even now strain to catch the last rays of the evening sun. And still I cannot forget that day two years back, a day of wild restless wind wailing under the eaves. And blinding snow that dashed itself in blizzard strength against the windowpanes, to hold me enthralled with its wildness.

There was a white spray like tidal waves of pure ice that raged and wheeled along the street below, holding these city houses in stranglehold as snow piled up and up again, upon each doorstep. Then reached as far up as the porches. I heard shovels scrape and click and thud as brave souls challenged nature. And with scarves whipping against their frozen faces, cleared the first mounds of this endless accumulation. While I with bated breath, watched their jerky movements, and prayed, perhaps out loud, to resign myself to face the foul weather. I must as a ritual leave the house first thing each morning for fresh air and a trip to the corner store.

I hid myself in the cocoon of my red coat. The one that has gone old, bought in a bargain basement at Sears, and now at the end of twenty years has seen better days. With an effort born of determined resignation, I braced myself against the wind. I stepped out into the storm unaware that this expedition would hence become a landmark, a historical milepost of my existence. My effort was concentrated, my footsteps unsure, and after five minutes I was no further ahead than when I started out. I was totally spent when an urgent voice behind me cut through the cold. I still remember the exact words, the cadence, their echoing.

"How you doing girl? What a morning!"

I need not have turned around, I knew after so many years at the window that it was Bibi, the West Indian who owned the house across the street. I saw her in my mind's eye, middle aged, no sign of grey. Her dark mahogany skin smooth as alabaster, her large eyes framed in lashes as thick as weeds. She would be smiling, her lips scarlet, thin and welcoming.

I turned to face her, her memorable image fixed in my mind. Her hands were bare, no gloves to shield her from the weather.

She seemed strong and capable as with great effort she swept sparkling drifts of snow from her walkway. Her hair dark and bright with winter's halo of white. I felt inclined to keep on going, but I, already was unsteady. My right hand clutched my left, and I was engulfed in sudden shyness. The sweetness of her Caribbean cadence rooted me to the spot. I listened attentively when she spoke again.

"If is shop you going, it not open."

"Oh," I replied, "Thanks. What's happened, bad weather?"

"No, is Mista Vincent and his old back problems."

"Oh" I sighed, uncertain whether to trudge on, when Bibi decided my fate.

"Come in for a coffee. It's cold out here. You is Vera yes? I hear people say that you live in that boarding house for donkey's years."

"Yes," I sighed, as my lungs filled with icy air. I tried to speak, but nothing came from my throat. But then it seemed that the wind nudged my feet, for I was steered right up Bibi's walkway.

'I'll only stay a moment." I chided myself. But once inside that home, I might as well had been chained or shackled, for I was captivated by the delectable aroma that wafted through the rooms. It brought to my mind a childhood long forgotten. The years when I was seven or eight, and my father, an English brigadier was stationed in India. Strange now, looking back through the passage of years to see myself that golden haired child amongst the chestnut dark skin children of Bombay. How curious that I wanted to be exactly like them, when my Indian Aya confided that all of them wanted to be me. It was back then that my passion was new for cardamom, cloves, peppercorn, ginger, cumin and garlic. How many years have I lived since then, confining myself to bland boiled cabbages, potatoes, eggs and occasional cheese. My taste harnessed and tamed.

"What's cooking?" I heard myself ask. I could not resist, I salivated.

"That," Bibi said with a flourish, "Is beef and pumpkin soup. Want some?"

"Oh please." I replied, unmindful that this early hour was normally reserved for tea or coffee consumption.

From Bibi's spacious living room, I could see into the elegant dining area that adjoined her large tiled kitchen. What a lovely home I thought to myself. There were shelves of well worn books, pictures in oval frames, an ornate fireplace and padded chairs pulled up to a prominent bay window that looked out like an eye into the storm outside. Next to that window, on a dark wooden coffee table, sat a pale vase of bright tropical flowers, their raucous colours more than slightly at odds with their sombre surroundings.

I sat trembling in anticipation, and watched Bibi in the kitchen as her steady hand carefully ladled two heaping bowls of soup.

"This is a Caribbean favorite." She boasted, "Its full of pumpkin, garlic, green onions, potatoes, peas, plus beef of course, and a dash of pepper. Oh, I should mention salt and thyme, but I also like to add a scotch bonnet pepper to add some zing, and some people also put in a dab of coconut milk if they so wish."

My taste buds turned summersaults in eagerness, and when Bibi placed the bowls between us, one for her and one for me, my heart raced. How long has it been, since I have had such a feast!

CLOSE THE BLUE DOOR

My grandfather told me I was fathered by a merman. He said he had always lived beside the Rio Conde and that he believed in spirits and knew the river's moods. During the course of his life, he had seen the river swell dangerously and become deadly many times. He had known its silences and had heard the raucous quarrelling of its currents when the spirits were angry. When the river became strong enough to sweep away houses, full-grown trees, animals, and humans, he became truly afraid. But more than anything else, he was in awe of the merpeople because he knew they occasionally mated with humans.

Grandfather said that his fair-skinned daughter, Saville, who was my mother, was chosen by the river's merpeople from the moment of her birth, for she was born with a thin membrane over her face, which was a true sign of the merpeople's ownership. That was why when she was a baby he took her down to the river to play in the shallows among the rocks and ferns, where she would delight in the little fish that came to nibble her small pink toes. Grandfather would sprinkle water gently on top of her head and ask the river spirits to spare her from drowning. Then he would brush her small feet with soft, dry sand, beseeching the spirits to keep her always on solid ground. My grandfather was a man who believed in nature spirits, and he never broke bread without giving thanks.

He said that spirits existed on the Earth to carry out the work of the Lord in heaven.

Saville was very much like my grandfather in appearance. For she, too, was fair and considered "red," which in our part of the island referred to blacks who were so light-skinned they appeared Caucasian. My grandmother, on the other hand, was as dark as the skin of a naseberry, and her hair as black as starapple seeds. There was an unmistakable bond between Saville and my grandfather; perhaps that was why her first word was "Da" and her first eager steps were taken toward him.

My grandparents were as dirt-poor as all the other riverside dwellers who lived in houses little better than shanties. They survived on the daily catch, sweet potatoes, cassavas and, occasionally, rice. My grandmother made a small living selling cassavas as a roadside vendor along the asphalt road that ran near the river.

As Saville grew older, she gazed down that road and wondered about the great distances it covered, and the marvels that lay beyond the horizon. She would light her kerosene lamp at night and give thanks for all those at home, never forgetting to ask the fire spirits to spare her family, always praying they would not follow the evils that surely existed along the road.

Saville did not attend school. My grandparents could not afford it, and besides they could not bear to be apart from her, for the school was many miles down that same road. Instead, Grandfather took her to see the mirrorlike water of the river on clear, still days, and in the evenings they would witness the return of the gaunt black fishermen who made a slender living from the sea.

My mother learned the ways of survival, never wanting more than she was given, but often she would fall into feverish trances, listening to the river's rhythms and murmurings.

When Grandfather saw her like that, he would become solemn and sad, his voice as soft as a whisper.

"Don't listen to the voices of the merpeople," he would warn. "They will try to lure you away and you will never see us again."

Hearing his words, Saville would cry great tears and promise never to leave him. "And always remember to close the blue door at night," he would insist, "for it is our only door that looks out over the river, and the merpeople will climb up the rocky riverbank and come in through it into the house to take you away."

***

One languid afternoon when Saville was fifteen she went down to the river as usual with Grandfather. He fell into a fitful sleep in the hot sun as he sat against a large boulder. In her loneliness for his company, Saville heard a strange whistle, unlike any she had heard before. She stepped over the sharp rocks, leaving her father's side, following the seductive whistling for more than a mile, almost to the mouth of the river. Coming upon a large moss-encrusted cave, reputed to be the abode of the merpeople, Saville thought nothing of it. Fearless, she crouched beneath overhanging vines and parted thick green river rushes, paying no heed to her father's warnings as she entered the cave.

When she returned to her father, he was only just waking from his sleep, brushing ferns and lily pollen from his hair. As his watery eyes fell on Saville, he sensed that something about her was not the same, but he was still too heavy with sleep to think exactly what it was. Soon the pleasant burble of the river assured him that all was well.

Saville took to seeking out the cave each time her father fell asleep on the riverbank. It was as though the river itself had consumed her, for she burned with a mysterious passion no longer satisfied with mere river murmurings.

But one day, on waking, Grandfather found her missing. His heart almost failed, he could hardly breathe, and a great pain lodged in his breast as his eyes misted with tears. He called out in terror to the river spirits, asking them to tell him where Saville was. Hearing no reply, he willed himself strength to climb over the rocks and weave a path through the ferns and rushes. More than once he thought he saw the wet outline of other footprints on the stones. When he came upon the forbidden cave, his heart filled with fear. "Saville!" he cried out, half hoping for no answer. Then, suddenly, he was deafened by the sound of a great thundering splash, and the thought of Saville among the merpeople filled him with great sorrow.

His trepidation vanished when Saville joyfully ran from the cave into his weary arms. He held her for a long time and cried freely. "We have to remember to close the blue door tonight," he told her. After that, Saville took to her mother's company, becoming solemn and silent, reminding her father of the river with its everchanging moods as she fell into household tasks. She no longer visited the river, though at night she found herself compelled to leave the blue door open after her parents fell asleep, and she would hear the strange whistling and the soothing stroke of the river against the shore. Her nights became dreamless, yet it seemed to her that she slept in the very arms of the dark river, for she felt its breath hot upon her cheeks, felt its currents and its foam penetrate her, felt its tongue warm against her flesh.

Grandfather was the first to notice Saville's changes. His daughter grew rosy, her lean frame straining to form new proportions as her thin, pale cheeks and her belly, month after month, blossomed like flowers.

"She is having a baby!" Grandmother exclaimed one morning. "Our poor child is having a baby!"

"I should have put a stop to it!" Grandfather thundered. "I should have boarded up that damn door! It is the work of the merpeople. She has been in their cave!"

By the time I was born, Saville no longer went near the river. Instead, she brooded indoors, always sitting with me in her arms by the blue door. Her eyes looked inward as streams flowed from them, baptizing me in river tears. And a wall grew up between her and her parents, surrounding them in loneliness.

Early one morning my mother jumped off a wooden bridge that spanned the widest point of the river and drowned herself. The river dwellers said she had returned to the merman in the river.

***

When I was growing up, a free government school opened near our settlement. I walked alone there, since both my grandparents had grown feeble. At the school I was called the River Child, though my true name was Lily, named for the flower that dots the meandering river. One day, when I was fourteen, I saw an old East Indian woman as I was returning home from school. She was bent under the weight of a bundle of sticks that she carried. Her eyes shone like coals and her wrinkled skin was almost translucent. My grandfather would have thought she was a fairy, but I knew she was human, being subject to her long, steady gaze.

"Good evening, child," she said, revealing discoloured teeth. A rope of grey-black hair was swung over her shoulder.

"Good evening," I replied, noticing her shaggy brows and unsteady hand. "Let me help you with your load."

She smiled, then painfully lowered the bundle to the ground, redistributed it, and gave me a load of my own. "Thank you," she rasped like a death rattle. "What is your name, child?"

"It's Lily."

"You are from the river settlement?"

"Yes."

"Well, I will tell you something I have told no one before."

Bearing our heavy burdens, we walked side by side in silence for miles, even as the sun dipped low in the sky and bathed the trees and shrubs in gold.

"It will be too late for you to walk back alone," the old woman finally said. "You will have to stay the night. I will walk with you in the morning."

My heart sank, for I had never been away from my grandparents for even a night, and I was fearful for them and for my missing them. We trudged on through bush and briar until at last we approached a small zinc house.

"Come inside," the old woman said. "Leave your sticks by the door." We entered the dirt-floor shack and she said, "So you are called Lily. It is a good name for someone as light-skinned as you, and look how your hair is long and dark. You could practically pass for a Coolie Indian like me. My husband and son were also Indian. But my husband, Vikram, was a heavy drinker and him beat us up all the time for no reason. And even when I love him, him beat me, anyway. That is why my son, Rajiv, run away. Rest your feet, girl. Sit in this chair. Is the only one I have. Let me just squat on this old pan and I will tell you all about him. My husband is dead now, choked on him vomit one night, and now I am alone. When I was young, people knew me as Gaitree Ladrin, but these days I am called Coolie Old Woman."

She grinned. "I loved my son so much. I spoiled him with love, for we had nothing else to give him. Look at me now, old and withered. You must find it hard to think of me as a beauty, but people say that is what I was. But, Lily, I am straying from the story. Is what we old people do. As I said before, Rajiv's father's drinking drove my son away. When him was seventeen, him found a cave down by the Rio Conde. Him did not know that cave was the place black people say is the merpeople's house, for we Coolies did not really mix with blacks. It was a godforsaken place a long way from here. But him did not tell me all I tell you. Him left a diary, which I, an uneducated woman, could not read. It is only through the goodness of the priest who read it for me that I know the story.

"Don't fall asleep in the chair, Lily. You have to listen, so others will know. Rajiv write in the book that one day him saw a beautiful young girl along the riverbank. She was very light-skinned, with hair the colour of honey. Him watched her daily while hiding behind the rocks. Then one day Rajiv whistle a tune on a tin flute, and she followed the sound as him led her away from a sleeping old man. Him dodge behind rock after rock, and she follow him right to the cave where him was living. The girl was a strange one. Him said she did not stop him hugs or kisses. And when him said, 'Take your clothes off,' she did. Rajiv said they met every chance they could, and him even manage to find her house among the shacks beside the river in the same settlement you are from. Him enter her room at night through a blue door, and though the girl lay with him night after night, Rajiv said him feel like she did not even know him was there.

"My son and me were close. And I know him had big dreams, because him had gone to school and had learning. Him dreamed of following the asphalt road to the city to make something of himself, and one night him did follow that road. Him quickly packed a few things by moonlight, so him daddy would not know. And with a kiss on my cheek as sharp as a hen's peck, him gone.

That night, Lily, Rajiv Ladrin was killed on the asphalt road, struck down by a market truck, and the driver get off, 'cause him say him not see Rajiv in the dark. And now I will never see my son again."

I turned my eyes away from the old woman as she tucked me in for the night in a bed of rags that at one time might have been her son's. I longed to dream of my grandparents, even as she caught me in her fierce black-eyed gaze.

"I had to tell someone," she said. "For my son was beautiful, so very beautiful."

THE INTERVENTION

It is the year 3089, and I Gabriel Angelo am a young keeper of old memories. I am one of the few people left on earth, who avoided the process known as the Intervention.

The Intervention was gaseous, and was designed to induce mass amnesia. It was released into the earth's atmosphere, and drinking water. As a result, memories of wars, riots, racial prejudice, deprivation, violence and even one's purpose in life was eliminated. Diverse races lost their sense of individuality, brotherhood took priority.

Two years ago, before the Intervention occurred, I came in contact with an old black woman named Rachel Malloy, and it was she, who passed on her ancient memories to me. Her persona had immediately captivated my artistic senses. It was not just her egg-plant coloured skin, or her wild gray dreadlocks, it was her warrior stance.

And since then, whenever she spoke about times prior to the Intervention, she would appear particularly animated. There was always a mischievous smile on her lips, and a sly wink in her eye as though amused at her ability to recall such contraband.

The day I first met her, had at first seemed like any other day. I was in my dwelling area, watching and interacting on my Autogram. This mandatory machine was in every dwelling, and between aged earthlings, such as I am, were obliged to immerse ourselves in all that it showed going on all over our planet. The images received were immediate, and we were required by law to report any matters considered out of line. Wars, riots, and even domestic disputes surfaced on the Autogram.

Our world was devoid of old world demarcations known as countries, and continents, all was now simplified into divisions known as East World and West World. The Autogram's unique perspective, would in ancient times be categorized as spying, and it sickened me. My late parents had felt the same way. In their absence, my duty was to maintain the Autogram, and the household. I might well have been under the watch of undisclosed benefactors or perhaps superior overseers, but at that time, I had no real reason to investigate, since food, drink, toiletries and clothing were always regularly provided.

My appointed time at the Autogram often found me dividing my time, indulging in sketching, though drawing was considered an antiquated pastime. However, an interest in art intrigued me, and with daily practice I came to understand how to use colour, shade, and perspective. I painstakingly smuggled small amounts of colour pieces, and paper into the dwelling, always fearful of being found out, since art produced by humans was condemned, since machines were said to be far more creative. I was fortunate that one could request washroom breaks from the Autogram, and only then, was one free from being observed. I was confident that these breaks offered a semblance of freedom so that I could indulge in my art. Though lately, as a result of this continuous deception, I began to receive messages on the Autogram inquiring about my well being.

But on that unforgettable day, when I met Rachel Malloy, there was no apparent reason but boredom from watching the Autogram, that caused me to wander away from my dwelling. I left the residential area, and walked past the nuclear power plants, the estuary of avenues and the underwater malls, on and on to the forbidden desolate area known as Meteor Plains, where a meteor had fallen years before. The meteor had destroyed a vast stretch of our landscape, and left it ravaged, stark and barren. We were told that there was no growth there except for struggling scrawny potted plants brought by enthused squatters now called gardeners, intent on restoring the natural habitat. I never questioned this standard description of the plains, and never wondered why the gardeners were allowed there, despite restrictions that bleared at the entrance to the supposed foreboding landscape. Pulsating purplish lights at the entrance warned of danger and pollution, and a declaration posted there read that one should enter only at their own risk. Even Autogram watchers ignored Meteor Plains, since nothing untoward was ever expected to happen there. I was to later discover that the gardeners were looked upon as the hope for our planet, since food in the city had become scarcer than anticipated by those who controlled society. I approached Meteor Plains, passed under the pulsating purple lights, and felt strangely liberated, as I climbed over a series of stone walls and entered the plain.

The air in Meteor Plains was better than I had expected, and though the landscape was said to be harsh, I found that it was not, it was strangely beautiful. Ferns and mosses caressed rock faces, and grew even more lush, as I progressed. I could not help but find it ideal for sketching. In the distance, jagged mountain ranges seemed to stand at rigid attention, as their peaks creaked against the sky.

Without hesitation, I sat myself down on a smooth boulder, and began drawing pictures in my mind, hoping I would be able to duplicate my thoughts on paper, and retain the immediacy of the effect. Then suddenly I realized that I was not alone, for on the horizon I noticed a girl about my age stumbling towards me. Her hair was long and dark, and even before she was close enough, I knew she was oriental. I was somewhat surprised to see an Oriental, since Meteor Plains for some reason unknown to me, had been said to have become a haunt of mixed race blacks like myself.

Then I noticed that not far behind the approaching girl was a woman. She was also dark haired, and seemed to have had difficulty keeping up with the girl's bold and determined pace.

Before too long, the girl stood directly in front of me, breathless and somewhat agitated.

"My name is Laureen," She said, a firm finger on her lips, as she cautiously moved closer to whisper, "Don't ask any questions, time is short," she continued, "they are bound to find us."

"Who's going to find you?" I stammered, suddenly jolted from my reverie.

"There's no time to explain. I am hoping that though you are brown, and not the same race as us, that we can trust you."

"You can trust me" I said, fearful of whatever it was that was causing such urgency in her demeanor.

"My mother is behind me. She's a scientist and as such, she has become aware of an undercover government operation, and as a result, she has been helping to build a secret shelter here on Meteor Plains. But as I said before, time is short. We need to get word to a woman who lives here, in a secret shelter, though we must at all cost avoid the authorities, for whatever it is they are doing, it will have huge international repercussions involving both East and West World."

I was so taken aback by what the girl was saying that I must have looked foolish. Then coming to my senses, I realized that just as the girl's mother drew abreast of us, a folded sheet of parchment was thrust into my hand.

"Sorry to have to involve you," Laureen said apologetically, "Please give this to the woman I mentioned who is living here. I had to use the old method of writing, since Autogram mail wouldn't have been private enough. To find the secret shelter you will have to go through the maze of caves, a half a day's walk from here, beneath the mountain ranges. When you get there, follow the red sand trail to the left, it will lead you to the entrance of a cave not unlike the others, but it is marked with a strange hieroglyphic that resembles an R. That is where she is, her name is Rachel Malloy. She has a brilliant mind though she is elderly."

The girl's mother came towards me, her appearance and posture marked by humility, as she held my hand in both of hers, and I was surprised at their warmth. Her eyes were weary and resigned, but she was more alert than I had given her credit.

" Laureen has given you the parchment." She said, her voice, a low whisper, "Guard it with your life! Hide it on your person, and here, take this also. It is a packaged lunch we brought, pretending we were here for a picnic. But they already know we are here, so there is no time left, none whatsoever. In fact, they should be coming over that rise in less than ten minutes, and you must hide!"

"Hide, where can I hide? The mountains are too far away."

"Sometimes one must hide in plain sight" She said, nodding towards the redevelopment area. "Hurry, go over to where the potted plants are. There are watering implements there, and large hooded aprons to keep off the muck. You'll fit right in with the other gardeners you're the right colour. Be quick!"

I hardly dared look back, for instinctively I knew I might be watched. I approached the gardening area, and noticed two or three squatters busy tending plants. None of whom even batted an eye, when I unhooked one of the heavy yellow aprons from a makeshift fence, and dressed quickly, before proceeding to water plants alongside the others. But through the corner of my eye, I glimpsed when a group of four men dressed in close fitting dark outfits, and some sort of covering that partially obscured their faces, came over the rise, and approached the two women.

I glanced up momentarily from the watering, trying to appear nonchalant, and was in time to see Laureen and her mother being led away in the mode of an arrest.

A good ten minutes passed, before I slowly removed the heavy apron, and cautiously began to head out of the gardening allotment. I was hardly even aware that my presence was noticed, until a medium built young man with dreadlocks, perhaps only a few years older than I, called over to me.

"Hi, I'm Luke," He grinned, "How's it going?"

I didn't reply right away, being somewhat taken aback by his attention. "haven't seen you before." he continued, as he held his hand out in camaraderie, "Are you a member of the Environs Patrol?"

"No, I'm not." I replied turning my head away, hoping to remain somewhat aloof.

"No? Well is the cultivation of new forests not of personal interest to you then?"

"Yes, but only in the sense that I like sketching from nature." My reply sounded somewhat false, and I found that I could scarcely look into his eyes.

"Do you know why it is that we are restoring the forestation?" Luke said, unperturbed by my answer, "It would give me the greatest pleasure to explain it to you. It is obvious from your appearance that you spend far too much time indoors. Your pallid complexion, for instance, I wouldn't be surprised if you are one of those Autogram watchers. Are you?"

"Give it a rest." I said, stepping away abruptly.

"You haven't told me your name," He said sounding sincere and apologetic. "I didn't mean to be rude. I just wondered if you even know the history of this godforsaken place."

It was a long time before I could get my dry mouth to move and respond.

Finally, I took a deep breath, ran my tongue over my lips, and I was surprised when words came out.

"My name's Gabriel Angelo. I'm mixed race. Caucasian and black. Perhaps that's why my hair is curly. My tan is not from exposure to the sun like yours is, it's my genes. Yes I'm an Autogram watcher. But in the old days, I would also have been considered an artist

"Be careful what you call yourself. Gabriel. You could be in danger because of what you say. We gardeners live under the radar, it keeps us more or less safe here."

"Does that mean you are defiant against whatever is going on in our world?"

"Yes" Luke replied, as he regarded me for the longest while, as though acquiring new respect for the likes of me.

But then without warning he shoved me forcefully against the fencing, his hand firmly on my chest as he spoke.

"The only reason I spoke to you, is because you look like us., and yet there is something about you that is different," He glowered. "My father was said to have wasted his time dabbling in art, and calling himself a master. But that was before they shut him down."

"What do you mean 'shut him down'?" I stammered.

"They killed him Gabriel, just like they will kill anyone who doesn't cooperate with the way they want this society run. You're from the city, aren't you? Haven't you ever stopped to think about how much of your life is controlled? We eat when they tell us, and only at assigned hours, and only of course, the food assigned us. We sleep when they say so, and we dress in the clothes they provide, and heaven forbid that we should step out from under their authorizations. You might not know it, but water is supplied to us for watering our crops, and small plants, but only in the amounts designated by the authority. Don't get me started Gabriel! There is a lot I could tell you, but then of course there is the reason we squatters are here, we are trying to rebuild the earth, though we are starting small. But it is the philosophy of what we are doing that will take root just like these small crops and simple plants we are watering. We are even introducing species that have not been known to survive in this part of West World. Take a look at this one for instance, it's an ackee tree, and it's doing very well, isn't it? The ackee vegetable was a favorite with blacks in years gone by."

"How so?"

"Folk used to make a meal with the ackee, it was cooked with salted cod."

"Seriously?"

"Yes, they used to soak the cod for a few hours to remove most of the salt, then dried it off to season it with thyme, Scotch-bonnet pepper and garlic. Then that was fried until crisp in coconut oil for a few minutes. After that they would add onions, chopped tomatoes, a pinch of black pepper and the ackee. That was fried together for a few more minutes then served plain, or with rice.

"Sounds good. Wish I could have had some."

"Perhaps you will my friend, that is what restoring the land is all about. But be careful though, mark my words, you too are under surveillance, don't be naive enough to think they have not noted the fact that you are here."

"But, who's controlling society Luke? Is it men, or machines? I was always provided for. I've never had to be concerned about such things. The focus of my attention has always been the Autogram, and my art."

"Well Gabriel, the reason you don't know who is in charge is because you've never used your brain to think things out, and so far, until now, you had not broken their laws. But be warned, your interest in art will sooner or later attract attention, and you will be punished. Those running society are the advantaged, and that is how they want things to remain."

I was still thinking about what Luke had said, a half an hour after leaving the gardening compound, and as a result I almost forgot the folded parchment concealed against my chest beneath my shirt. Only when the parchment threatened to dislodge while I was walking, did Laureen's words suddenly come back to ring loud and clear in my memory. Without hesitation, I set my sight on the distant mountainous horizon and

without a backward glance, I began my trek to find Rachel Malloy.

The sun was directly overhead, and I regretted not wearing some sort of headgear for protection. Beads of sweat stood out on my forehead, while streams ran down my back.

Fortunately, the landscape was a constant source of inspiration. I worked out in my mind, colours and shading for new art pieces. I never seemed to tire of the ragged gullies, the canyons, jagged rocks, the biting air, and the feeling of being totally alone on the earth.

The landscape changed dramatically towards evening, becoming almost semitropical, with lush palms, ferns, and the occasional citrus tree. After a while, I heard the busy sound of insects, and in the sky I witnessed the passage of a hawk and then a swallow. This evidence of natural restoration must surely be the handiwork of the squatters, I thought to myself, as I approached a grove of apple trees. The world is indeed reverting to the way it used to be. I don't know how often I had heard my own father speak of locations similar to where I now found myself.

After the long journey through the unfamiliar landscape, exhaustion and hunger began to set in. Then remembering the packaged lunch from Laureen's mother, I wolfed down the four meat replacement sandwiches, laced with tomatoes, lettuce, mayo and mustard, and washed it down afterwards with three water pellets included in the package. Then I munched on fresh apples from the orchard, which were far better than any apple I had ever had in the city.

By nightfall I was at the foot of the mountain range, I was awed by its austerity, and I couldn't help but feel insignificant as I stared at its massive peaks that seemed to pierce the sky. A riddle of caves dotted the mountainside, alongside hundreds of crater-like indentations, and rude holes, set there as though by an unseen hand.

A cool wind blew, as gloom gathered, and I heard a low mournful humming. It sounded like a trumpeter of death and it sent a chill running through me. My first thought was that it was a possible forewarning of a disaster yet to come. To my relief, I realized that the mountain itself with its many deep indentations and hollows acted as an instrument that gave voice to the wind.

Mesmerized by the star dotted sky and the yellowing moon, I finally I averted my attention, and noticed a trail of red sand beneath my feet, visible even in the half-light. I examined a handful, and was surprised to find that the sand was composed of small pieces of red jasper. It brought to mind, something my mother used to say. "He who bears the Jasper stone becomes possessed of passion and strong emotion. For he who bears the Jasper stone is engulfed in love."

The trail led me through a rocky crevice in the mountainside. When after what seemed like hours, I emerged on the other side of the mountain, I found myself inside a strangely quiet secluded valley, surrounded by massive mountainous ranges. There was such a sense of tranquility there, I couldn't help but feel that I had finally found my true home. That peaceful abode was indeed the zenith of my deepest desire, and I found myself easily giving in to exhaustion. I laid down under the stars on what felt like some sort of moss-covered carpeting, and the last thing I remembered, was curling into fetal position before I fell asleep.

Shortly before dawn, I was startled to awake to the sound of a rich resonant female voice singing. I was not alone, as I had thought. I turned over on my back, and stared wide-eyed at a strong looking black woman who stood there unflinchingly, as she leaned on a white staff. She wore a long loose purple tunic that billowed dramatically about her. My artist's eyes couldn't help but notice her thick graying dreadlocked hair, tied in colourful strips of cloth, that looked almost serpent-like in the morning light.

"What you doing here boy?" She said, roughly. "How is it, that you found this place?"

She was a figure of absolute authority and I was left speechless, even as she forcefully jammed her staff into the ground near me

"I'm looking for Rachel Malloy..." I stammered, "I have information to give her."

The woman stood tall before me, her face stern and craggy.

"And who want to give Rachel Malloy information?" She demanded, giving me a sharp nudge with her sandal.

"I'm Gabriel Angelo, an Autogram Watcher..." I said weakly. "I have information given to me by a girl named Laureen, and her mother."

"And when since Laureen and her mother start sending things to me, with somebody as beige and scrawny as you? How far you come from?"

"I'm from the city...I'm an Autogram Watcher"

"Okay, okay boy, you don't need tell me that again, just give me whatever information you have, and I might even offer you something to eat."

I hastily reached into my shirt, the folded parchment was still there, and I handed it over to her.

Rachel Malloy held the parchment up, and the first rays of sunlight seemed to illuminate the written words. I watched her expression grow dark and her brows furrowed as she read the words, before holding me in an embittered gaze.

"Come!" She commanded, "We are just about out of time!"

I staggered to my feet, and felt her cool hand, as she practically dragged me across the valley to a distant maze of caves. The hieroglyphic that Laureen had mentioned was above the entrance to one of the cave. It must, without a doubt be the entrance to the secret shelter, I thought

Bending low, we proceeded into the cave. The interior was as dark as a moonless night. After a few meters, the tunnel widened, and strangely enough I found myself becoming more accustomed to the poor light.

"It's beautiful here." I whispered, as I saw sedimentary rocks, embedded with bright quartz crystals. Rachel Malloy did not respond, her grip tightened as we plunged further into the mountain's depts.

I heard the musical sound of water running over stones, and saw beautifully formed rough granite, limestone, dolomite and even gypsum slabs. The tunnel was lit not by any manmade power source, but by bioluminescent mosses and fungi.

"We are there." Rachel Malloy announced, as she pressed her palm against what looked like a large flattened agate embedded in the cave wall. "This is the shelter."

If I did not know better, I would have thought I had been miraculously transported back to the city, for the interior of the shelter was spacious, modern, and well equipped, even with an Autogram. "Sit," Rachel Malloy said nodding towards a table with a woven cornucopia basket brimming with fruits that spilled on to the tabletop.

"Help yourself, the fruit is quite fresh. There is much that I have to tell you."

I was midway through a nectarine, when she spoke again. Her eyes seemed somewhat unfocused as she sighed, and began her story.

"Laureen's mother's name is Dr. Ivy Chan," She said shakily, "She was one of the greatest scientific minds that this planet has ever known. We met years ago, became friends, and were considered renegade. Different races did not form friendships back then. But while Ivy trained as a scientist, I grew proficient in the natural arts, finding since childhood that I had powers and capabilities that no one else even guessed at. But enough of that!

The parchment you brought has information that will change the whole damn world forever. You and I, might well be the last humans to remain in the state of mind we are in today.

You see this shelter, Ivy and I built it, we knew that a day would come when we would need to seal off from the rest of the world. That is why we install special insulation, generators, oxygen suppliers, and stocked up on crates of water pellets, foodstuff and other things necessary to last us for months. Ivy's daughter is the only other human who knew about our plans.

Ivy found out that scientist were interested in stopping racial riots and the conflicts it generates, by using chemicals to control minds. The experiments they used with rat and chimpanzees went well, so they decided to use it on humans. Ivy was afraid that they didn't develop the chemicals well enough, and something could easily go wrong, because according to her, she noticed that the rats started to act foolishly, and the chimps were not doing anything but play. But other scientist told Ivy that she was being ridiculous, because that kind of behavior is a normal development in such inferior mammals, and the main thing is that the animals stopped being violent. Now, the parchment you brought informed me, by my calculation, that they are going to release that chemical into the earth's atmosphere and drinking water at noon today The resonance will last about three days. That means, starting then, neither of us must dare venture outside of this cave. It is the only way to avoid the effects of what they are calling 'The Intervention'. I only hope Ivy and her daughter are alright."

The weight and magnitude of what I heard left me reeling. I dropped the nectarine I had been eating, and tears threatened. "Ivy Chan and her daughter have been arrested!" I spat out.

We remained sealed inside the cave for eight days, and learning of my artistic interests. Rachel Malloy introduced me to the craft of using grounded herbs and dried flowers to produce vegetable dyes and colours. As a result, I spent entire days planning murals, and deciding on colour placements and unique points of perspectives. Thus, the time in the cave passed unnoticed. I drew sketches of our city's skyline, and began to include the dramatic true landscape of Meteor Plains, and included people, representing the different races from East and West World. It was then, that I thought about Luke, and I drew him.

One morning I awoke to find Rachel Malloy rolling back the barrier to the cave entrance. "The worst has passed." She sighed heavily, "We are pretty safe now. Our heads have not been tampered with. Thank God, we can go outside again. But Gabriel, you know of course that you can stay here for however long you choose, and you can do your paintings on all the cave walls, because here, you'll never be short of surfaces and material to work with."

What a relief it was to once more step outside into fresh air. I felt enraptured by every birdcall, every breeze, and even the rustle of leaves, and how wonderful the sun. I told Rachel Malloy

I would return by late afternoon, though I knew I would be a lot later, and headed towards the gardening compound in search of Luke, for his words haunted me. I wanted to tell him that I had not once resumed my duties as an Autogram Watcher, and that I was setting about being creative, despite the danger. Most of all, I wanted him to be proud that I was now using my brain.

When I arrived there, the gardening compound, seemed less cared for. Plants were drying in the baking sun, and the watering implements were hanging untouched. I walked a good deal further south; and followed the sound of laughter and voices, and that is where I saw him! Luke, with his dread locks flying, was twirling and prancing in the company of a group of young multiracial men. They were holding hands and skipping, I overheard the words of their song, and couldn't believe my ears! "Ring around the roses, a pocketful of poses."

I screamed his name. "Luke! Luke!" But he didn't seem to hear, in fact he might have been beyond hearing. His grin like all the others with him, was broad and engaging, as like a circle of children they indulged in the game, unmindful of all else. Only then did it occur to me that what I witnessed, was, as a result of the Intervention. The world had indeed changed beyond recognition, and the Luke I had met mere days ago, the defiant, clear thinking Luke, was lost forever.

On impulse, I returned to the gardening compound to retrieve the ackee plant, hoping I could save it. What if it had died. But I need not have worried, it was still alive, its leaves were green and glossy. I gathered it up, and made the long trek back to the secret shelter, with it held securely in my arms, my thoughts racing to the future when this stalwart plant would bear fruit and once again feed people.

Rachel Malloy was waiting at the mouth of the cave, her staff held high, and a welcoming smile on her lips.

"Thank God you are home Gabriel" She said joyfully, "We will be safe here. I discovered that the Intervention had absolutely no effect on all of earth's vegetation, or salt water habitants. Gabriel, you wouldn't believe what the Autogram is showing. It would seem the whole world has lost its senses."

CHAIN LETTER

My Abuela Rosalee claimed that we must have been the only two people ever to answer such a letter. I wasn't exactly a chain letter, although now that I think about it, it was passed on in much the same manner. I will never forget the day it came, although I couldn't have been more than nine years old. It was on of those sticky June days that used to find me rushing home from school thirstily looking forward to one of the wonderful lime drinks my Ecuadorian grandmother used to make. She used to say, "Give me a couple of limes, a clove, a knob of ginger, and a dollop of brown sugar, and I can make a better drink than Kool-Aid" Her concoctions were legend in our tiny household.

Back then, we lived on College Street in Toronto, and at seventy-five years old, Abuela Rosalee, though speaking no English, was magnificent at negotiating deals in Kensington Market. She used to go there every Wednesday morning to invade the fruit stands. With only a few dollars she was able to provide Mama and me with the most exotic fruit punches.

My mother Carmela was thirty-five. Being a widow, and with her job starting at six am, and ending at six pm, she was more than grateful that Abuela Rosalee (who was her mother-in-law) had come to stay with us. Abuela helped with the housework, and with me.

Most afternoons I could count on my Abuela to be on the front porch busily knitting and rocking. She always seemed to have a sweater on the go. But I suspect, that she intentionally sat out there, so that she would be the first to catch a glimpse of Mama as she returned from her Dufferin Street factory job. "Carmella," she used to say, "You look tired, it's not easy for a single woman these days. There's rent to pay, food to put on the table, and the boy needs clothes for school. You and I can do with little, but not the boy. It's hard for him."

I remember bounding up the rickety porch steps that afternoon. Abuela Rosalee was rocking as usual, her thick hair silver in the sunlight, but her black brows were pulled together fiercely, and I sensed something unusual, since she was not even knitting.

"What's wrong Abuela?"

"It's this letter." She said fretfully, turning over a white envelope in her hand. "Don't know what it says, but I hope its not bad news" Abuela sighed.

I glanced apprehensively at the envelope, and read the large letters printed on it: TO OCCUPANT.

"I'll open it," I said excitedly, "I'm an occupant."

Abuela Rosalee sighed deeply, her hands fell into her lap, and her jaw went slack. "Okay, read it," she replied, "But try not to frighten me. I tore open the envelope to find a small greenish card folded over once. There were words printed on it in bold type, which I immediately translated into Spanish for Abuela Rosalee, who closed her eyes and held one hand over her heart.

"My peace I'll give to you." I read, "My peace I'll bring to you, if you will shelter me in your home. for one week, and after that, I will move on, and you in turn must pass this note on to a stranger."

"Where did the letter come from Abuela?" I asked.

"Oh Juan, I don't know," she shook her head. "I heard a noise out here, and I came to see if someone was breaking in. I was so scared, me being an old woman. But all I saw was this letter on the doormat. Whosoever left it, was long gone, by the time I got downstairs. "

"So maybe its serious, maybe we should say yes Abuela."

"Yes, we should child. What have we to lose, one never knows the ways of the Lord, and maybe it's about time something good happened."

That night, our next-door neighbours came over. Mama didn't mind visitors, as long as they didn't overstay their welcome. Dominic and Fatima Costas often came to play cards with her. It was customary that Abuela Rosalee kept out of their way. Abuela claimed that young people needed time to themselves. I found her in her room praying the rosary, so I waited in the shadows until she was finished.

"Abuela," I said. "Do you think that anything will happen?"

"Ah child," she replied, "Who knows the Lord's plan."

I climbed up on her broad bed and pressed my fingers into the softness of her quilt. "Abuela." I began, "should we tell Mama?"

"No sweet one," she smiled, "This way she won't be disappointed."

"That's true."

"But off to bed with you Juan, you need your rest."

I slipped off the bed obediently, but just then I heard the doorbell ring.

"Abuela, did you hear that?"

"Go see who it is at this hour."

I took the stairs two at a time. "I'll get it Mama," I shouted knowing that Mama and her friends were still playing cards in the kitchen. I opened the door a crack, and peered out into the darkness. "Who's there?" I asked softly, my whole body electrified with excitement. "Whose there?" I repeated, and was amazed to make out the figure of a stranger. He had a radiant smile that shone, despite the dimness. I caught my breath, and was surprised at just how blue his eyes were. They were even more blue than the morning glory wall paper in our kitchen. His honey coloured hair, fell well below his shoulders.

"Good evening," he said, "I am here to see your grandmother."

"Who're you?" I stammered, but before I could say another word I heard Abuela Rosalee on the staircase behind me.

"Come in, come in." she smiled. Then she bent down and whispered into my ear in Spanish. "Perhaps he is a messenger or an angel of the Lord."

"Peace be to this household," the stranger said, as he passed his hand in blessing over both our heads. Abuela fell to her knees, and tugged at me to join her there.

"Rise up in peace, little ones." He said, this will be my home, and you will be my family for a little while."

'My mind was in sudden turmoil'. What would Mama say, especially with one more mouth to feed. Where would the stranger sleep? Would he be sharing the upstairs bathroom, or would he use the dingy one in the basement? Would he watch TV, and would he rather have wine than fruit-punch? But worst of all, would we all have to go to church everyday?

As though reading my thoughts, the stranger smiled in my direction. "Peace be with you." he said, "Sleep well, and may angels watch over you."

When I awoke the next morning, the stranger was still with us, having slept on the couch downstairs. I tiptoed down the staircase, trying not to disturb him, but it was useless, since he sat up as soon as my bare feet touched the floor.

"So, you're at St. Helen's School," he said brightly.

"Yes sir," I replied, rubbing my eyes. "Does Mama know you are here?"

"Yes," he replied, his eyes fairly twinkling.

"Does she know who you are?" I asked testily.

"Do you know me?" he replied, answering my question with his own query. "Your mother might know, but since it is only four thirty am, let her sleep. She needs the rest."

"You speak Spanish!" I cried out, suddenly realizing.

He held me in his blue gaze. "I speak many languages." He replied with a smile. After that, I had no idea where the time went, for in the early dawning we talked about school, sports and even food, and before I knew it, Mama was up and preparing for work. I could hear her shoes through the ceiling above us. When she came downstairs she looked particularly animated.

"Juan," she said, "you're up already! I hope you didn't wake our guest. Offer him some tea. The best kind, the kind we have from Ecuador. Pour him some juice too. He must be thirsty."

The stranger smiled, but said nothing.

Our front porch looked out onto College Street, and Abuela Rosalee began to spend her mornings out there in the company of the stranger, their two chairs rocking side by side. Even the neighbours began noticing our serene visitor; and it became increasingly difficult to explain his presence. Even the streetcars took to slowing down as they went past our house, and I don't know how often I saw faces pressed up against car windows staring out at him. To me, his smile grew more radiant with each day. Our lives were not in the least disrupted by his presence; on the contrary, we seemed to become more caring for each other, and the people around us. And in spite of our meagre fare, he seemed satisfied. I need not have worried, we didn't have to go to church every day, and he never asked for wine, since he enjoyed Abuela's fruit drinks as much as I did.

The end of the week came all too quickly. We all knew instinctively that soon it would be time to say goodbye. On the last day Mama made codfish cakes before she left for work, and a steaming pot of coffee which we washed down with cream. We all drank in silence. Then finally the stranger spoke.

"I will not forget this house," he said, "I will not forget you Carmela, or your boy and Abuela Rosalee. Surely this house is blessed."

It was Abuela Rosalee who thought of giving him a parting gift. She pulled out an old photograph of us all together at Christmas three years before.

"This is to remind you of us." She said huskily. The stranger accepted her humble gift, his face lit with joy.

"Goodbye dear friends," he said, "Be kind to all your fellow men, as you have been to me, and yours will be joy in heaven."

The last I saw of him, was when he stopped at the front door to bless the house. "Bless this house." He said, looking skyward. "If after I leave, anything of mine is ever found by this family, I give my permission to you all, to keep what ever it is." What an odd thing to say, I thought at the time.

The house was unbearably empty without him, yet I sensed him in all that we did, felt his presence in all the rooms. Although none of us said a word; we were aware that he was ever present, in each other's thoughts.

When Abuela Rosalee pulled out the couch where he slept, she found tucked in under the cushions, a slip of paper which turned out to be a lottery ticket. Across the back, a note written in Spanish said, 'For the little family'

Abuela Rosalee immediately passed on the 'chain letter' to the man at the fruit stand in Kensington Market, and that night, we all waited with bated breath for the results of the lottery.

LONG NIGHT UNTIL MORNING

Chapter 1

One Morning

It has been three long weeks since my beloved twenty one year old son Eduardo, passed away. Three long weeks of grief, mourning and tears, and I who had been such a weakling has had to be strong. I am full of memories that will not let go. I remember when I was younger and perhaps more foolish than I am now, I was as wild as the wind that rustles in the pampas, and my reputation was known throughout San Miguel City. But that was before I met and married Claudia Vasques, Eduardo's mother, a show girl. My life changed, I was hopelessly in love, though she did not seem to reciprocate my feelings. She said she preferred the gypsy vagabond existence of show business to upper class domesticity, and it wasn't long after Eduardo's birth that she left us as stealthy as the night.

As a young child, Eduardo was eager to be shaped and guided, but I was depressed and emotionally internalized, being the one rejected, and I allowed my aging but able father, Rinaldo Gomez Torres, to raise my son. My father, a womanizer was as feisty as a bull, and even in his later years had not been tamed. It was no surprise that by strange osmosis, Eduardo grew to be exactly like his grandfather. I admired their devil may care temperament while I myself needing time to heal allowed them freedom.

My father, solid as granite, was rejuvenated by Eduardo. He relished in Eduardo's liaisons and celebrated his conquests, but his strength eluded me. I never saw him falter until the news of Eduardo's car crash came. The news came in the person of an Inspector Perez of the San Miguel police force, who arrived unexpectedly at our door at eleven o'clock one Friday morning. I could tell instinctively from his military bearing that he was armed with words that would break my heart. And not wanting a dramatic or emotional scene at the front of the house, I invited him inside to the breakfast room. There are large windows there where one can easily rest their eyes on the view of grassy fields and mountains beyond the house. Perhaps I thought those views would have a calming effect on the inspector.

"Senor Sebastino Torres," he said, with a slight hitch to his voice, as he crossed the wide hall and entered the breakfast room. "The news is not good." I followed his eyes and saw that he looked neither left nor right, as though unimpressed by my belongings. "Senor," he continued and he sounded as hollow as the caves at the far end of the city. "Please, this is not easy for me to say."

"Would you like a coffee?" I said, delaying the inevitable, as I pulled out a chair for him.

"A shot of brandy might be more in order." he muttered under his breath, but I pretended not to hear, as I called out to Beatrice, a young Amara Indian servant girl who has since left my employment. She had been at work in the kitchen, and her eyes were wide with surprise when she saw the inspector. But her expression softened when I asked her to prepare the bitter sweet drink for our unexpected guest.

Inspector Perez wasted no time waiting for coffee. He leaned against the breakfast table as though it were his own. What would he have thought if he knew how valuable an antique it was? It was purchased in Lima Peru years ago for a small fortune. But he however never once examined the table; instead his eyes drifted to the copper pots hanging from the ceiling, the dried herbs on the countertop and the clay figurines and crucifix on the sideboard, and then finally his eyes rested on a single photograph in a silver frame, a photo of Eduardo. In the photo, Eduardo smiled out bravely at the world, his hair jet black, his eyes light brown and his very handsomeness brought sunlight into the room.

"That's your son?" the inspector asked, tapping his index finger on the hard mahogany beneath his hand. He swallowed hard, and I nodded in reply, fearful of words to come, as both Eduardo's portrait and I waited with frozen eyes to be jarred by Perez's declaration. Then slowly my tongue loosened, "Is this about Eduardo?" I asked, "Has he been drinking and carousing with the girls again?"

The inspector didn't answer, for he was momentarily distracted as Beatrice brought in the rattling coffee pot with two tall ceramic mugs on a wooden tray that was carved by Amara Indians like herself. She immediately took up post next to the coffee pot as though awaiting my command, but Perez proceeded to pour his own coffee unmindful of her. What poor manners, I thought.

"It certainly is about your son," Perez said, slowly drawing the steaming liquid to his lips. "In fact, this is quite serious Senor Torres. Eduardo was involved in a devastating car crash. It is a miracle he is still alive!"

I heard a dreadful ringing in my ears, and the room seemed to revolve drunkenly around me, the coffee pot, the fields, the crucifix, the cups, everything including Perez and Beatrice. I made an attempt to stand, but my legs buckled and inadvertently I knocked over the coffee pot and it fell with a metallic clatter and a hiss. I heard Beatrice scream, though my eyes were fixed on the dark liquid that oozed out to of the pot to leave an ominous stain on the rug, before settling into the crevices of the cold red tiles of the floor. It was Perez's steady hand that guided me back to my chair, and next thing I knew Beatrice was on the floor with rags and a bucket cleaning.

"I'm sorry," Perez said soothingly, "This is the worst part of my job, being the bearer of bad news."

"Thanks," I said hastily, "But I must see my son before…" I couldn't bring myself to finish the sentence, for I couldn't face the consequences, and I shut my jaw and bit down to prevent moisture from spilling from my eyes. Then Beatrice, ever vigilant, produced a small tumbler of brandy. The brandy stung my lips and tasted as harsh as the news I had just heard, though it slid easily down my throat. But suddenly I was jolted when a voice boomed from the top of the stairs.

"What's happening in this house?"

It was my father Rinaldo Torres, he must have heard the clatter and Beatrice's scream, and he was standing ramrod on the wide stair. His smooth face belied his eighty years, though his hair was thick and silver.

Inspector Perez rose from his chair, and with an outstretched hand went to the bottom of the stairs in the living-room to address the old man. His voice was soft and reassuring, but there was no putting out the fire in my father's eyes. It was a fire that even I at my age forty one could not easily quench. It was no surprise that the next thing I heard was bellowing,

"Eduardo is made of the same steel that I am. He will be well in no time!"

I hastily crossed the floor and it surprised me to see that my father's pale fingers looked clammy as they trembled against the dark mahogany banister.

"Pappa lets go to see him," I said urgently, but my father ignored me and brushed past with watery eyes as he unhooked his suit jacket from a peg beside the front door. And although it was unseasonably hot in San Miguel city, I too felt a chill in the air.

****

I should not have seen Eduardo the way he was in that hospital. He was pale and broken, and his swollen limbs were swathed in bandages and his beautiful eyes encircled in dark pouches. Yet his skin was translucent as though already seeking companionship with death. Only a wayward strand of his dark hair that tickled his cheek reminded me of the Eduardo I knew.

I held my emotions in check, though I felt hot bile rise in my throat, and I was fearful of alarming Eduardo as he had alarmed me. But my father placed a cool hand on Eduardo's forehead, and held me close with his other, "My sons," he said raspily, and I felt him quiver, but managed to stop him before he collapsed. Just then, Eduardo's eyes blinked open, bloodshot and yellowed.

"Father" he moaned

"Hush" I replied, trying to spare him further hurt.

"Father," he repeated, "I love you."

I gripped him with my free hand and squeezed back tears. "You're my beloved." I said

But even as I spoke I could feel my own father limp and wasted leaning against me for support.

"Grandfather," Eduardo wheezed, "I've let you down."

Eduardo died peacefully that evening, and my father suffered a stroke. I alone took charge of funeral arrangements, and my beloved son was buried in an inner city cemetery. How often he must have passed that place without thought of finally resting there. His funeral was well attended, it seemed as though the whole city was there, all the daring young men, and the strapping girls mourned the loss of his arms around them. Children came too, for they all knew and loved Eduardo. The old were there, for Eduardo knew them all by name, and knew their ailments, and their tears, and he knew the old widow who spoke of his grandfather as her first love.

"What a waste, what a waste," an unknown beggar woman sighed, clutching her saddened children against her bosom as Eduardo's coffin passed her by, his face iridescent with light like an angel.

My father Rinaldo who was confined to the hospital woke up as if from a deep sleep a day or two after the funeral. I was fortunate to have been sitting beside his bed when his eyes shot open.

"Sebastino," he said shakily, "Sebastino, I'm alive."

And with slow but deliberate motions he tried to lift himself out of the bed.

"Cuidado Pappa" I said, "Careful, your doctor feels you've had a close brush with death."

"What do doctors know?" he said raspily, "I'm not dying, I feel electricity in all the fibers of my body. Doctors condemn us to death long before we are ready. I'm not ready to die! There's not a woman in San Miguel who has not known my caress and even now my loins ache for female companionship."

"Pappa, take it easy." I pleaded seeing his face redden.

"Send the car round!" he hissed, "Tell Eduardo to buy a jug of wine, and we will drive down the main street together and feast on the sight of women. Where the hell is Eduardo anyway? He should be home by this time. And what's this place with all this white around me? White sheets, white walls, even the women are in white. Where the hell am I?"

"Pappa," I cried, "Cuidado, your blood pressure will go up!"

"Nonsense!" he shouted, "A good woman and good wine can cure that."

The next time my father woke up, he was more rational, more restrained, yet more childlike, and full of confession.

"Don't call the priest." he whispered, "I don't want him to know my sins, and I don't want him to know that these past twenty years I have not been wild, and have not even had a woman. San Miguel would be disappointed in me."

I couldn't help but smile, and wonder at the many times I had turned a blind eye when lights had gone off far too early in the servants quarters, and I had imagined him there in Beatrice's arms.

"What about Beatrice?" I heard myself ask, before I could stop myself.

"Where the hell is Eduardo?" he suddenly bellowed, "Ask him, for he's the one who fell in love beneath his station. He didn't want to be as haunted as you are by love lost, so he kept up the charade of being in love with every other woman but Beatrice, though she lives in his heart. Bring Eduardo to me, I'll tell him to confess. Where the hell is he?"

My father proceeded to beat his fists violently against the wall beside his bed, and the sound of it brought two nurses running. I was ushered out of his room, but I could hear his hacking cough and his heavy breathing even from out in the hallway becoming heavy and urgent. And I heard when it all went quiet, and somehow I knew that my father had passed on.

I sat in quiet in the hospital chapel, unable to comprehend the reason for recent events, for I had often heard it said that God has a reason for everything. But I could make no sense of things. After what seemed like hours, I finally left the hospital and stepped out into fresh air. I felt like a fish drowning in air as I walked briskly past open air markets where Indian women in bowler hats sold fresh fish, fruit, and house-wares as well as paraphernalia for creating magic potions and spells for sorcery.

I crossed over the busy street on impulse, stopping momentarily to glance at the distant mountains that rose into the clear blue sky, and I bent my head once more in prayer for the souls of my father and my boy. Strangely enough, my feet led me to the inner city cemetery where Eduardo lay, perhaps because it is a place of peace and tranquility. Huge monuments obscure the city beyond its wall, bird song and butterflies linger there, and blossoming shrubs in the warm air perfume the atmosphere.

I was about to make my way to Eduardo's resting place, when something intangible stopped me. I stood perfectly still beside an unusually large statue of an angel of resurrection, and I was shielded by its gigantic wings. Just up ahead I made out the figure of a woman with her back to me kneeling beside Eduardo's grave. She couldn't see me, but she was swathed in a black mantilla. Her face seemed golden though darkened by her tears. Then I noticed the wonderful ripe roundness of her belly. It looked as soft as the mound of roses she had placed upon my son's grave.

When she turned to leave, I clutched my heart realizing that it was Beatrice the Indian servant girl, for she had let her mantilla fall around her shoulders, and it let loose her long black hair. Her hair moved like pampas as it framed her beautiful face, a face I had not taken time to notice while she was in my employ.

She did not see me as she walked silently amongst the graves. She did not know about my explosion of tears, or see when I turned away to face a long night until morning.

****

Chapter 2

Long Journey

I left the cemetery bathed in tears of shame and hope, and with sadness that a grandchild of mine would be born into illicit poverty. Surely such a fate was unbearable. I swathed my face in a white handkerchief and longed for advice from the father I had so recently lost, and had been remote from. But my tears resisted the white harness and flowed freely. I walked for several blocks amongst city monuments, office edifices, market squares and then the slums. Murmurings in my mind grew loud and escalated as I told myself to find the girl who carried my son's seed, though I battled with myself resisting.

Two days later I was not the sole mourner at my father's funeral, for though he had outlived his close friends, a few women came to wish him a fond farewell, but it was I alone who walked with him and laid him to rest. After the service, my feet led me to the terraced tumbledown villages where the mountain Indians dwelled, and I made haste to find her, though not knowing where in the landscape of rundown dilapidation she might be.

In the end, I gave up hope even as village children nipped and tugged at my heels demanding handouts, threatening to steal.

My father, my precious father would have known exactly what to do, he would have given them the few sticks of gum I carried, but I ignoramus that I am, fled with a chorus of beggar children's voices loud in my ears. Were it not for an old washer woman who spoke sharply to them, I might have been trampled and robbed on the cool mountainside that overlooked the city. "Who are you?" the woman demanded sidling up to me with her wrinkled eyes and basket of laundry; as the children scattered,

I told her my name, and she shook her head in despair, a knowing look in her eyes. "She refuses to give up the child." was all she said; standing ramrod, and I knew exactly what she knew. "She will not bend" the woman added, "Her lineage is from the same stubborn tree as mine, the same proud stock."

"So you're related?" I asked.

"Are the llamas on the mountainside one family?" she coyly replied, and I lowered my eyes from knowing.

"I just want to talk with her." I said, seeing the dark cavern of her toothless mouth, and the way her mouth became like a rosebud as she spoke, and I realized that words were my only weapon. "My son might have loved her, had he known."

"Bullshit!" the woman fired back, "your son probably sired a stream of children from here to Santiago! You aristocrats live only for your own pleasuring, not for the long haul like us. See those shacks behind us? They're all built from broken hearts..."

I felt shame for Eduardo's foolishness and ashamed of myself. I was about to wander off, when the woman's hand sharp as a claw stopped me. "She is leaving," she said urgently,

"She wants to make a better life in America."

"When is she going?"

"A week from today, she will take a train to Mexico."

"And from there?"

"From there she will find an encampment where with the help of human smugglers she will wait for a train to take her out of the country up through New Mexico and beyond."

"It could be dangerous."

"What's more dangerous than sleeping with a rich man's son? Beatrice will risk everything for the child, no one can stop her."

"But I can give her money… Set her up in a home…."

"Stupid man, just as I said, you aristocrats bah! What about dignity! She'll refuse you just like I would."

"But such trains are nothing but danger, especially to a woman in her condition."

"She knows the risks; she is travelling with an old friend."

"Who?"

"Maria Soarez a relative of mine."

"Tell me where and when is her train leaving from and I will pray that the Blessed Lady protects her."

****

In the end, I decided to assist the Blessed Lady, and with some roundabout inquiries managed to cover both train fares and guaranteed seats for the two women. My generosity did not go unnoticed. It was met with suspicion by the station clerks whom I advised to refund the women's monies, using what ever excuses they could come up with, without mentioning me.

To her credit, Beatrice put up a fight at the station. But the clerks finally managed to convince her that for the sake of her child, they were providing her with seats that had become available as a result of a last minute cancellation. So there was no sign of suspicion in her dark eyes when her payment was returned. I disguised in the garb of a peasant watched and smiled.

Both women wore broad hats that effectively hid half their faces, though not even that intrusion could hide their beauty. I was taken aback; Maria Suarez's features matched Beatrice's like a twin, the long dark hair, healthy chests and fine figure. 'Same stock' I repeated to myself as the women swung themselves aboard the train, Beatrice as agile as her companion. Careful, I whispered to myself, careful don't take chances with Eduardo's child.

It must have been my thoughts of the child that spurred me, because all of a sudden, I found myself rushing back over to the station clerk and purchasing a ticket for myself. It wasn't a moment too soon for the train was pulling out as I hastily clambered aboard, with my wallet strapped to my chest under my shabby shirt. "This is for you Eduardo." I mumbled to myself as I settled into a seat one carriage behind the women. But I was hungry, and thus somewhat regretful of my spontanaety. Looking around I saw that the carriages were all full, and that people had brought their own food aboard.

It wasn't long before the next stop where vendors surrounded the train selling tortillas, cane juice, coffee and empanadas and fried plantains. But trying to appear frugal, I bought only one tortilla, which I carefully checked for cleanliness and greasiness, while managing to burn my fingers on the hot food. There were no plates, no napkins, only a piece of banana leaf. I couldn't help but wonder if Beatrice and her companion had eaten. How I wanted to watch them, but avoiding suspicion I kept to myself and ate in silence my bandana pulled low over my eyebrows.

I must have dozed off, but I awoke to the wild swaying motion of the train as it chased through the thick jungle unmindful. The interior of the train was dark though it was still daylight, and I realized that it was so because so many of us were aboard, and some people were even dangerously clinging to the outside of the vehicle. Not a chink of light came in at the windows and worst of all; I could no longer see Beatrice or Maria if I wanted to. Mother Mary protect them I whispered, are they alright I wondered; though I daren't desert my seat.

I pressed up close against the widow and somehow managed to glimpse the jungle outside, it was denser than I had expected, and it seemed to swallow us up in one gulp. Mother Mary pray for us I whispered as we sped on,

Hours passed, some of the people who had been clinging to the train, seemed to have fallen away into the bush, but more than likely they must have been beaten off with the stout clubs of train officials. We crashed through dark foliage that blocked out the sun, and our hot bodies, eager and illicit, brushed against each other in the dimness as I clung to my chest guarding my wallet. Hours and hours went by and the unforgiving jungle would not let go it's stranglehold, as the train serpent-like slid in and out of mountainous crevices, tunnels and lonely stretches of unrelenting wilderness. 'Lord deliver us' I sighed, as the train finally slowed, and clanked to a halt. The babble of voices around me ceased and a man in a shabby uniform came down the isle ringing a loud bell. "We're at the encampment." he announced, and all around me there was a flurry of activity, live chickens in cages were squawking, and suckling pigs squealing as bags, bundles, sacks and parcels were removed from the floor and the shelves, and it was I alone who had nothing to carry except my pounding heart, and my hopeful soul.

I saw an old man struggling with a cloth bag, and I helped him carry it off the train, his toothy grin was my reward. Once on the ground he shook my hand, "Thanks, I'm Jose he smiled, "My daughter Cornelia will help me from here on." he said, nodding at the handsome woman two steps behind him.

I wanted to immediately wanderer off to find Beatrice, but I was obliged to share a coffee from a tin cup with the old man and his daughter. All the while, my eyes were on our surroundings. We seemed to have found a cesspool of humanity, naked children ran in and out of the bushes, ragged barefoot men hauled wood for a fire, and women with skirts hitched up boiled clothes over one fire and stirred a large soup cauldron on another. The jungle floor was littered with garbage, and makeshift hammocks dotted the tree branches. Like a beehive, it would seem that everyone had found work to do. As the women fired words at one another, I saw that Beatrice was assigned duty at the soup cauldron. Other women from the train were assigned to set up bedding, while others were sent to find edibles in the bush. "Cuidado" I sighed, "Cuidado."

I was assigned to help to collect and boil dirty laundry, in order to keep ticks and lice down, and that night I slept under a tree. It rained that first night, but I was sheltered. By day two I was unrecognizable, what with mud and dirt on my clothes and skin, as well as swellings from tick bites. "How long will we be here?" I asked a young man, who was eerily reminiscent of Eduardo. "The guides are coming today." he replied, "Those of us who can pay, can choose the best of them; otherwise one has to take your own chances. But the train that will smuggle us to the border will pass through here tomorrow night."

"Is this one of its stops?"

"It doesn't stop…you have to hop on with the help of your guide."

"Good Lord, that's brutal."

"It is our one chance,"

"I suppose you are right…What's your name?"

"Julio"

I didn't see Maria until the last moment, she was sent to help to collect the last of the sun dried clothing with a team of us, but she looked spent, dark circles brooded under her eyes, "Let me help," I said, "I'm acquainted with a relative of yours,"

"Who do you know old man?" she replied with a sharp tongue.

"It doesn't matter, just let me help. You'll need strength for the rest of the journey."

She reluctantly handed me her load and accepted my assistance before admitting that she needed rest. "Is the other woman with you alright?" I ventured.

"Morning sickness is taking its toll." she replied as though it was obvious. .

"Poor thing, pregnancy can be rough." I said turning away reluctantly. "I'll say a prayer for her."

"Thanks."

"By the way the guides are coming soon. Are you hiring one?"

"With what money old man?" she retorted before walking away purposefully, never once looking back, proud and dignified.

At noon the guards came to negotiate, there were two dozen of them, all lithe of frame and nimble. Transactions were conducted in the interior of a makeshift tent. No one knew who was paying or who was declaring their right to take chances. I knew I was in good shape, but could I jump trains?

In the end I hired a guide, but most troubling was the fact that Beatrice might not be able to hire one. My guide said his name was Oliver, but who knew, since none of us used our real names; mine was Frederick. I spoke with Oliver far longer than was allowed.

That afternoon, chickens were slaughtered, and soup made. I paid the equivalent of five dollars for a bowl feeling that I would be well nourished without having to resort to the usual yams, potatoes and cassava. My eyes searched the campsite for Beatrice and Maria, but they were no where to be seen, and who knew when the train would be arriving. I was filthy dirty, no wonder Maria thought I was an old man, perhaps even a beggar. Thank goodness I still had my wallet and my dignity.

I was sitting alone near the encampment when I heard leaves rustling, and Jose joined me. "Hola," he said, "Good luck on your journey; this is as far as I'll be going."

"Is that so?"

"Yes, my daughter will send for me when she gets to America. She is strong and ambitious and intelligent."

"I see."

"You take care. Hope you find what you are looking for."

"Thanks, I hope so too.

I smiled with gratitude as the old man limped away, though I couldn't help but wonder if he would even make it to America.

Then all of a sudden, I heard an awful rumbling, it was a train approaching over the mountain, so I hurried back to the camp. Everyone was rushing about with their belongings as the guards rounded us up. We waited expectantly as the train approached. It was a cargo train and it deliberately slowed as it drew abreast of the camp. The guards immediately sprung into action hoisting up women and children; then I jumped on and held on fast with all my strength as the motor purred and pulled beneath me. I watched the loading of human cargo as the wheels clacked and clanged near to me, whispering certain death, and that was when I saw Oliver. He mounted the moving vehicle as though accustomed to the risk, with Beatrice held fast in one strong arm. I sighed with relief; he had kept his word.

The train charged on as the strongest of us clambered up to its roof, and that was when I saw Cornelia. The train was bucking and shaking though her strong hands held fast. How wild and beautiful she seemed with her hair the colour of pure honey rising and falling in the breeze, but it was her dark doe-like eyes that held me. "Hola" I said, as I pulled myself up alongside her. "Cuidado." We both laughed as our muscles strained against the machinery. "I cannot help but be careful," she grinned, "Otherwise I'd easily slip off."

I found some comfort in her companionship, and it wasn't until an hour later before I again glimpsed Beatrice. She was held fast in Oliver's firm grip alongside other travelers on top of a car parts carriage. As for Maria, it was with great surprise that I finally saw her. She was hanging precariously to the side of the train, and she was trying desperately to gain footing to the roof. Without thought to my own safety, I inched my way to where she was with the wind howling and longing to claim me as its first victim. "Give me your hand.' I shouted as I crawled nearer. I saw fear in her eyes, as she stared back at me, yet in the end she chose to trust me as I grabbed her. I held her firmly and pulled with all my might, though it seemed she swung at the side of the train like a rag doll. "Brace yourself!" I shouted, "We are coming up to a tunnel."

There must have been a miracle available that day, for when next I tugged and pulled her, Maria was hoisted up beside me inside the pitch-black tunnel. "Stay still!" I hissed, "We should be out of here soon." But despite my encouraging words, all I could see ahead was sheer blackness and it was clammy, as the engine's noise became more acute than ever.

"Thanks" I heard Maria whisper close to my ear. "You saved me."

"Nothing of the sort," I replied, "I was just being of assistance."

Finally, we came back out into the sunlight, I had to shade my eyes, and only then did I see that Cornelia had joined us. "I was thinking that perhaps you needed help." she said, and I saw that her muscled arms were strong and capable. "But Senior, you're far stronger than I suspected."

"You're not an old man, are you?" said Maria sounding somewhat suspicious as she stared at me with fresh eyes. But how could I tell her that I was the youngish grandfather of Beatrice's unborn child. In the condition that I was in, who would have believed I was Eduardo's pampered well to do father, wasn't I covered in mud and rags with a crusty beard coming in? My only reply to Maria's question was a smile.

That evening, the two women and I shared a few guavas and some fresh green peas that Cornelia had brought along. Maria slipped off her shoulder bag to present us with two ripe mangoes which Cornelia cut up with a pen knife for us to share. As I feasted, I saw that in the distance Beatrice was eating what looked like a slice of papaya. Good, I thought to myself, papaya is good for the digestion; we can't have her suffering an upset stomach just now. It also confirmed that as instructed Oliver had provided for her, I was glad since I had paid him well.

Our throats felt parched as the sun burned overhead, but at sunset, we relished the descent of the cool evening, dreaming of long droughts of water. None of us had had a chance to bring water. But in any case, in exchange for guavas, some travelers near us were kind enough to offer each of us a sip of cold coffee from a thermos. The drink was bitter but most welcomed.

It was another day's journey with a diet of fruit and sips of coffee before the jungle eventually spat us out and the train seemed exposed not only to the elements but to those who patrolled territories near the border. That afternoon a woman lost her footing and fell from the train and perished, and I couldn't help but be grateful that it wasn't Beatrice. As the day wore on people became both restless and fearful, and they began jumping off the train to begin the next leg of the journey. At first, they jumped two at a time but then it escalated. All the while I kept my eyes on Oliver awaiting his signal, then there it was, he waved a yellow handkerchief, and jumped with Beatrice in his arms, as others followed. My heart stopped as I watched them, Beatrice, the baby and Oliver. Watch over them dear God I prayed, and then all too soon it was me, Maria and Cornelia rolling down a grassy mound where we landed in a heap as the train sped on. Unfortunately, Maria landed badly and twisted her ankle.

"I wonder if it's sprained." I said, as I grasped her slim ankle in my hands and examined it.

"It will be alright," she protested, as she pulled her leg away and struggled to her feet. "Maria, you're walking like my father." Cornelia said sounding concerned, "He has a very bad limp you know."

Before I could say a word, Oliver came hurrying towards us. "There's a place near here that's not patrolled. I'll take you across the border there. After a mile or so you can hook up with my friend Jeremy. I've written instructions as to how to find him. He will take you the rest of the way. But before we set out Beatrice will need to rest. She has not slept in days."

"Is she alright?" Maria asked. "Yes, she is." Oliver replied, "She was in my care, wasn't she? The baby's good too. Beatrice ate well, she had cassava cakes, papaya and cane juice. But now we all have to be careful. We have to cross arid land. Don't worry, I brought water, we'll fill another bottle from a stream along the way."

"Are you sure it is not patrolled there?" I asked, looking around furtively and alerted to every sound.

"I'm certain. Don't forget I've made this same journey several times before. But if by chance there is a helicopter, I will cover us all with camouflage cloth if we can't find shelter. Understood?"

"Perfectly Oliver, now take us to Beatrice."

We found Beatrice curled into a ball asleep under a tree. "She's exhausted," Cornelia sighed, "Here, let me cover her with my poncho."

While Beatrice slept, Oliver took me aside and whispered. "It is dangerous out there." he confided, "Because even though we will be in United States territory, we might as well still be in Latin America. There are trackers, not with dogs, but with helicopters. The women will have to trust our judgment, yours as a matter of fact."

"But I know nothing about survival, and helicopters and where to hide."

"You will have to learn. This could be life and death."

"Don't speak to me of death," I said softly, "It has visited my heart too many times lately."

When Beatrice awoke, she wet her lips on a sip of water, but refused to deprive us of the precious drink we would need later. "I seem to know you." she said, shooting me with a glance.

"I'm from the camp, you saw me there. It is not likely that you'd know me."

"Never the less, you remind me of someone, I wish I could remember who."

Thank God for the beard and my scruffy appearance, I thought, as Oliver leaned closer to listen.

"Up ahead is a corn-patch." he said under his breath, "It's wild corn, just help yourself, and try to make it last. We have to eat it raw though."

Each of us took some corn, and it filled Maria's shoulder bag and I offered to carry the load. It was a good walk before we came upon the stream Oliver had mentioned. We were parched and unable to resist its seduction, se we waded in then drank our fill. There were snails and water-spiders in the shallows, but none of us seemed to care. Cornelia scrubbed her face until her skin glowed pink then she dangled her beautiful hair in the water and shook out the wet accumulated dirt and dust, and the other women followed. I didn't dare wash for fear my true identity would be revealed. It was only when we were standing there in the water that I noticed that Maria's ankle had swollen to twice its size. "Are you alright?" I asked, but she brushed off my question, insisting that she was fine,

"I'll be leaving you here." Oliver said, "Don't forget to keep to the trees, and don't under any circumstance deviate from my written instructions. If all goes well, it should be a day's walk. My friend Jeremy will meet you at the appointed place. I called him on my cell."

I was about to question him further, but Oliver quickly disappeared into the bush, leaving me in charge.

"He left the water bottles." Cornelia said, coming towards me, "I had a feeling he wasn't going to stay with us and now with Maria's ankle and Beatrice exhausted we are not likely to make it to find help."

"You don't trust me then?" I said hoping she would contradict me, but she smiled softly, "It is not you that I don't trust, it is our circumstances. Something tells me you are a good person, but I can't help but feel that you are hiding something."

I didn't dare answer her, for she was far too astute for my lazy brain. "Come, we have to check on the others," I said, "Maria will need a bandage, but we'll have to use banana leaves and some soft bark to tie it with."

Beatrice was quite concerned when we returned to her, "Maria's in pain," she said, "How's she going to walk all that way?"

"I'm going to bandage her leg. It will ease the swelling."

"Where's Oliver?"

"He left."

"He left! How are we to find this person Jeremy?"

"You'll have to trust me."

Cornelia was kind enough to lend me a hand as I bounded Maria's ankle, and as we labored together, Beatrice was there watching my every move with suspicion in her eyes. "Are you trained in First Aid?" she asked.

"No, but I had a s… a child."

"You have a child! Why aren't you with your child?"

"My child passed away." I said solemnly. And my answer must have stung her, for I saw when she lowered her eyes, and I heard her faintly whisper, "The father of my child has passed away too.'

I wanted to crush her to me and weep hot tears for Eduardo, but instead I went to collect the shoulder bag pretending as though I was devoid of emotion. "We'd better get going," I said, "darkness is coming. You alright Maria? You could lean on me."

"I'll be fine." she shot back as she grabbed Cornelia's arm.

You alright Beatrice? Just say the word."

"I'm ok."

Chapter 3

A Long Night

We were like insects in the night, moving swiftly under the sparkling stars, though of course my ears were sharply alert for the sounds of helicopters, For the first hour we were fine, and I began to feel a rush of confidence even a touch of pride, from my being flanked by three beautiful women on a starry night. This must have been how it was for Eduardo I thought, though he would have been well scrubbed and fresh smelling had it been him.

The tree-line thinned out and the land, even at night appeared raw, exposed and bare, much like a desert devoid even of pampas

"Let's stop and have some corn." I said as we approached a lone clump of trees. "We could rest a moment and rest out backs. It doesn't seem there will be too many more trees this size up ahead,"

"What ever you think is best." Beatrice sighed hardly disguising the tiredness that had come over her.

I took out two ears of corn from the shoulder bag, and Cornelia handed me a penknife "You might want to shave off some of the corn," she said, "We'll have to be frugal." "Thanks" I replied as I scraped off corn for each of us with the knife. But before returning the instrument, as a precaution I hacked away, and managed to cut down some of the lower tree branches. "Why are you doing that?" Maria asked, and I was about to reply when we all heard the unmistakable sound of an approaching helicopter. "Lie down!" I commanded, and the women immediately fell to the ground in a heap. "I'm going to cover you over with branches; then I'll crawl under to join you.

The women remained perfectly still as I quickly covered them, and dragged a large leafy branch over myself. Too bad we don't have Oliver's camouflage cloth I thought. But we all remained still as the helicopter passed over twice with search lights beaming down. None of us dared even breath until finally it darted off into the black sky.

"Everyone okay?" I said nervously, knowing that if the helicopter had been any closer it would have blown off the flimsy branches.

"You saved us," Cornelia smiled, wiping her eyes, "you and those branches…Thanks, and to think I thought you were foolishly going to make a fire for the corn."

We all laughed nervously as I shared the corn amongst us.

After a quick rest, we walked for three hours sipping water as we traveled. Then finally we slept fitfully out in the open and awoke with the sun to find ourselves still in the desert.

"Did we walk in a circle?" Beatrice asked. "Not likely" I replied, "There's a line of trees ahead of us, about an hour's walk.

The walk was brutal, the landscape was hilly, but offered no shade as the sun bore down on us unrepentantly and our water was running low. My worst fear was to be caught out in the open before we reached safety and shelter. It was an hour and a half before we arrived at the trees thirsty and bedraggled. There was no water insight except for that which had collected in a hollow stump. "Wet your lips but don't drink." I said, "There has to be water here with all this vegetation." We followed the tree-line for a good twenty minutes before we suddenly came upon a small stream. We were so parched and exhausted we drank our fill, and replenished the water bottles even as the women again ladled water over each others head. I did not object when they included me in their game, although all of a sudden Beatrice, who had gone to find a tree to rest against, screamed. "My water broke!"

I was filled with a barrage of emotions, delight at the impending coming of my grandchild and fear from not knowing what to do concerning the birthing. It took me a while to get my bearings, but when it kicked in, I assured Beatrice she would be alright even as Cornelia removed her own petticoat and told her to lie on it. Poor Beatrice moaned for about an hour and I, though feeling helpless patted her forehead reassuringly trying to remain calm. Then suddenly Maria hissed, "Someone's coming."

Fear washed over me as an all terrain van came speeding towards us. It is all over I thought even as Beatrice moaned louder despite the nearness of the two women crouched beside her. We joined hands and waited, only to hear footfalls crashing through the foliage. It felt like the longest ten minutes of my life. I braced myself and couldn't help but feel akin to a wild lion protecting its herd, as I glanced up jaws clenched.

"Hi it's Jeremy." A friendly voice said in Spanish, and I looked up to see a tall well built Caucasian man with a wide grin. "I'm Jeremy Grant from Canada. I'm here to collect the tomato pickers for the farm in Leamington Ontario. But hey, what's happening here?"

"This young lady Beatrice is about to give birth," I said nervously.

"Oh my God...Well let me get a blanket from the van and a first aid kit just in case we'll need to disinfect anything, Who's in charge?"

"Me."

"Any experience with childbirth"

"No."

"Then let me take over, okay? I've some experience. You'll have to trust me now young lady, try to relax, the pain will come in waves, but you look strong enough to ride it out. The pain's coming again isn't it?

Beatrice nodded and gripped my hand, perhaps because I was closest.

"Yes, it hurts so bad I want to scream."

"Then scream, and if you feel like pushing grab on to someone and push as hard as you can. I will be right back." said Jeremy with a toss of his head, and by the time he returned with the blanket and the first aid supplies, Beatrice was racked in pain squirming and moaning.

I felt almost heady with excitement as hope once again filled my very veins. Imagine I was to be witness to my own grandchild's birth. O Eduardo, my beloved Eduardo, if only you could have been here. My heart pounded like a drum as Beatrice held fast to me muttering and whaling.

In less than half an hour the baby was born, pink and robust. Jeremy had guided it out, and Cornelia cut the umbilical cord with scissors from the first aid kit, and Maria almost fainted.

"It's a boy!" I cried out with gusto, unable to contain my exuberance or hold back tears for the boy was as beautiful as Eduardo and as radiant. Cornelia joyfully laughed a throaty laugh as Maria helped to nestle the child in the blanket beside Beatrice. "What are you going to call him?" she coaxed.

'I wan to name him after his father."

"What's his father's name?" Jeremy asked, beaming with pride.

"It was Eduardo. We loved each other very much. But we were like Romeo and Juliet, his middle names will be Romeo Sebastino. I'll not forget my love."

"But why Sebastino?" Cornelia asked, but Beatrice didn't answer she snuggled closer to the child and continued nursing him under the blanket.

****

For the sake of Beatrice and the baby we remained in that oasis for two days, and the van quickly began to feel like home for Jeremy had stocked it well with supplies such as juice, pop, water and canned meats and vegetables, and fortunately for Beatrice there were clean rags that were quickly fashioned into diapers.

"We have to get to a store." Jeremy said solemnly, "The baby will need clothes and proper diapers...but it will be a day's drive at least."

"We set out early the following morning chasing the sun across the barren desert until finally we came to a highway.

"I have fake ID for everyone but the baby." Jeremy said, "So when we get to the Canadian Border, we'll have to hide him."

I had paid Oliver well, and it was clear to see that Jeremy too had come through with his end of the bargain. As I glanced over at Beatrice, I could see the horror of endless negative possibilities in her eyes, "Where will we hide him?" she asked clutching the baby tighter to her breast.

"There's an opening under my seat just the right size."

"Won't it cry?"

"Not after a tiny sip of beer."

"Are you sure my baby will be alright?"

"Positive."

"But beer, do we have to use beer?"

"Yes."

"I'm so afraid for my baby, but if you're sure..."

The desert was brutal; the sun boiled down on the van and practically baked us. We drove until I was exhausted. I wondered how Jeremy kept his sanity and how Beatrice kept the baby from disturbing us all. Maria laid her head on the open window and sang a love song and we all joined in the chorus, all except for Jeremy who kept concentrating on his surroundings. He was right too, for the highway cut through precarious regions. We eventually stopped for cool water from a swiftly moving river, and all of us waded in to wash off our accumulated sweat. And when Cornelia immersed her hair in the water, she put me in mind of an angel, she was that beautiful!

"Anyone feel like eating Barbeque?" Jeremy asked as we made our way back to shore, "My girlfriend Montrice and her family usually have a meal waiting for me and my van loads. They're a close-knit black family, lots of good food and good loving."

"Really!" I said out loud hoping Jeremy did not pick up on the surprise in my voice when I learned his girlfriend was black. "Where does she live anyway?" I said conversationally.

"She's right here in Texas. She refuses to relocate to Canada though we have two kids. She says Texas has everything she needs. Her house is about twenty miles from here. I'll call her on my cell."

****

When we arrived at Montrice's house there was already a crowd in the large back yard. It was clear that a party was in full swing. A chubby black woman ran out to greet us, it was Montrice. "Welcome to Texas" she said in Spanish, and it made us feel right at home. She threw back her head and laughed and tugged at two young mulatto children with blondish hair. "These are ours she grinned, "They're happy to see their daddy home, aren't they Jeremy honey?"

All around us was a sea of friendly black faces, as we enjoyed chicken ribs and macaroni and potato salads, and we began to feel even more at home. Maria mingled with the crowd and with her halting English seemed to make friends easily. But shy Beatrice was amazed by it all, and I saw when Montrice handed her a bundle of baby clothes and she seemed quite taken aback. "No point me keeping these anymore,' Montrice said, "Jeremy and me have all the children we need, just look at how sweet they are."

"Thank you, Ma'am, thank you Ma'am" Beatrice spluttered bowled over by the generosity, and I saw tears escape her sad eyes. "Thanks so much, you and Jeremy are the best."

Later that afternoon Jeremy pulled me aside, "I bet you're wondering why I don't settle down here with Montrice. The truth is this place is racist, it would be hard for us here as a couple. Canada is different, but Montrice would hate the winters, so as a compromise I come to see her every chance I get. I love her very much."

"Love is a strange thing." I said under my breath noticing that Cornelia was standing not too far off from us.

Later still, the women all helped with the washing up while some of the older men went to smoke on the verandah. I was delighted to speak a little English but being a nonsmoker, I went to sit with some men around my age in the living-room. I found myself without naming names, talking about Eduardo and my father. "There is no love like a father for his son." I said hoping I wasn't offending anyone. But just then Cornelia and Beatrice passed through the room and I held my tongue. I couldn't take my eyes off them and the baby, and I knew I was in love.

That night Montrice and Jeremy slept together in one of the bedrooms while the rest of us camped in the living room. Maria who had fallen into conversation with one of the young men known as Fitzroy, was the last to settle in.

In the morning after I washed, I asked to use the phone. My beard had grow in, and I was sure that even my lawyer whom I called in San Miguel, would not have recognized me if he could have seen me. Afterwards we were all taken by complete surprise when Maria announced that she had decided to stay in Texas. I knew immediately that her decision had nothing to do with her recently injured ankle, so it must be something to do with young Fitzroy. "I'm sorry Beatrice," she said, "But I see a good opportunity here to start a new life." But the rest of us without saying so out loud had already decided to continue on to Canada with Jeremy.

That morning with much thanksgiving to Montrice and her family, we once more set out on the road, this time without Maria, and headed for Louisiana. The two women fell asleep in the back of the van almost immediately, and I sat up front with Jeremy.

"So, what did you think of them, my Texas family I mean?" Jeremy asked with a smile in his jaw

"They were wonderful." I replied.

"I know," said Jeremy, "And that is why last night as I made love to Montrice I finally had her agree to come and live part of the year in Toronto, so we can be together more often. God, I love that woman. Next time I pass through Texas, she and the kids will be leaving with me."

"How'd you meet her anyway?"

"She used to help to smuggle families into the States. But now she's resigned to looking after her own family. She adores me you know. She's a journalist, she writes for a Black focused magazine."

"What a lucky man you are, she's wonderful in everyway isn't she?"

"Yes she is, but by the way, which of these women are you in love with, Beatrice or Cornelia? My guess is it is Beatrice the baby seems to mean a lot to you."

"Hush, I'm not in love with any of them…I'm just fascinated with the baby."

"Is that because you lost your son?"

"Yes, I suppose so, since the baby reminds me of him. By the way, what do you know about Fitzroy? I'm sure Maria decided to stay because of him."

"I've known Fitz for a long time. He works in a vegetable store. He lost both his parents when he was quite young. He's a good lad, seems to have made something of himself. He lives with a disabled Aunt. Maria will like it there, they're good people. But what do you know of Maria?"

"Absolutely nothing, we just met, but she seems strong. Beatrice knows her."

"What do you know about Beatrice?"
"Nothing to tell the truth."
"And Cornelia?"
"The same big nothing."
"Why do I get the feeling that you'd like to know them better?"

****

With Jeremy as the only driver it took us days to travel roads through Louisiana, Mississippi, Alabama, Georgia, the Carolinas, Virginia, Pennsylvania and finally New York State. Because of the baby we stopped often for rests, diaper changes and for us to use restrooms facilities and to buy food and gas. I had never imagined that outside of San Miguel there were such extremes of poverty especially amongst the hoards of blacks visible in most of these States. There were times we didn't feel entirely safe, since there seemed to be an underlying hostility towards us as Hispanics, and that is why Jeremy chose back roads even though he knew it would make the journey much longer.

Chapter 4

On to Canada

When we arrived at the Canadian Border we were exhausted, and even the baby was asleep in the false bottom of Jeremy's seat. Jeremy acted as our spokesperson. He told the guard we were tomato pickers he was transporting to a farm in Canada, and he showed our fake IDs and papers. The papers were carefully scrutinized then finally met with approval; though luckily, we were not interrogated. We waited fifteen nervous minutes with the baby beginning to rouse from sleep, and my heart stopped beating. Beatrice must have wanted nothing more than to nurse him, but that would have compromised us all, but then a miracle occurred. The guard, after some deliberation decided not to search the van. Everything must have seemed legitimate, and he waved us on. What a relief it was, that in a matter of moments we were speeding down a Canadian highway and breathing freely again.

Hours later we arrived in Toronto, and I found myself missing the mountains of home. The city was modern and imposing and seemed to stretch for miles. "There are people from all over the world here." Jeremy said just before he dropped us off at a hostel on Parkside Drive called La Casa: The Spanish Speakers House. We were welcomed by the staff and given access to hot showers and offered small tidy rooms to stay in. The windows of La Casa overlooked the tree-lined street that bordered on to a huge park called High Park. At a glance the lush landscape was reminiscent of the better parts of San Miguel, but then at second glance it was unmistakably Canadian with its tall Maples, with not a palm tree or pampas in sight, but there were lush perennial gardens and three storey homes for families and renters alike all in a row.

Jeremy had more than earned his payment before waving goodbye and going off to his Roncesvalles Ave condo. But before leaving he assured us that he was available if we should need him for anything. Thanks to the staff at La Casa I was able to contact my lawyer and arrange a transfer of funds to Toronto. Beatrice and the baby rarely left their room, perhaps she felt safer there, or she preferred to hide out inside to mourn Eduardo. Therefore ,it was Cornelia and I who were thrown together to explore the park and the neighborhood.

Every Wednesday a doctor came to the hostel to examine the household. We were thankful for the service though Beatrice confessed to him that we were in-fact refugees and that the baby was born on route to Canada. It was that doctor, Doctor Ira Patel who provided the baby with its first set of papers. He also insisted that Beatrice should rest for the next four weeks.

"It is quite pleasant here." Cornelia said one afternoon, "People seem to mind their own business. Anyway I have let my father know that he can stop worrying about me, because I'm being well cared for, and the people at La Casa are even going to help me to find work. My father said that it took so long for me to contact him that he thought I was lost somewhere in the jungle." She laughed.

"Allow me to cover the cost of the call," I said, "I at least owe that to the old man. I liked him the moment I saw him. But did you tell him I am here too?"

"No, I didn't; but what about me, did you like me when you first saw me, or were you somehow hankering after Beatrice? Anyway, there was really no need to tell my father about you. I know exactly what he'd be thinking."

I couldn't help myself, I laughed out loud. "I have no feelings that way for Beatrice. It is her boy that has stolen my heart. And another thing, you should tell your father I'm here, he's a sensible man he'd know I'm a gentleman."

"You might be right, but enough about my father. What I want to know is why has the baby stolen your heart? Isn't he nothing more than a stranger to you?"

"Cornelia I won't say anything else regarding that matter, but baby Eduardo seems to have given me back my life. I recently lost my son and my father."

"Yes, I gathered as much, and I sympathize, but what an unusual man you are, to be so moved by a stranger's child."

"Cornelia, one cannot help who you fall in love with. Just look at Jeremy and Montrice."

"I suppose you're right; one cannot help these things. I myself…oh never mind."

"Never mind what Cornelia?"

Oh, it's nothing really."

It was the warm days of summer and I got to know the park quite well, I even knew its hidden nooks and crannies. But some days I wandered down to the lakeshore imagining myself back in San Miguel, and every now and again I'd imagine the baby there too, and then there was Cornelia. I seem to have harbored her in my thoughts, though these days I chose to spend more time alone.

Then one afternoon the staff at La Casa came to find me to say that Beatrice was not well. It would appear that she was missing home so much that she was making herself ill. Cornelia was not available, since she was out on a job cleaning houses. Therefore, it was I alone who went to speak with Beatrice.

"Hello Beatrice," I said cheerfully, though she looked quite despondent. It almost seemed that she couldn't find it in herself to utter a single word. But that was until I offered to hold the baby. Her eyes lit up and she appeared relieved as she accepted my offer and handed me the baby. I felt the weight of it in my hands and my heart almost burst from the love I felt holding it near.

"What a beautiful boy." I whispered huskily as I held him and watched him breath. Then I searched his tiny face, to see shadows of my own Eduardo, and I was not disappointed.

"I don't want to stay in Canada." Beatrice sighed, "I miss San Miguel like one misses a lover. My lover Eduardo used to come to my room at the back of the house where I worked as a servant. His grandfather always kept watch so that no one would find out about us or disturb us. Eduardo was afraid of disappointing his rich father whom he loved more than anything. Come to think of it, you sort of remind me of him, but he was more officious, though he was as handsome as you. But in any case, I couldn't imagine him doing the things you do, and another thing he never had a beard like you. Do you know Eduardo always said that one day we would find a way to be together, but he didn't know how? In fact, he used to spend his days driving around San Miguel flirting and pretending to be a womanizer, but he always came home to me at the end of the day. What sweet loving we shared before he died in a car crash. I felt like dying too when I heard of his accident. I remember I was in the breakfast room about to serve coffee at the time, but the worst part was I knew I was pregnant with his child and I couldn't say a word about it. So, in the end I left my position at the house before my condition would become common knowledge and bring disgrace to the Torres family. You know how it is at home don't you? But now his child has brought me my greatest pleasure."

I couldn't hold back the tears that welled in my eyes, and I longed to hold Beatrice and comfort her. I wanted to ask her forgiveness and reveal my true identity; but somehow, I held back on any revelations as I reached out and took her hand and kissed it.

As fate would have it, that was the very moment that Cornelia arrived home. She did not flinch or show any emotion as she confronted us. "I'll take the baby for a walk outside." was all she said, though her eyes seemed weary after a hard day's work.

I could barely bring myself to let go of the baby, and it hurt my heart to hand him over.

Then as Cornelia left with the baby, my thoughts were filled with guilt about the kiss she witnessed. I wondered what she might be thinking, but then again there was Beatrice in tears begging me to help her find a way to go back home again. I knew even then that nothing would appease her, though I told her I would try my best to help her.

I remained with her until finally she fell into a fitful sleep sobbing on her bed. I left her room quietly and closed the door behind me wondering what she would think if she knew I was indeed Eduardo's father.

Half an hour later I found Cornelia sitting in one of the garden chairs at the back of the house cooing to the baby. She looked up as I approached. I wasn't sure if her eyes were shiny or if they were hiding tears. "Hello," I said, "How's the boy? Do you know his mother wants to go back to San Miguel?"

"She's not the only one." Cornelia snapped, "Life here is hard, and I don't want to have to always depend on charity."

"Cornelia, my dear Cornelia, are you sure you're not upset about anything."

"Of course not. Oh, maybe I am, but the baby seems to appreciate me, perhaps I'm bonding with it. But by the way, why the hell were you kissing Beatrice's hand?"

"Cornelia, the poor girl is having a tough time; I didn't know what else to do."

Sure, I don't see you being that attentive to me though I'm having a tough time too. I'm a receptionist not some darn house cleaner. I know I don't speak English well enough yet but I guess you know that already, don't you?"

"Cornelia if you ask me, I'd say you're jealous."

"Rubbish; I'm just mad at everything"

"Then let me take the baby, I like holding him."

"There you go again, but it is my turn to hide behind the baby."

I don't know what possessed me, but I took Cornelia roughly by the shoulders and would have kissed her had I not heard Beatrice behind us.

"Well, well what am I interrupting? Sorry but it is time to feed the baby."

Cornelia's eyes darted wildly as though disappointed, and then she attempted to hand over the baby. "I owe you a kiss." I whispered in her ear as I took the baby from her arms.

"You don't owe me anything." She said out loud as she released the child, and allowed me to hand him back to Beatrice.

The next morning, I awoke to someone calling my name urgently at my door. I threw my covers off and sprang out of bed and opened the door a crack. It was Beatrice. "What's the matter?" I asked.

"The baby's sick. He's running a high temperature; Doctor Patel can't come so I have to take him to the Emergency at St. Joseph's down the road."

"I'll come with you, let me just call a taxi. Did you tell Cornelia?"

"No there's no time to tell Cornelia and besides, she has to go to work."

In a matter of moments, we found ourselves being dropped off at the hospital, and after that it was a two hour wait to see a doctor. For me it was almost as though I was transported back to San Miguel as memories of my father and my Eduardo in hospital came back to haunt me. I prayed that little Eduardo would be alright even as I saw his mother buckle with fear. Only then did I realize that she might be as ill as the baby.

I was right too, for as it turned out both Beatrice and the baby had an infection, and though Beatrice was prescribed antibiotics, the baby was not. We were told that the baby would have to switch to formulae until his mother recovered; but meanwhile he was prescribed only medication to lower his fever.

"It's a nasty infection," a nurse whispered, "but what else can one expect from a house full of refugees." I heard another nurse whisper, and for the first time I felt ashamed.

As we were preparing to leave the hospital, I saw Cornelia bursting through the crowded waiting area looking worried as she tried to find us. "I just woke up" she said when she saw me, "the La Casa staff told me you were here. Is the baby alright?"

"You should have gone to work;" Beatrice said sounding exasperated, "you could lose your job. Anyway, the baby and I have an infection. He's going to have to go on formula, and we have to pick up medication."

I glanced over at Cornelia and saw hurt tears in her eyes, "Poor baby" she sighed, and I slipped my hand into hers. Surprisingly she made no attempt to release her hand even as we headed for the dispensary.

Cornelia went into work later that morning and I took over looking after the baby while Beatrice rested. I relished those moments of feeding and changing little Eduardo and I never once neglected to tell him how much I loved him. It was almost as though the love I poured down on him in conjunction with the medication was instrumental in helping to lower his fever. I was never more mesmerized by his beauty.

That week, very evening when Cornelia came home, she would gently take the baby from me, and I would sit and read the paper to Beatrice. Her illness seemed interminable and I began to wonder if she really wanted to get well, or if she dreamed of joining Eduardo on the other side. Doctor Patel said that she needed a will to live. From what we gathered Beatrice had no family back home. All she had was the baby.

"Beatrice, you are young and beautiful, love will come your way again." I often said to her, but she would only shake her head in disbelief. Perhaps she had seen how sunken her eyes had become.

I insisted that once a day she and I and the baby wander over to the park for fresh air and exercise. Mostly I enjoyed going because the wildest parts of the park put me in mind of the outskirts of San Miguel, and I was beginning to suffer from homesickness. However, one day while we were there, I decided to fetch Beatrice a hot dog from one of the vendors, and when I returned with it, I found her in deep conversation with a young man and his sister. He was called Enrico and his sister Stella. They were Canadian Latinos and had never been to San Miguel or South America for that matter. Before I could ask questions of them, they laughed and told me that what had attracted them to Beatrice was her wonderful baby, and her beautiful but sad looking eyes. I liked the two of them immediately not only because of their laughter, but because they brought a smile to Beatrice's wan cheeks.

It soon became a daily ritual of ours to meet up with the young people and to share an hour or two of fun with them. As the weeks went by, I saw Beatrice gaining strength and looking forward to their companionship. It wasn't as though Enrico was handsome, far from it. He was bone thin and his teeth looked too large for his mouth and his hair was a mop of unruly spikes, but it was his sense of fun that was exactly what Beatrice needed. And whenever Beatrice spoke about returning to San Miguel, Enrico would ask if he could accompany her. At first, she used to laugh at the prospect, and then she realized that he was serious, and she surprisingly began to explore the possibility; and I knew then without a doubt that she was falling in love with him. There was a time that Beatrice would have cringed if anyone suggested there was any attraction between them. Firstly, she was three years his senior, and with her exotic looks, she would perhaps have been able to attracted another handsome Eduardo type, but life is full of surprises. I began to see a softer side of her, and a sweet unmistakable gentleness, and I wondered if her feelings for Eduardo had been only as a result of the obsessions of first love.

Beatrice literally blossomed with this new friendship, and on more than one occasion I glimpsed Enrico gently holding her hand. He even began to take her on short trips downtown in his car without us; and as a result of these sojourns Beatrice grew more radiant and I was thankful.

Cornelia too sensed the changes in Beatrice, and she was delighted when once again she and I were left to our own devices and were able to undertake various explorations together. It wasn't as though Enrico totally neglected us, for young gentleman that he was, he still occasionally would take us all in his car to explore Toronto. One such evening while sitting in the back seat of that car with Cornelia, I was overcome by her beauty and the wonderful aroma of lilacs that she wore, and I drew her to me and kissed her passionately. Her mouth was as soft as velvet, and it was as though a whole new world was opened to me when she responded in kind. It was a long time since I had felt so alive, and I held her close, afraid to let her go for the rest of our journey.

Strangely enough, Beatrice never seemed to take much notice of my and Cornelia's blossoming romance; perhaps because her own relationship was growing by leaps and bounds. Then one day I noticed that she seemed even more satisfied than ever. I imagined that perhaps things had started to pay off for her. The connections she had made through La Casa had borne fruit for she obtained legitimate travel documents. I was happy for her, and was taken by complete surprise when she informed Cornelia and I that she and Enrico had secretly got married at Toronto's City Hall. I had at first regarded it as a marriage of convenience, but I soon was to change my mind after seeing how devoted to each other the couple had become. Their eyes were joyful and there were always explosions of laughter, and the baby thrived in the union.

"I can't wait to show Enrico San Miguel" Beatrice smiled, and I knew immediately that the time had come to follow the baby home.

The next day Stella, Enrico's gangly sister brought a bottle of Champagne to the house. We and the staff were invited out to the porch where she popped the cork in celebration. She then toasted the bride and groom and said a few words:

"Congratulations to Enrico and Beatrice on this very special occasion. I am so happy for my brother he has brought me a wonderful sister. Don't anyone of you think I'm going to be missing him too much, because come September I'm going to study art in Madrid, I've always wanted to do that and I have just been accepted into a school there. Some of you might not know it, but though my brother and I were born and raised here, our parents are from Spain. Mom and dad would have wanted to be here for Enrico's wedding but they are in Spain looking for a place to spend their retirement, and Enrico is so in love, he didn't want to wait a day longer to claim his bride. Neither I nor Enrico have ever lived in a Spanish speaking country so it will be quite an adventure for me, and I suspect for Enrico too. I must say that Enrico has never been happier, and I know you are all happy for him too. He works as an accountant and with his substantial savings he plans to buy a small house in San Miguel where Beatrice is from. So not only will he be speaking a lot of Spanish, but it looks like I'll have a place to stay when I visit them. My brother, from the look of things has inherited you all as family. How lucky he is that beautiful Beatrice and her adorable son Eduardo has accepted him. And on that note, I must again extend my warmest congratulations."

That night, as usual I complimented Cornelia on her beauty, and I asked her if she would like her father to come to visit us in Toronto or if she would rather that we went to see him in San Miguel.

"Is there something special you want to ask him?" She replied suspiciously with a toss of her hair, "Before you meet my father again, there is nothing I want more than for you to tell me who you really are. I've been completely honest with you, but I can't help but feel that you have not been entirely honest with me."

Though she laughed nervously, I saw such pride in her eyes I felt ashamed of my deception.

"Well I must admit you have a point Cornelia," I said cautiously, and I reached for her and kissed her hard, and she felt soft against me. "I have not been totally honest with you," I whispered. "So, let me start off with my real name, it is Sebastino Torres."

"Sebastino! Isn't that the baby's middle name? What's going on here?"

I was surprised she remembered the baby's middle name, but all I could do was hold her closer.

"I didn't choose the name, Beatrice did. She wanted to name the baby after its grandfather"

"So, are you saying the name is a coincidence? Or is there something more to all this?"

"There isn't anything more than the fact that Beatrice just wanted to remember what she construed as a doomed relationship with the baby's father."

"But why your name, come on Sebastino or whosoever you are, there has to be more to it than that. Come to think of it, did she know who you were all along? Don't you think I deserve an explanation? Sebastino, I have been thinking, and perhaps, depending on what you have to say, it could be our relationship that's doomed."

"Cornelia, there is no reason to be fatalistic. I will tell you everything, though it is a long story about fathers and sons."

"Go ahead tell me, long story or not."

"Well since you insist, here goes: Years ago when I was a much younger man I was full of the fire of youth. I was born into a wealthy family, and lived in the best part of San Miguel but I used to scour the seediest parts of the city searching for God knows what. I ended up defying my widowed father and marrying a cheap show girl from the lower classes. Her name was Claudia, and it was impossible to domesticate her, she was wild and crude. Life with her was all about lack of basic morals. I soon discovered that there wasn't a decent bone in her body. Needless to say, she quickly grew bored with me and refused to settle down despite my wealth and social standing. It was no surprise when she left me for another man soon after our son was born. We then divorced, and I never heard from her again, although rumors have it that she died from dysentery.

After that, I was so tormented that I regret to say that I hardly had time for my own son. Although fortunately for me, my father was there and he stepped in and raised my boy. Those two were as close as apples in a basket. And though I was in charge of a house full of servants, I was so remote from them that it surprised me when my grown son fell in love with one of them. She was a young girl who always kept her head down in my presence, perhaps from fear and guilt about my son. But sadly, my son died tragically and I'm not sure if he knew that the servant girl was pregnant with his child. To make matters worse, my father passed away not long after my son, though I now have the distinct impression that he had known a thing or two about my son's affair. When I finally learned of the pregnancy, I decided to try to somehow make amends and help the girl and her child anonymously. I suspected that she would have been too proud to accept any assistance, so when I learned she was leaving San Miguel, I made a spontaneous decision and followed her here. Any way; I suppose by now you realize where this story is going, and that the servant girl's name was Beatrice and my son was the Eduardo she adored."

"What! But how is it that Beatrice didn't recognize you?"

"My hair wasn't long back then, and I didn't have this beard."

"So are you going to tell me you've been disguised all along? If so, it's really pathetic, and it makes me wonder what Beatrice would think if she found out exactly who you are?"

"I don't really know if it would make any difference, but so much time has passed that now I don't know how to tell her."

"Perhaps it would be more appropriate if we both talked to her. But anyway, your story was so moving. I cannot even imagine how you continued living after all that happened to you. I would have been a basket case. What a fool of a wife you had; is that why you've been afraid to trust another woman? Now I know why it took you so long to kiss me? I wanted you to from the first moment I saw you. How handsome and strong you looked carrying my father's bag."

"You must understand my dearest Cornelia that I was always afraid of upsetting the applecart, but thank goodness there are still good women in the world like you."

"Sebastino my dear, I can't help but feel that you should make every effort to be close to your grandchild. I really think that would be as good a reason as any, for us to return to San Miguel, besides the fact is, I'm longing to see my father."

****

A month after that conversation, I was to find myself under a steel gray Toronto sky and there was no doubt in my mind that summer was over. The air already tasted of the coolness of fall and somehow. I dreaded the coming of winter. I had thought that by that time we would have been back to the warmth of San Miguel, but not all went as planned. The first thing was that Beatrice moved out of La Casa with the baby and went to live in Enrico's family's home in Cabbage Town. Apparently, Enrico decided not to leave the country without his parents meeting his new wife, and receive their blessings. Fortunately for him they were scheduled to return to the city within weeks. But I however began to wonder if he and Beatrice were reconsidering their decision to return to San Miguel.

The second thing that caused plans to be reconsidered was that with Cornelia working steadily with a cleaning company, she was considered to be a fulltime worker and was therefore no longer eligible for residency at La Casa. She came to my room in tears explaining her new status, and I wondered how much longer I myself would find shelter at La Casa. Then to make matters worse, she received a letter from her father saying that he wanted to come to Toronto to see her. He apparently thought it wouldn't be fair for her to give up her job to come to visit him just when she was getting established.

"I have to find a place to live." she said, "But Sebastino I cannot afford to spend all my earnings on rent, and Pappa will need a place to stay." She sobbed.

"I know," I replied, "I will help you to get a place, though it would simplify things if we got a place together."

"Yes, that might be so, but what about my father, he would be quite upset to find us living together. He's old fashioned you know."

I could hear a tremor in Cornelia's voice and I saw that her eyes were teary, and I hardly knew what to say. But then I cleared my throat and words tumbled out.

"I realize what you are saying Cornelia, no doubt he'd object to the living arrangements. My father would have been exactly the same."

"Well Sebastino, who's to stop us moving in together after his visit, we could share the finances."

"You would do that? Is that what you are saying?"

"I'm saying I could uphold your honor if I have to."

You would you do that just because of my father?"

"No, not for his sake my dearest, but for your sake, haven't you guessed that I have fallen in love with you?"

That same afternoon we began in earnest to search for an apartment, and since we were both fond of the High Park area, that was where we started to look. At first all that we were directed to were dreary basements, and noisy above store flats. But I wanted to find something that would make Cornelia proud, and I began negotiations with one of the local banks that contacted my bank back in San Miguel. We became so caught up in the planning that Beatrice, Enrico and the baby rarely entered our thoughts. Then the day came when we were to be shown a condominium at the top of Roncesvalles Avenue near Dundas. The moment I saw the condo I knew immediately it would be exactly the sort of place that would be suitable, there was even room for the old man and lots of space for Cornelia and I when finally, we would move in together. It is no wonder that my heart was joyful.

Time went by faster than I anticipated and it came as a great surprise when Beatrice called me at La Casa to let me know that she had met her in-laws, and as such was welcomed into their family and received their blessings. She then proceeded to tell me that Enrico's parents had convinced her that she should make contact with the baby's grandfather in San Miguel, so that he too could be welcomed into the family. She then confessed that she had taken the liberty of calling his house many times but was not able to reach him.

There was a huge lump in my throat as I listened to her, and I would have given anything to blurt out exactly who I was, but instead I kept my lips sealed. How can I tell her now I wondered? But it was clear to me that she hadn't a clue who I really was. "Perhaps I can reach the grandfather," I said confidently, "Tell me exactly what you'd like him to know, and I will see that he gets the message. My lawyer has a way of making contacts even when at first it might seem impossible."

"Well tell him his son lives again in the eyes of my baby, and tell him that all that has happened is water under the bridge. Tell him I'm longing for the day when he can hold the baby in his arms. And tell him that we as a family could grow to love him, especially the baby, and I hope he won't take offence that me a mere servant girl is insinuating myself and my family on him."

"I am sure he would be delighted to hear," I replied, "For I am delighted as it is, as well as full of confessions."

"What sort of confessions? If it is about how you feel about Cornelia, we have all already guessed that you are both in love."

"Beatrice....it is not about me and Cornelia, though you are right, we are in love, it is about Eduardo's father. I have to confess to you and the priest that he and I are one and the same person."

"You are Eduardo's father Sebastino Torres!! This is unbelievable, it must be a miracle!"

"Yes," I replied shamefaced, "I am the man you probably hate...."

I expected reprimand, but instead I saw that Beatrice was smiling, she looked lovelier that ever as she approached me. "I have come to know you, and I could never hate you, not now Senor Torres. Eduardo wouldn't have wanted that, especially after all the amazing things you did for all of us. We are all forever in your gratitude and I can't wait to tell my dear husband about you."

JUST A SINGLE WORD

Mars always had a strange, mystifying attraction for her. Even as a child of ten she talked about seeing unexplained long stretches of an alien landscape. She was so positive that the landscape was real that people had a hard time shrugging it off as no more than a lucid dream. She even described the exact brick and mortar rusty shade of red that at times would unexpectedly engulf her in a cloud of thick dust which settled into her pores and threatened to choke the life out of her. Then without warning it would retreat to expose a landscape measured by endless mountain ranges, larger than any on earth.

The first time that she had found herself on this alien world, a rusty sky had hung menacingly over the broad horizon, the landscape appearing splintered into the recesses of cavernous caves and multitudes of gigantic rocks and boulders. "I must be on Mars", she thought, shielding her eyes from the glare, and realized that her clothing was stained in magenta, and her long hair, now coated in a varied pallet, had fallen into rat tails.

She looked around furtively, hoping to find something that would make sense of what was happening to her, but all she could remember was a faint voice that had whispered something in her ear. She couldn't recall what it had said. She opened her mouth, hoping that by some osmosis her mouth might repeat the words, but all she heard was the sound of silence. Hoping to find the source of the phantom voice, she turned entirely around, only to find that the landscape looked exactly the same in all directions. Ankle deep in maroon red particles as brittle as salt, she stood stock still in contemplation. "How did I get here?" she wondered, then was startled to find herself back on Earth.

Yet, again and again she visited Mars. She was never afraid, for she felt she belonged in that barren paradise devoid of the distractions of foliage, water sources, animals and even insects. It occurred to her that her visits had a purpose, but what that purpose was she did not know.

Like an ant dwarfed by an Olympic stadium, she always trudged onward not knowing if going right was better than going left, or if certain directions were to be avoided. Like falling snow, the cadmium dust changed the face of the landscape from moment to moment, and she believed she had no choice but to press on over endless obstacles.

In all her visits she was never hungry or thirsty, though time passed slowly, for something in the very atmosphere must have sustained her. The weight of being the lone human on the planet encouraged her, made her want to explore further. Despite falls, scrapes, and bruises she never slowed down. She sensed how bedraggled she had become and knew that she no longer resembled the young girl who sometimes lived on a blue planet that hung like a tiny lantern in the distant sky, and it set her mind to wondering. Was that planet keeping secrets from her? Was it watching her?

Sometimes she dimly recalled that her father, an archeologist, had traveled all over Earth with her in tow. His devotion to her never dimmed through years, though he lived in sadness and sorrow knowing that his daughter often disappeared, only to return looking contented, yet curiously worn and stained with scarlet dust that spilled from her clothes and shoes, with no palpable explanation to account for her condition.

And she knew that some day, she would not return home.

ACKEE NIGHT IN CANADA

Everyone has some kind of addiction. I'm no different. Mine is my relationship with Dave. I allow him to consume me, though I know I might be better off exorcising him from my life. Initially I was attracted to him because he was so different and allowed me glimpses of another perspective on reality. But I am weary now and long for freedom in body and spirit. As for Dave, he's forever threatening to leave the city. He has this dream of heading out west. He feels things will go better for him there. He doesn't mention the fact that his old school friend, Nino Giovanelli, lives out there, or that Nino is now married and on welfare doing a little art work on the side. No, Dave likes to think that when he gets there things will fall into place, that he'll find a suitable room. One that isn't dusty or wanting for heat in the winter. One where his single bed won't squeak at the slightest touch. One where the noises from passing traffic won't overpower him. And one where, if there are people downstairs, they'll be good people and considerate, too, not like the ones where he is now, who are out to get him.

Dave isn't that fond of people; he likes being alone. Meditation is what he calls it. He spends his mornings in the park, thinking and assuming postures. On more than one occasion he's been approached by gays. Dave hates being bothered, especially by gays. Can he help it if he's lithe of frame and attractive? Heck, he's thirty-eight with the body of a twenty-one-year-old.

By afternoon he's exhausted but spends what's left of his energy practising on his bass guitar. He plays well but doesn't accept compliments easily. Dave is a perfectionist. He spends most evenings playing in dives around Toronto in a band called the Saltys. He despises all the band members, calls them assholes, and hates having to jam with strangers who always insist on using his equipment. "Why the heck," he says, "do 1 continually fall into the trap of thinking I have to be Mr. Nice Guy to these jerks?" He values isolation the way some people value possessions, and you dare not call him when he wants to be alone. If you do, he won't be rude outright. Instead he'll hardly say a word, speak monotonously, and practically slice you off the phone with his silences.

He enjoys a good feed, though, and can handle the spices in West Indian and East Indian cooking. He swears he's a vegetarian, but hasn't been known to refuse a good serving of meat. He heaps his plate at each meal as though it were his last, and without fail can find something or other wrong: too much salt, too little gravy, not enough potatoes, et cetera. He's one strange dude. You constantly get the feeling that if you were to push all the right buttons to please Dave, then he might stay in your life, and he might find it in his heart to reciprocate affection.

But then, with almost no warning, he'll pull what I call his St. Francis thing. He feels that people should have only the barest of possessions and live lives that are spare. Then, in the same breath, he'll reveal that if he had money, he'd have the right and might to live the sort of life he dreams of. He buys lottery tickets in the hope they'll take him off welfare and allow him to buy a new bass guitar, not like the one he has now but like that old black one he shouldn't have traded ten years ago. He would like a good flute, too. But never mind new clothes. He can manage with what little he already has. He would definitely get a haircut, though, because it might give him a better shot at meeting interesting women. He would also like tools. It has been too long now that he's been wanting tools to practise his cabinet-making. Manpower put him through a course fraught with frustration and assholes. But he came out clean in the end, producing three or four fine pieces of furniture.

There are times when I wonder if I had known Dave's track record whether I would have let him into my heart. A heart he handles as he would a meal, constantly searching for that telltale fault, that might-have-been, that if-your-custards-were-thicker-I-might-have-stayed sort of thing. For someone who wasn't supposed to be staying, Dave has stuck around for a long time. Ten years have come and gone, and he's still in danger of leaving. He still manages to wrench my heart with talk of getting up and going, and no amount of good cooking, good loving, or just plain goodness will persuade him to stay.

When I first saw him, he was as lean as he is today, with the same stained teeth I had attributed to tobacco but have since discovered is from all the tea drinking he does. He drinks six or more cups a day, a habit he acquired from having been born in Scotland where, whenever it got cold, which was most of the time, he was always reaching for a hot drink.

Dave once had nose surgery to improve his breathing. No, it wasn't by choice. His doctor told him the air passages were blocked in his nostrils because they were underdeveloped. But Dave swears it's dust that caused the problem, plus improper diet. He feels his doctor's a quack, and insists he's going to sue the guy for violating his nose. Trust me, there's nothing wrong with Dave's nose, not now, anyway.

"Sylvie," he says to me, "check my profile. Does my nose look crooked or anything?"

"No, Dave, it doesn't."

"It's got to. It doesn't feel right."

"Get a grip, Dave. Your nose is fine."

"Maybe I should be eating more green veggies and sunflower seeds. The vitamin content is quite high. It's gotta be good for healing and stuff."

It's as if Dave needs this nose thing to talk about all the time.

"You know, Sylvie, all the dust in my room is getting into my nose. I'm going to have to spend a week disinfecting the walls and floor."

"Sure, Dave."

"Hey, you weren't the one who had to have surgery."

He swears I should have known he was coming into my life. Swears I shouldn't have got married or had my three kids, even though all that happened long before I met him. And he wasn't joking when he said I should have seen him coming.

Sometimes he makes me feel guilty about owning a home; it's the St. Francis thing with him. Looking almost Christ-like with his beard and longish hair, he insists we should all live as frugally as possible.

"When I first saw your paintings," he often says, "I was blown away by the way you paint eyes. All those eyes seem to jump out of the canvas and follow you from room to room. It's freaky." Sometimes Dave is as innocent as a child, and it's at those times that the room seems to be filled with his beauty, and tears spring to my eyes. "You are one talented mother," he says, embarrassing me.

Quite often I steer Dave into the kitchen and cut him a slice of cornbread. It's his favourite, and it isn't something his granny used to make back in Scotland. It's uniquely mine.

"Love your baking," he always tells me, hunger lighting up his hazel eyes. "What's for dinner?" he asks now.

And I think, God, I wish I could come up with the right combination, that single ingredient, that one thing that will make him stay and never leave me.

I decide on ackee and cod; it's Jamaican like me. Ackee is a vegetable, delicious but potent, and poisonous if eaten unripe. It is fabulous with Canadian cod, and it's extra-fast to prepare. Dave will like it. I am outwardly calm, but my heart turns cartwheels.

Dave leans over the pot. "This will hit the spot," he says, and I hope he never realizes what hit him when the unripe ackees I have used kick in.

WHERE DID SANTA GO?

George and Dora Stevens were retired, they lived in a small four floor apartment building overlooking a Toronto schoolyard. Unknown to many locals, especially children, George was the man who played Santa Clause in one of the city's best department stores at Christmastime. He was perfect for the part. All his assets were genuine, his beard was thick and white, his cheeks ruddy, his frame portly, and even his eyes seemed to twinkle. You couldn't have found a better Santa look-a-like.

George and Dora were known to keep to themselves, as though deliberately shielding themselves from constant comments and inquiries regarding George's unique appearance. It was Dora who did the shopping, and any other daily chore that might involve leaving the building during daylight hours. But George was no slouch, his days were spent helping with the cooking, cleaning and other general chores around the house. As a result, many of the other apartment dwellers were hardly aware that George existed; and that was exactly how the couple wanted it.

One sunny morning, after breakfast, George pulled his chair over to the window to take advantage of the sunlight. He had been reading the newspaper, as was his habit at that time of day. The window was slightly ajar, and he couldn't help but hear the high voices of the children in the school yard below. The boys and girls below were playing hopscotch, and George was pleasantly surprised, to see them playing an actual game, and not an electronic one. The sight of it brought back memories, as he smiled to himself, and watched for a few minutes. He couldn't help but notice, that there was a small boy squatting down, apart from the others. Even from three floors above George could see that the boy was staring at a patch of dirt. There was no doubt in George's mind that perhaps the boy was watching ants or other crawling insects. He kept his eyes on the boy, and saw when a winged insect flew out from the boy's hand. The insect seemed to dance in the air; then soared out of sight. The boy stood up quickly, and at that precise moment, looked upwards, only to meet George's eyes in the apartment above.

George would have stepped away from the window, but he was riveted. He watched as the boy below craned his neck, this way and that, determined not to lose sight of the flying insect. Surprise was written all over the boy's open face, and it was clear that the boy was not searching for the insect. He was amazed by the sight of George. George immediately recognized that well known look of wonder that he had seen many times before on children's faces, while he worked as Santa. He instinctively placed a finger over his lips, hoping to silence the boy. It would not do, he thought, if somehow the other children were alerted. The young boy responded to his signal, with a smile, then with a shy wave, he ran off at the sound of the school bell.

A day or two later, as George was sipping coffee beside the window, he found himself involuntarily seeking out the boy. Several children were playing Tag, in the school yard, but the boy was not one of them. Then as though from out of nowhere, the boy stepped out from behind the school wall. There was expectancy written all over his face, as he looked up at George's window. George quickly waved, coffee cup in hand; then stepped away. But he couldn't help himself, he returned to the window. The boy was still there, he was flashing a broad smile, as George waved back. These small encounters continued for at least a month or so, and George had not mentioned a word of it to his wife considering it a trivial part of his day. He wondered however if the boy had ever mentioned him to others, and he also wondered whether the boy had friends, since he was always alone. Despite these brief wonderings, George didn't dwell on the subject. His days were full, and he and his wife found such pleasure in each other's company.

One morning, after Dora had left to do the weekly shopping, George went over to the window, and searched out the boy. His eyes followed several groups of children at play, but there was no sign of the boy. George had not been feeling all that well, and he thought that the sight of happy children at play would cheer him up. But as he stood there he felt somewhat dizzy and nauseated. He could feel his breath coming in short gasps, and it became difficult to breath. He pried the window open about an inch or two, with the hope that fresh air would settle him. But despite the fresh air, there was no denying the strange feelings that doubled him over, He was so light headed that he had to grab at the windowsill for support, and he glimpsed the boy running towards the building, arms waving frantically, and shouting "Santa! Santa!"

That was the last thing George saw before he keeled over. He was not to know that it was the boy's urgent cries, and determination to stand his ground that brought a teacher running. "Santa has fallen down!!" the boy screamed over and over, as tears spilled down his cheeks, his finger pointing at the slightly open window above.

At first, no one believed the boy. How on earth, could Santa have fallen down; was it a picture, or a Santa ornament he meant? But the boy shook his head stubbornly, and was so insistent, that a 911 call was made. Paramedics arrived with a wailing sound that filled the air, with hope and fear. It was the boy who pointed out the apartment to the small crowd gathered below. "Santa fell there, and he did not get up!" the boy wailed.

One could almost hear from that distance, the pounding of the heavy boots of the paramedics as they navigated the building's third floor. The crowd swore that they heard the jolt that resonated when they gained access to the apartment. But all they really heard was silence, even when the paramedics found George sprawled on the floor.

"Is he conscious?" They wondered, and "Is he alive?

By the time Dora returned home, George had been taken away. Neighbors congregated at the front of the apartment, and in the hallway waiting to inform her about the drama that had taken place. Dora was distraught, she wrung her hands and quickly sipped from a glass of water offered to her by a neighbor. "Where did they take him.?" She inquired, "Please call a cab. My poor dear George, I have to be with him!"

Just then, another concerned neighbor generously offered to drive her immediately to the hospital where she would find her husband.

At the hospital, Dora was soon to learn that George had suffered a stroke. He was likely paralyzed on the left side, and was not expected to return home any time soon, and he would have to undergo rehabilitation.

Dora, filled with love, wept at his side, and slipped her hand in his. She saw that one side of his face had sagged, and his hand felt cool, and she knew instinctively that he was unable to speak, though there was a slight smile on his face, and she was comforted.

"I'm here George," she whispered, "You must be exhausted, I'm glad you seem to understand what I am saying. I love you George, and you know what, a lot of folk were kind to me just now."

Dora wiped back tears as she continued, "The neighbours told me that a little boy saved your life darling. Things could have been worse. I am very grateful to him." And there again, she was sure she saw a ghost of a smile on George's face. "I'll have to thank that boy properly. Won't I darling?"

Dora rested her head near George's soft pillow, and after what seemed like hours, she awoke to find George still there, though she had fallen asleep. She looked around, suddenly recalling her unaccustomed surroundings, and she saw a young woman she had never seen before sitting in a chair near the bed. "Are you a doctor?" Dora asked wearily.

"Oh no," the woman replied, with a smile "I 'm Claire, I'm a teacher from the school beside your building. "We are all so glad that little Neil was able to save your husband's life." She continued, "Would you believe that all the children at school are saying that Neil is a hero. But just imagine this, when I spoke to Neil, all he wanted to know was, 'where did Santa go'? so I told him that I would come to see for myself, and I would let him know."

"What a sweet boy" Dora chimed in. "and how nice of you to come. Thank you" Dora's voice shook with emotion, but there was strength in her, as she leaned closer to George. "George, "she whispered, "we owe a lot to that boy don't we. You and I are soulmates, so I know exactly what you would like to say to him, and Clair here, will tell him."

Claire pulled her chair even closer to the small bed, her young face almost luminous as she listened intently.

"First of all." began Dora, "You must tell Neil thanks from the bottom of our hearts. And tell him not to worry, Santa will be back at Christmas. He will be dressed in his red suit and bells too, and his beard will be whiter and bushier than ever, and just you wait and see Neil, thanks to you, Santa will lead the parade as always, there will be laughter, and fun, and Christmas trees, gifts and stockings, and special wishes. But Neil, Santa just needs a little time to get all those things ready."

ROBERTA ON THE BEACH

How far the distance from a childhood of poverty in the blazing tropical sun to where I stand today, a creative young man equally at home with pen or brush, defiant of raging snows that whistle and sting, even as I write, pressed against a frosty window, determined to capture the essence of a past that haunts me. My pen wields tears like ink and guides my hand as creases in my brow awaken wells of remembering. I recall her well, Roberta, my beloved sister, the enigmatic subject of my painting Roberta on the Beach.

—Caleb Douglas

The way some people thought you would expect everyone from Montego Bay to be either lucky or rich. This was probably due to the town's location on the picturesque Jamaican north coast where many of the locals benefitted from a thriving tourist industry.

It was in this supposedly idyllic setting that Roberta Douglas was born. She was not representative of those who were indeed lucky or rich. Her family was part of what might be termed the working poor. Roberta herself felt hard done by and often wore an expression of defiance on her otherwise attractive face.

When she was sixteen, she would sashay down the main street with an air of affluence. It was a game she enjoyed playing. After all, who was to know that her bright clothes were mainly hand-me-downs? No one looking at her noticed her clothes first, anyway; it was her long reddish hair, pale, lightly tanned complexion, and startling green eyes that grabbed attention. Even more of a curiosity was the fact that her brothers and sisters were all black.

Like most Jamaicans, Roberta could trace her ancestors to various origins, in her case, Scottish, Jewish, and African. Roberta's looks were said to be like those of the Scottish greatgrandmother on her father's side of the family. Her father, George Douglas, was the son of a Scottish immigrant named Trevor Douglas, who came to the island in the late 1800s. Eventually he married a local woman named Edith Oliver. Edith was from a long line of proud black Jamaicans with impressive full lips, broad nose, brown eyes, and short-cropped curly hair. It was an ideal marriage; Trevor delighted in Edith's simple ways, and she in his sophistication. Unfortunately Edith had never been a strong woman and was plagued by epileptic seizures. She conceived a child, and because of improper medical care, only lived to see him reach his first year.

Trevor, a young man of twenty-four, resigned himself to raising the child on his own and eventually broke all ties with his homeland. He was a devoted father who saw to his son George's education and care, and he lived to see his child grow up to marry a local girl named Hannah Weiss, delighting in the birth of six of their children. George, a self-taught accountant, took on freelance work to supplement his family's income. Employment was scarce, and the home was often reduced to the most meagre fare. Hannah, a handsome woman of Jewish and black descent, wore her long black hair in a coil down her back. She was goodhumoured and sympathetic and expected the best of others. And, although it was a financial hardship, she took in occasional washing to make sure her children were educated.

Roberta, the eldest girl, often spent her days at Cornwall Beach, a popular tourist haunt, where she sat and listened to foreigners converse about their faraway homelands. For Roberta, names such as Helsinki, Copenhagen, Glasgow, and Hammersmith became an enchantment. She would close her eyes, dig her toes deep into the sand, and let her imagination take her to unexplored worlds where neither the sea, nor the salty breeze, nor the cry of wandering seabirds could disturb her reverie. But it seemed to her that all too soon she would have to return to the reality of scarcity and the cramped cottage with its pathetic cardboard walls, creaking floors, and crooked windows. She could hardly remember a time when she hadn't slept three to a bed. It was much the same for the others, since her parents shared one room. Slim and Caleb, her older brothers, shared another, and she and her sisters, Sheila, Georgina, Elaine, Lorraine, and Maggie, shared two rooms where double beds in each room restricted movement. The tiny living room offered the only respite, but it was really part of the kitchen where there seemed to be a constant stream of family.

The cottage's location just outside town was an excellent one. It overlooked the blue Caribbean Sea from a rocky perch. At the time of its original purchase by Roberta's now-deceased grandfather, Trevor, arid land such as theirs was considered to be of little value and therefore a poor investment. It was with much foresight on his part that Trevor still went ahead and bought the land with the cottage on it, even though he couldn't afford to replace the dilapidated building.

Roberta could remember running along the rocky pathway in front of the cottage, catching the wind in her hair, tasting the expected sharpness of salt in her mouth, and hearing the rhythmic call of the sea. As a child, she chased butterflies in the sunshine and hunted fireflies during the long evenings. The ever-watchful Hannah would wring her hands in constant fear that one of her children might fall from the treacherous path into the swirling sea below, and was grateful that it never happened.

For Roberta's eighteenth birthday the family held a modest celebration: a virtual feast of cake, ginger beer, rice and peas, and chicken. Even Roberta, who was usually discontented with what the household had to offer, had to admit that this was a fine celebration, which was not only for her birthday, but also for her graduation from high school.

Long into the night, when the rest of the family had retired to bed, Roberta lay awake, contemplating her future. She felt unfulfilled. Slim and Caleb had recently started work in one of the local hotels, but their salaries weren't nearly enough to offer any security. If her Grandpa Trevor were alive, she thought, there would be no cause for uncertainty.

She lay rigid in the shared bed where, being closest to the window, she had a good view of the cliffs outside. She could see where the land, like a pointing finger, jutted into the sea. She could have easily been mesmerized by its beauty, but hushed whispers from the living room reeled her in like a hooked fish, and with a jolt, she returned to the reality of the cramped bed.

Reluctantly she turned her head away from the beckoning horizon, her ears straining to hear the whispered conversation. It was her mother and father. Never did night noises seem louder to her. The rattling of the wooden window frame in the night breeze was an annoyance, the buzzing of insects a discordance, and the sea quarrelling with the rocks below deafened her.

"She might not want to go," her mother whispered.

There was a long silence before her father answered. "Hannah, she'll want to go. She'll be right at home over there. Haven't you noticed how she craves the company of the tourists?"

Noticing how sure of himself her father sounded, Roberta sat bolt upright. "Papa!" she called out as if in warning, swinging her bare legs over the side of the bed. The hushed whispers died as she steadied herself beside the open door, heart racing. "Is something wrong?"

Her father looked up wearily, fixing his eyes on her startled face. "Sit down, Roberta." As Hannah patted him gently on the shoulder, he smiled weakly. "We were talking about you."

"Yes, Roberta, your father and me have news. I got a letter from your Aunt Melanie. Is my older sister who go away to England as a domestic but become big businesswoman."

"What's happened to Aunt Melanie?" Roberta asked.

"Nothing happen," her mother replied. "But out of the blue Melanie write and offer something too good to be true. She want to educate one of you children in England. Slim and Caleb like their jobs at the hotel, so we think of you since you the oldest girl. Aunt Melanie think one of the family might be interested in nursing."

A thin sweat broke out on Roberta's pale forehead. She felt faint. She clutched at the edges of a stool to steady herself. Her throat was so dry she could barely speak. Imagine, a chance to go to England, she thought. She didn't much care for nursing, but she would have agreed to anything that offered a way out. Her green eyes blazed in the darkness. "Papa," she whispered, "it's what I've always wanted."

It took six months for all the arrangements to be finalized. There were long lineups in the passport office, a passport photograph to be taken, and a suitable person found to sign the documents. Hannah mentioned their need for clothes at the local church. Roberta would have died of shame had she known, but she was so caught up in the excitement of the planning that much of the details washed over her.

At Montego Bay Airport the rest of the family were full of concerns: Would she be warm enough? Why was the plane so small? Would Aunt Melanie be able to recognize her? Roberta brushed aside their fears; like a racehorse, she strained for the excitement of the race.

Hannah clung to her only momentarily and hid her swollen eyes behind her long black hair. And her father squeezed her hand so tightly it felt like the embrace of a shackle.

"You're the first one to go," he said gruffly. "Try to help out the others. Don't be like my father who never looked back to his homeland and family. Roberta, we love you." With a final squeeze of his daughter's hand, he shuffled over to Hannah's side, feeling like an old man, and reached with trembling fingers for his wife's steady grip as his green eyes swam with unshed tears.

"Hannah, my darling," he said, "I have the strangest feeling I will never see Roberta again."

Hannah arched her brows and pursed her full lips to silence him. "Don't be silly, George. She be back. It's your Scottish blood make you so superstitious."

In spite of her reassurances, Hannah's heart skipped a beat. She feared George's prediction, since on more than one occasion in the past he had been right. He wasn't wrong this time, either, for less than a year after Roberta's departure, he succumbed to a fatal heart attack. The family was devastated, and Roberta was immediately notified. Slim and Caleb suddenly found themselves responsible for the rest of the family, and they made sure Roberta remained in England. Aunt Melanie saw the wisdom in this decision, realizing that her niece's interest in nursing was flagging and any break from the program could spell the end of it.

In England Roberta felt like an orchid in an igloo. Nothing could have prepared her for the incessant damp and cold. Layers and layers of clothing were never enough to alleviate her constant shivering. But by sheer determination she swore she would accustom herself to the weather, just as she accommodated herself to living in her aunt's home with the modern conveniences of hot running water and a proper living room with a television. She even had her own bedroom and full run of the rest of the house. Aunt Melanie's brisk, efficient, organized manner impressed Roberta, though. It was so unlike her mother's easygoing ways and ready laugh. Time and again, Roberta missed the closeness of home, and couldn't help but wonder if her formidable aunt, who appeared to be such a tower of strength, might have a softer side.

For Roberta, London was overwhelming, with its churches, castles, monuments, shops, crowds, double-decker buses, and the Underground. There were days when she would wrap herself in her warmest blanket and watch television by the fire for most of the day, but Aunt Melanie would subtly steer her back to her studies.

After the news of her father's death, Roberta pretended that life for her hadn't existed before going to England. In doing so, she shut off the harsh realities in the lives of those left at home, and decided not to write her family or read their letters.

Because of shyness, she had, at first, remained aloof from her fellow students, but eventually she began to study in the student lounge where a number of her colleagues gathered. One of them, Suleika Ramsaroop, a bright, friendly girl from Bombay, introduced Roberta to her circle of friends.

One day, when Roberta was immersed in conversation with students from Malaysia and Burma, a pleasant Scottish burr attracted her attention. It sounded so much like Grandpa Trevor's that she caught her breath sharply and saw, framed in the doorway, a tall blond young man with blue eyes. He came over to where she was and introduced himself. His name was Chester Daley, a doctor from Scotland.

During the next few weeks, Chester and Roberta struck up a close friendship. Aunt Melanie quickly became accustomed to his presence in her home. She watched with mixed feelings as her niece blossomed under the ever-watchful eye of the young doctor and knew without doubt that the two young people were falling in love.

Melanie Weiss had never married or had children, and now, in her late fifties, looked back with much regret at the chances she had missed. She recognized in Roberta a certain sassiness that she herself had possessed as a young girl and hoped her niece wouldn't make the same mistakes she had made. Being a regular churchgoer and a well-respected member of the black community, Aunt Melanie was surprised when Chester, after six months, instead of proposing marriage, suggested that Roberta and he move in together.

Roberta felt mature enough to make her own decisions, therefore she and Chester found themselves a flat close by. Aunt Melanie's only demand was that Roberta not give up her studies, not realizing that she had nothing to fear on that account because, under Chester's guidance, Roberta buckled down to her training.

Roberta's new home was a small flat with a tiny fireplace and only four rooms to move around in, but with Chester beside her, it felt like a palace. Her mail was forwarded from Aunt Melanie's place and quickly, without being read, became fuel for her fireplace. Her life was too perfect to be interrupted by the sadness and depression of those across the ocean.

Aunt Melanie remained a part of their lives. Sunday-afternoon visits with her became a ritual. Chester, too, enjoyed the roast beef, rice and peas, and hot hams she always seemed to have on the table. Her thirty years in England hadn't diminished her preference for Jamaican food.

As time passed, Chester's letters to his parents in Scotland were more frequently punctuated with the names of Roberta and Aunt Melanie. As a result, his parents grew impatient to meet the girl who had won their son's heart. It was inevitable that Roberta would eventually see Scotland, the land of her ancestors. She had long decided on this, even before meeting Chester. Now, with his encouragement, they immersed themselves in travel brochures and plans to visit his homeland.

They decided to take the train. Roberta was as restless as a puppy, and even three suitcases weren't enough to hold her Beach down. But on the train she sat glued to the window, observing the landscape flash by mile after mile as she held tightly to Chester's hand.

She thought it was magical when they crossed the Scottish border. To her, it was destiny fulfilled. She strained her ears to hear distant bagpipes and church bells, and in her elation imagined she did.

She was fascinated with her surroundings: heather-covered hills, meadows, fields, castles around every bend, and countless herds of sheep, all of which set her blood racing. She wasn't at all prepared for the surprise of Chester's parents' country estate. By estate standards, it was only modest, but for Roberta it might as well have been Tara in Gone with the Wind. It was called Hawthorne Hold and was set amid rolling green hills and a welltended garden. The Daleys, broad-minded and middle-aged, welcomed Roberta with open arms, and she, who had never been inside a home such as theirs, was quick to compliment all its finery.

Mrs. Daley showed them to their rooms and somehow managed to keep out of their way until suppertime, giving Chester ample time to escort Roberta around the estate and point out things he remembered fondly. First, they explored the grounds and what must at one time have been stables, then they wandered in the small woods behind the property and later investigated the lush garden.

Once back inside the main building, they settled in the parlour. Mr. Daley popped in just as they were catching their breath and offered them both a nip of Scotch to welcome them. The shaggy-haired gentleman seemed unassuming, but when he asked Roberta about her family and home in Jamaica, she felt self-conscious and determined not to disappoint him. Without anyone to contradict her, she effortlessly embroidered stories about her origins. Grandpa Trevor Douglas became a rich Scottish immigrant, her parents' little cottage became a villa, and even the rocky cove became an exclusive beach. She related half-truths about the closeness of her family, surprising even Chester.

That evening at supper, when Mrs. Daley mentioned over boiled cabbage and pot roast that their guest must be more accustomed to exotic and expensive food, Roberta hid her eyes behind her hair, a habit she had learned from her mother. She realized she had betrayed these good people and longed to escape. The remaining days of her visit couldn't pass quickly enough. Her silly game had ruined Scotland for her. Finally she convinced Chester to leave a day early.

After returning to London, she continued to ignore the many letters from home. Fear that her invented past would be exposed became an obsession. She immersed herself in study, becoming so self-absorbed that she hardly noticed on her regular Sunday visits to Aunt Melanie that her aunt was showing signs of physical weakness and seemed unable to cope with the house. She didn't even notice that the sparkle had gone from her aunt's smile.

Melanie Weiss had known for a long time about tumours, which at first appeared in her breasts and then spread to her lungs. She was well aware of her impending demise and, wanting to do something worthwhile for her sister, Hannah, had offered to help educate one of her children. She wasn't at all prepared for the great burst of love she felt for Roberta, and constantly chided herself for not confiding in anyone, especially Roberta, about the true state of her health. Nevertheless she trusted in the Lord that with Chester on the scene Roberta would be looked after.

Then, one weekend when the usual Sunday-dinner invitation didn't come by telephone, Roberta and Chester decided to visit Aunt Melanie, anyway. Roberta let herself into her aunt's house where silence met them, and it was evident that Aunt Melanie hadn't been there for days. Roberta used the phone to call the few friends of her aunt's she could remember, but came up with nothing. It wasn't until Chester ventured next door and made inquiries that a Mrs. Bowles from Trinidad and her family came forward with information. However, by the time they made it to the hospital, Aunt Melanie already had both feet planted in the next world.

Aunt Melanie's minister, the Reverend V. Robottom, officiated at the funeral on what Roberta felt to be a particularly cold and damp Wednesday morning. She was particularly moved by the many Londoners who came to pay their last respects to her aunt, the popular grocery store owner, and was grateful for the support of Chester's strong arms.

Aunt Melanie's will was read the following afternoon in the presence of a solicitor. Melanie Weiss proved more than generous, leaving her niece the tidy sum of twenty thousand pounds while proceeds from the sale of her home and business were to be given to her sister, Hannah Douglas. Hannah was, however, not to be informed of any of this until after the actual sale of the properties. In addition, many of Melanie's personal effects and furniture were to be donated to charity at Roberta's discretion. Afterward, Roberta spoke with the solicitor until well into the evening regarding these personal details and others, which she wished to be clarified.

For the next couple of days she spent her time sorting through her aunt's personal effects. Charity stood to gain considerably, since Roberta couldn't store the belongings elsewhere. She chose only to keep the mahogany dining-room table and chairs that she and Chester and her aunt had used so many times. The strain of these sad duties weighed heavily on her. She turned only to Chester for comfort, since she chose not to inform her mother about the recent death. So she hardly had time herself to recover from the initial shock when, while clearing out Aunt Melanie's house, she received a fateful phone call.

The call was long distance from Jamaica. Roberta's heart pounded uncontrollably. She calmed herself, assuming it might be a friend of her aunt's, but it was Roberta's younger sister, Elaine. The voice, sounding hauntingly familiar, crackled over the line. "Hello, Roberta, is that you? It's Elaine."

The lilt of the Jamaican accent sounded painfully quaint, and it caused childhood memories to flood through Roberta's mind.

"Roberta, are you still there? We haven't heard from you for so long that we decided to phone. I'm calling from a neighbour's house. We still don't have a phone."

Roberta gripped the receiver hard, feeling, on the one hand, comforted by the familiar voice, and on the other, embarrassed by its rustic intonations. Had she sounded like that? she wondered. "Is something wrong?" she finally asked out loud. "Has someone died?" All the while, she imagined Elaine at the other end of the line being impressed by her English accent, but Elaine replied so quickly that Roberta knew there was no time for her sister to fully absorb anything Roberta was saying.

"No one's dead, Roberta, but Mama's quite sick, and she wants you to come home."

Cheeks burning, Roberta bit her lips as her eyes brimmed with tears. "Did she hear about Aunt Melanie?"

"Hear what?"

"She died a week ago," Roberta said, not bothering to soften the blow since, after all, this was Elaine, who was as strong as an ox.

"What! Why didn't you call us?" Elaine demanded, an angry edge creeping into her voice.

Roberta sunk her nails into the flesh of her palm and lied her way out of the predicament. "Things were too busy here—ministers to see, solicitors, real-estate brokers, funeral directors to talk to, decisions to be made, and even teas."

"Did you do all that alone?" Elaine asked, sounding more sympathetic.

"Well," Roberta replied, "my boyfriend, Chester Daley, helped me, but mostly I did it alone."

"Roberta, you must come home, especially now. Mama is so ill. We're afraid of losing her, and now we can't even tell her about her sister. It would be too much of a shock."

Then and there Roberta decided to go home for a month. Aunt Melanie's passing had taken its toll on her, and she realized that the home from which she had shielded herself for so long had finally caught up with her.

Two days was all she had to wait for the departure. And when she told Chester of her plans, he was pleased, then surprised her by deciding to join her there after her first week with her family. Roberta was panic-stricken, trying to figure out how to explain away her fabricated stories.

Any amount of years away from home changes one's perspective of what home was really like, and Roberta, feeling more English than Jamaican, arrived on the island wearing a drab brown English summer dress, which was at odds with the vibrant colours of the island. She was surprised at the many changes around her. Her eldest brother, Slim, had shaken off the family nickname by becoming a strapping young man. And Caleb and her sisters were no longer children. But judging from their speech and well-worn clothes, Roberta imagined that nothing had happened in their lives. The thought of Chester among them terrified her, and a hot flush stained her cheeks with shame.

The cottage was smaller than she remembered, and much shabbier due to neglect. Even the garden seemed abandoned to weeds. She found her mother propped up in bed with two soft pillows. Roberta's impression was that Hannah had aged a hundred years, because her once-proud jaw looked slack and her lush black hair was streaked with white. Sobs escaped Roberta as she held her mother in her arms, then she suddenly released herself from the noose of her mother's caress and backed away from the sick bed.

"Chester will be coming next week," she said as her large, disappointed eyes swept the room.

Hannah read her thoughts. "You both can have this room," she said weakly. "I stay with the boys. It won't be for long." Her mother's simple solution brought another flush of shame. Roberta lowered her lashes, as if that action alone would prevent her mother noticing. But Hannah wasn't finished with her yet. "Why don't you tell me about my sister? Is Elaine who tell me. I know something wrong. What's the matter, girl? You forget where you come from?"

Roberta turned away in confusion. The problem wasn't in forgetting; it was in remembering.

Over the next few days Roberta went about the cottage with a critical eye. There were creaky floors, loose shingles, and lopsided window frames. Her vigilance, inevitably, got on the nerves of the rest of the family, with all her complaining. Nothing, as far as she was concerned, was as good as she had had in England. Sheila, Elaine, and Lorraine avoided her as best they could, then giggled behind her back at what they perceived as her phony accent, since Jamaicanisms were already creeping back into her speech. Maggie and Georgina had had enough, but felt compelled to be nice to her, since she had been away for so long. Slim and Caleb, who were out of the house for most of the day, were glad not to be directly involved in the quarrels. Only Hannah thrived in the tense atmosphere. It was as if the mere presence of Roberta caused her eyes to shine and her cheeks to glow as she endured the girl's complaints.

By the fourth day, a more relaxed Roberta decided to provide the family with some of the necessities they lacked. Juice glasses, guest towels, and cutlery were purchased with the intention of using them upon Chester's arrival. She hired a handyman for repairs and painting. She couldn't alter the actual size of the house before Chester's arrival and, to her dismay, realized that the washroom needed an overhaul, as well as the kitchen. But all she could do to cheer things up was to paint them in bright colours. In spite of her efforts, the thought of Chester's imminent arrival made her positively ill, because nothing went according to her plan. Her attempts to improve things began to feel like trying to stop Niagara Falls with a Band-Aid. There was no stopping the army of cockroaches that inhabited the house, and no matter how much was done, invariably, there was always something more. And then there was the garden...

The night before Chester's arrival, after clearing away things, Roberta was unable to sleep. She swung her feet over the side of the bed where her soft, downy English slippers awaited her. Unlike the night of her eighteenth birthday, there were no voices to disturb her; the rest of the household slept peacefully, unaware of her turmoil. A walk in the cool air could be just what she needed to calm her, for already there was a terrible knot in her stomach. She kicked off the slippers and padded softly across the uncarpeted floors, careful not to disturb anyone.

Only a drowsy Hannah detected her movements. She turned from her sleep, full of concern, and whispered softly in the silence, "That you, Roberta?"

Roberta felt years of pent-up resentment die in her throat. There was never any privacy at home. She should have known better. But somehow this time it felt good having someone near caring about her. "Yes, Mama, it's me. I need some fresh air." She listened as her mother moaned softly and went back to sleep.

That night the wind was wild and raw. Roberta stepped out, and it greeted her with such fury that it whipped her light gown against her lean frame, revealing all that was fragile about her to the wicked night. She held tightly to her clothing and climbed down the well-remembered rocky path. The salty wind stung her eyes, almost blinding her, but she hurried on, impatient for the beach below where her toes would soon sink into the cool sand.

The beach was dark and deserted. There were no sounds except for the lapping of waves. Her feet were washed by the water, then her knees were covered. Before she knew it she was waist-deep. Feeling light-headed, she sang to herself and waded farther out into the darkness where the sea, like an everpatient lover, waited in silence to receive her fully. Thrilled by the rushing water, she thought about Chester and raised her fist defiantly against the miles of ocean that separated them. She heard the urgent call of a lonely seabird, sensing its desolation. In a moment of total abandon she imagined reaching out for Chester through the starlit water, offering no resistance when waves crashed around her, then closed furiously over her head.

XXX

On the afternoon of Chester's arrival, brilliant sunshine lit the skies, and even the wind had dropped considerably, as though it, too, stood at attention. When the tall blond man with the friendly blue eyes arrived at Montego Bay Airport, a sense of festiveness was in the air. Throngs of local people awaiting relatives from

England crammed the waiting areas, and Chester found himself desperately searching the sea of faces for Roberta, unaware that a massive hunt for her had already been undertaken. Disappointed, he gripped his luggage and started toward the taxi stands and the overzealous drivers vying for his fare. He had gone only a few feet when a dark young man approached him. Chester, assuming that this was one of the drivers, handed over his suitcase. But something in the tilt of the young man's chin and the curve of his brow made him pause.

"Are you Chester?" Slim asked.

"Yes, I'm Chester Daley," he replied a little too quickly. "Where's Roberta?"

"I'm her brother, Slim... Roberta's been missing since last night."

Chester was soon surrounded by Roberta's brothers and sisters who had come to receive him. Caleb, having borrowed a car from a friend, made the long, weary journey back to the little cottage. The spectacular sweep of landscape was lost on Chester, and he hardly heard the mocking laughter of the sea as it crashed against the jagged rocks. Later, all he was to remember of that journey was the end of it, with Hannah standing tall in the doorway of the cottage, arms held wide. To Chester, her cascading hair and high cheekbones suggested a beautiful dark goddess. She looked stronger than he had expected, but when he gathered her in his arms, he felt her quiver like a broken butterfly.

Roberta's fluffy slippers lay where she had left them, and Chester, recognizing them, blinked back mist from his eyes. He found the little room prepared for him pleasant and, full of unexpected exhaustion, threw himself down on the clean sheets.

Later in the afternoon when he awoke, he stared at the ceiling, not daring to move or even to breathe, hoping that during his rest things had been sorted out and all was well with Roberta. But the house was too still, too expectant. A sudden commotion brought him to his feet. It was Caleb, breathless and wild-eyed. "Mama! Everybody! Come quick!"

The house almost shook out of its foundations from the scampering feet. But Caleb only paused momentarily in the little kitchen before heading out again. "Come down to the beach!" he screamed.

As Chester made his way with the others down the rocky cliff path, the sight of a fishing boat on the shore sent a shiver through him, and his last remaining hope died in his throat. Even before he got there, he could see flame-coloured hair matted with seaweed hanging over the bough, and knew that the body covered by the sailcloth was Roberta's.

Hannah collapsed in the sand, years of wringing hands over Roberta finally culminating in tragedy. The children were struck down one by one, carrying their grief like sirens on the wind. When Chester eventually saw Roberta's face, she looked like a pale water nymph. And when he dared to touch her cheeks, he found them unbearably cold. So cold that he crumpled into the sand, his heart breaking right on the beach. After that he remembered the warm hands of Roberta's sisters leading him back to the cottage where Hannah, the goddess, held them all fiercely in a bond of love.

Chester's short stay extended to six weeks. He moved his things into the little living room under protest from Hannah, but she finally gave in when he wouldn't have it any other way. Everyone in the household drew strength from his presence.

During the long days, he remained close to the house, helping out with chores and seeing to minor repairs. But in the hot evenings he became a solitary figure wandering along the rocky cliff path, forever staring out to sea, as though answering the call of the lonely swallows who hid among the cruel rocks. Sad hazel eyes watched his every move, silently willing him back to safety, but when, on the wildest days, he meandered aimlessly along the treacherous cliffs, unmindful of danger, the sure-footed Georgina would always be sent to lead him back home safely.

The family found that by the time he was to return to England they had developed a bond with him and would surely miss him. After his departure, a London solicitor contacted them with news about their windfall. Roberta's entire inheritance from her aunt would be equally divided among her brothers and sisters. And Hannah was shocked to learn of her own inheritance.

It wasn't until three years after Roberta's death that Chester Daley returned to the island. He had found it impossible to shake off the memories of the time he had spent with the Douglases. Many times in London he would suddenly feel a twinge of something in the air, hear a certain sound, or perhaps even feel the wind blow just so, and he would be transported back to the Jamaican cliffs, with the wind at his back, and feel a pair of soft, loving hands lead him on and on. There was no denying the urgency. He had to see it, feel it, all again.

He didn't inform anyone about his arrival, didn't search out anyone in the waiting crowd. Filled with unexpected buoyancy, he welcomed the squabbles of the higglers and taxi drivers, and a rush of memories flew along with him in the cab as the salt on the wind exhilarated him and the spectacular cliffs, palms, hibiscuses, and roaring sea all seemed to greet him. When the cab pulled up to the Douglases' property, the run-down little cottage was gone. In its place stood a large modern home surrounded by a well-tended garden. Chester's heart leaped into his throat. They must have moved, he thought, and was about to ask the driver to turn around when he made out, under the aquamarine sky, the figure of a young woman tending the plants. Quickly paying his fare, Chester added a hefty tip and, with suitcase in hand, hurried headlong from the cab as though driven by something intangible and irresistible.

Approaching the young woman, he was struck by her fierce, dark beauty. It was Georgina. Sunlight danced in her long curly black hair, and when her large, surprised hazel eyes met his, Chester knew what had brought him back to this tropical family. He smiled as dimples stood out in Georgina's cheeks, and she held out her slim arms in welcome.

XXX

I, Caleb Douglas, had always wanted to be an artist, but my dreams were secretive and private. I longed to create, though cheap lead pencils were my only tools, and I hoarded discarded brown wrapping paper, clean backs of old greeting cards, and leftover ruled sheets from exercise books to use for my sketches.

My free moments were spent sketching, and this solitary pastime might well have gone on indefinitely had it not been that on reaching eighteen I accepted a paying position as kitchen help in one of the Montego Bay hotels. With my older brother, Slim, already working there, I knew the job would be menial, but in our circumstances three pounds per week was inviting.

Most days it wasn't until late in the evenings before Slim and I could hurry home, anxious as roosting birds and so worn out that immediately after our meagre suppers we would fall asleep while the rest of the family engaged in conversation.

During lunch hour, I often wandered away from the hotel compound. One such afternoon, feeling particularly restless, I followed the meandering shoreline of the hotel's beachfront. I ignored fences and barriers and strayed into adjoining properties until I came upon a rustic strip of sand known locally as Pelican Beach. The shoreline was dark and muddy, supporting the growth of wild mangrove trees and straggly coconut palms. I saw driftwood, hotel refuse, and the skeletons of abandoned boats and paddles scattered in the surf, and I felt as abandoned as the litter blowing along that hot beach. Lonely, I imagined myself a solitary figure in the wind, when a sound, like that of the cracking of a whip, startled me. A sudden flight of swallows and seagulls beat the air with their strong wings. I knew I must have disturbed them, or someone else was on the beach. Instinctively I turned and saw that an artist was setting up her equipment beneath the mangrove overhang.

I approached cautiously. Something other than my usual timid self prompted me. The artist was so intent in her work that she wasn't aware of me until I was almost level with her. She was fair-skinned and wore a wide-brimmed straw hat to protect herself against the sun, and a white Sea Island cotton shirt that billowed in the breeze over her cutoff denim shorts. Her legs were long and shapely, and her freckled arms looked strong. Her brushstrokes were sure, and around her wrist I glimpsed a strand of purplish Job's tears seeds. Why would she wear such a bracelet, I wondered, since all of us locals were reluctant to wear them, feeling they would bring bad luck? I concluded that she was foreign.

"Hello there," she said, looking up. "You gave me a shock!"

From her speech I could tell she was Jamaican like myself and not a tourist. "I'm sorry," I said shyly. "I shouldn't have come over." My words were stilted and formal. She smiled and stood away from the canvas, affording me a better look at her work. I didn't say anything; words were stuck like plum seeds in my throat.

"So what do you think?" she asked confidently, nodding at the painting.

What did I think? Oh, I wish I could have told her. The painting was extraordinary. In fact, her eye for detail was uncanny. She hadn't missed the browning palms, the choppy sea, the boats, or the conch shells.

"It's good," I said, finally managing to speak. "It's quite good."

She threw back her head and laughed heartily, and I had a rare opportunity to really look at her. She seemed about twentyfive, her complexion was flawless, and her eyes were pale grey. "You wouldn't just say that, would you?" she asked, bursting into my thoughts.

"No, I mean it. It's really good." I searched her oval face for something that might miraculously prolong our chance conversation.

She laughed. "Well, it's not really my work. It belongs to a student who's about to graduate. I'm just the chaperone for the girls from Kingston Art School."

"Well, it's brilliant, anyway. But if you're the chaperone, as you say, why are you out here alone?"

"The students have gone farther down the beach for a break. I was just helping to spread some glazes for this student, you know, to help bring out the colours."

"You shouldn't stay out here alone. Know what I mean?" "I know what you mean, but so what? Artists should be able to work anywhere without being disturbed by nosy people like you!"

"Well, excuse me," I said, instinctively stepping aside. "You're wrong about me. But as for you, how come a smart, good-looking woman like you doesn't know the first thing about being careful on an isolated beach? You don't think you'd attract men?" I turned away, heart pounding, before she had a chance to respond.

"Wait!" she called out after me. "I was rude. I apologize."

She held out her hand. It was a slim, pale hand that seemed to reach across years, for when I looked at her more closely, it occurred to me that perhaps she was older than I had first thought. There was even a possibility that she could be over forty! I wasn't sure what to make of her, but when she reached out so tentatively, her fingers touched my hand and I knew I had to forgive her.

"It's all right," I said, turning away again. "But I better get back to work."

"Please wait," she insisted. "My name's Valerie Ingram. What's yours?"

I stopped. There was such a presence about her. It was almost as though she were the wild sea itself. I felt myself drifting, drowning, fighting against her tide, until at last I lay frozen in the warmth of her half smile. "My name's Caleb Douglas."

"Come here often?"

"Not really. What about you?"

"Sort of." She laughed, covering her mouth with her free hand. "I usually come here with students from the school in Kingston every second month or so."

I hardly heard what she said and was surprised to hear myself speaking my thoughts out loud. "Why do you wear Job's tears? Don't you know they bring nothing but bad luck and only tourists can get away with wearing them?"

She snorted. "Nonsense! Don't tell me you believe in that backward mumbo jumbo."

"Yes, I do. Mark my words, those things bring tears." "What about John crow beads? Do they bring John crows?"

"Don't make fun of it," I warned, walking away and feeling foolish as her cool eyes stung my back. I was glad she couldn't see my face, glad I couldn't see hers, since she must have guessed at my poverty and poor education. I supposed that as far as she was concerned, I must be totally backward. And I wanted nothing more than to prove myself to her.

"By the way, do you paint?" she called out after me.

"No!" I called back sharply, then softened. "I draw. I'm always drawing."

"You what?" she shouted, deafened by the roar of the sea.

"I said I draw!"

"I'd like to see your work," she said, leaning into the wind.

"I have to go," I protested. "I work over at the Sea Horse Hotel in the kitchen, and I'm late already."

"Well, how about bringing some sketches with you tomorrow, same time, same place?"

I was suddenly nervous, full of the fear of criticism, exposure, and rejection. What if she told me I was only wasting my time. I held my head down in anguish, unable to meet her eyes, but the wind spoke my reply. "Yes! Yes! Yes!" it cried. "Tomorrow," I replied. Then, remembering my lack of training, I turned self-consciously to face her. "Nobody's ever looked at my drawings. I never had any instruction, so you might not like them."

I waited for her reply with a pounding heart and hoped that its loud beating wouldn't expose me for the idiot that I was. Then I watched in a trance as she put the varnish brush and her hat aside. I saw her auburn hair float like a sail on the breeze as she cupped her hands and called above the sea's roar. "That's even better, because it means you're an original."

And I didn't know whether to laugh or cry.

XXX

That evening at home my thoughts were in confusion, one moment hopeful, the next full of dread. I searched out my drawings one by one, retrieving each from its hiding place: under a floorboard or a mattress, in a drawer under clothes. Then I rolled each piece into a cardboard tube, careful to choose only those that excited my senses. Black strands of my hair fell across my eyes, and I prayed that I would be calm and not let myself down.

The next morning I rose early as usual. I was aware of a certain stillness except for the occasional clink of a teacup against a saucer. And I knew that although the rest of the household might still be asleep, Papa was up and having his cocoa. I held back momentarily, too wracked with insecurity to emerge from my room. When I finally crossed the threshold, Papa's eyes met mine across the kitchen table where the hot pepper pickle jar, Pick a Pepper sauce, guava jelly, Andrew's Liver Salts, and Milo tin crowded one another on bamboo mats.

In middle age Papa's face had settled into a handsome cast, only a whisper of grey invading his thick, dark hair. He looked tired, almost resigned, but one glance from him pinned me to my chair, and my grip automatically tightened around my cardboard tube of drawings.

"Morning, Caleb," he said, smiling, his blue-veined hands lying solidly on his place mat, his dusky countenance brightened by the unusual green of his eyes.

"Morning, Papa," I said. "Morning, Mama," I added, suddenly noticing her by the stove.

She glanced sideways at me. "Morning, Caleb." Smiling, she quickly poured out another cup of the steaming liquid. "Here," she said, coming over to the table, "have a cup before you go to work."

"Thanks, Mama. Where's Slim?" I asked, hoping the question would act as a diversion and shift the focus from me and, ultimately, off my drawings.

"Slim going stop off at the post office before him go into work," Mama said, continuing to heat the cocoa. "Miss James, the postmistress, say we get mail, so somebody must come pick it up."

"I just hope it's not some bad news," Papa said, bending low over his second cup. Mama's eyes narrowed, a smile hidden in her cheeks.

"George, don't you go setting your mouth on things. You Scottish people have 'goat mouth,' and we know that mean you can make things happen that wouldn't normally happen, so just you be still."

Papa responded with a wink and a good-natured click of his teeth. He might have laughed, too, had two of my sisters not come bouncing into the room.

"Mama, Mama!" the youngest one, Maggie, wailed. "Elaine took away my hair clasps and I wanted to wear them to school, and now she making monkey faces after me."

"Calm down, you two," Mama scolded. "Whatever happened to 'Good morning'?"

"Good morning!" both girls chimed, coming over to sit with us.

Elaine sighed heavily, then smiled coyly. And I wondered if Papa would be taken in. She moved closer, her hair cascading around her face.

"Look, Papa," she coaxed, "my hair's a mess. It's thick and ugly and full of tangles. Can I cut it?"

Papa's neck muscles stiffened as he glared at her. "You can forget about cutting your hair. I like my daughters to look like girls, not plucked chickens." There was a hint of a smile in his cheeks as Mama chuckled over by the stove. And when I turned away and caught Maggie's eye, she, too, was smiling. But Elaine wasn't finished yet.

"Please, Papa," she pleaded.

But Papa just leaned heavily on his elbows and lifted a finger to his lips. "Sssh! Never start a day off with an argument. It bound to spoil the rest of your day. And another thing, tie back your hair. Go get a piece of ribbon from Mama. It will help tame your lovely hair if anything can."

Elaine did her best to conceal the smile that slowly spread across her face as she basked in the light of the indirect compliment. Then, turning to Mama, she sounded almost triumphant. "So can I have some pieces of ribbon?"

"The first thing you do is plait your hair," Mama said. "You're right about one thing. Your hair's thick, but it's very pretty. A long braid down your back will suit you to a T."

Maggie had sat quietly throughout the whole exchange, but as I glanced over at her, I could tell she had quickly lost interest in the turn of events. "Where's everybody else?" she asked, addressing no one in particular.

Mama looked up from the cocoa. "Sheila and Slim had to leave early, so you better go wake the others. Tell them the cocoa's ready."

"Do I have to?" Maggie whined, but one glance from Papa set her on her feet.

I gulped down my cocoa, grabbed my drawings, and went to wash up quickly, then headed to work. By the time I got there, the cook was already on duty and putting the finishing touches to breakfast. I put my drawings away in one of the supply cupboards and settled into my tasks. I knew that Slim made it in on time, as well, because I saw him walk past the kitchen, but there was no opportunity to speak with him, so I kept the pent-up excitement about my appointment with Valerie Ingram to myself.

By the time afternoon came, I was impatient to leave. I didn't have to return to work until two o'clock. Therefore, I would have enough time to get to Pelican Beach and back. I followed the same route as the day before, only this time my impatience was apparent as I raced headlong across the sand. High in the blue sky, I noticed a flock of John crows circling. The air was putrid, filled with the stench of a dead animal, and I wanted nothing more than to be out of the downwind.

As 1 drew closer, I saw Valerie in the company of some young artists. They were sitting astride wooden donkeys, sketching. I was terribly disappointed. I had hoped she would be alone. Then she saw me and came over immediately.

"Caleb, did you bring your drawings?"

I told her I had and waved the cardboard tube at her, delighting in the pleasure I saw in her eyes.

"Good. Let's get away from here." She glanced briefly at her companions before we headed down the beach and stopped under the shelter of a spreading mangrove.

"These are just a few of my pieces," I said nervously, my throat dry and tight. Valerie carefully extracted the roll of drawings from the tube. My heart refused to beat, and I searched her face for any expression that might disclose her thoughts.

Digging my toes into the sand, I was afraid of revealing the trembling that gripped me. When Valerie glanced up, I wasn't sure what to think. Nothing betrayed her thoughts. "You have a gift," she said throatily. "I wonder if you realize you have a natural understanding of perspective. Your lines are beautifully uncluttered."

"What you mean by that?" I blurted, regretting my words the moment I said them.

She laughed, as I knew she would. "It means you're darn good!"

I was stunned. I honestly hadn't expected praise, and I sat there like a slack-mouthed idiot.

"Mind you," she continued, "I'm not a teacher, but I've been around enough art and artists to know good stuff. I'm a patron of the art school. Basically, what that boils down to, is that besides being on the board of directors and acting as chaperone to the students, I also have a say in major decisions, you know, stuff like who gets admitted, who can get scholarships, and such. Have you ever thought about applying?"

I shook my head absently, too embarrassed to meet her direct gaze.

She leaned closer and smiled. "Why don't I think before I say things? It's the money, isn't it? Would a scholarship offer change your mind?"

"I couldn't," I replied, managing to ease the words out of my parched throat. "My family...we're poor."

There was no need to say anything else. Being Jamaican herself, Valerie was no stranger to how tough economic times affected families such as mine. She bit her lip as though attempting to swallow words that might get in the way, then grabbed me by the shoulders, her face aglow with renewed excitement.

"Listen, you should paint. I'd really like to see what you could do with colour. I can supply you with proper sketch pads and a set of watercolours and brushes."

"Why?" I asked suspiciously.

She didn't answer right away. She sensed my pride, sensed protest rising in my throat and, armed with only a smile, managed to cut off any further opposition on my part. "It's really nothing more than my way of thanking you for sharing your work with me. And you know what? I have a whole lot of art supplies here. I won't be coming back to Montego Bay for a couple of months, so until such time, you could show me whatever you manage to come up with. You owe it to yourself to be the best you can be."

After she put it like that, I couldn't help but share her infectious laughter.

That night as Slim and I walked home from work I was tempted to tell him about what had happened. But he was too excited about local news he had overheard discussed at the tables: sugarcane farmworkers were on strike in the Eastern Parishes, and the Farmworkers Union was trying to get them back out to work; the bauxite industry was really taking off near Mandeville; and the price of sugarcane had gone up in Europe. I barely commented on the situations because I was too caught up with observing how beautifully the breadfruit, poinciana, and tamarind trees were silhouetted against the night sky. All I could think about was taking out my recently acquired bundle of art supplies, so I could begin painting in earnest.

The evening, in spite of its normalcy, concealed something ominous in the air. The feeling was nagging me when Slim suddenly halted.

"Look," he said, "all the lights are off at home. That's unusual." His words hung like icicles in the cool night air. Following his gaze, I saw the cottage in darkness. Were it not for a flickering glow in the front room, the cottage would have been invisible. It was blanketed by crouching darkness, imperceptibly pressed against the black rock face that jutted into the sea.

"Poor Mama," Slim said. "She waited all day to read this letter and now it's too dark at home for her to read it."

"You're right!" I said, remembering the letter that had been discussed briefly at breakfast.

Slim pulled the envelope from his pocket and pondered it in the moonlight. He weighed the envelope in his hands, as if that would reveal its contents and satisfy our curiosity. "Wonder who it could be from. The postmark's London, England, but it doesn't have a return address. And it's definitely for Mama."

An involuntary chill ran up my spine, and I couldn't help feeling that it might have been better if that wretched letter hadn't come. Slim sensed my misgivings and smiled. It was the same way Papa had of smiling in the face of disaster.

"Hurry up," he said with a grin. "The sooner we get home, the sooner we'll know what it's about."

We raced up the path, and the resulting crunch of our shoes on the gravel alerted Mama, who met us at the front door, storm lantern in hand. "You don't know how glad I be to see you both. Don't worry. Everybody okay. We have a power failure.

Your sisters gone to bed and your father step out to buy a bun. I was hoping he meet up with you two."

"It's a moonlit night," I said, trying to ease her agitation. Was she worried about the letter?

Then, as if reading my thoughts, she asked, "Slim, did you get that letter at all?"

"Yes, Mama, I have it right here."

"Thanks. Let me just serve both of you some beef soup. You must be hungry. It's so late. Then I sit down and try to read the letter by the lantern."

I will always remember the patterns of light that flickered across the kitchen's stucco walls as Slim and I sat hunched over our bowls, hardly daring to look up, our eyes peeled for crawling insects and flying bugs. Mama sat at the head of the table, her face illuminated by the lantern's glow. For a long time it seemed as if she were holding her breath. Except for the occasional click of our spoons against our bowls, silence reigned.

"But wait," Slim said, "you're not going to open the letter?"

The silence was broken, and I glanced up quickly, noticing that Mama had already opened the envelope. Her sure fingers caressed the folded sheets of blue paper, and I watched as she slowly straightened each page. Something of my anticipation brought to mind my recent encounter with Valerie, and I reached down beside me and felt my little bundle of art supplies, experiencing a rush of pleasure that they were real. The joy of my pounding heart drowned out all sound, and I could have sworn Manna's voice was coming from a long way off. Had I fallen asleep? I looked up, suddenly jolted back to consciousness as I realized she was talking about the letter.

"You won't believe this," she said. "It be from my older sister, Melanie."

"Is that so?" Slim said, craning his neck toward the letter.

"Yes," Mama said. "She live in England for years, though she never keep in touch. She run a grocery store in London, and it looks like she do well. Because here it is. She offer to send for one of you children to go to England to study. Imagine, a chance to study over there. Everything paid for and a place to stay. Well, how about it, Slim?"

Slim's spoon fell with a clatter. He quickly pulled his chair away from the table, the wood screaming against the smooth floor. Suddenly the golden glow of the lantern was no longer comfortable. "Not me, Mama," Slim said, shaking his head in desperation. "I'm settled in my job at the hotel, and who knows, I might even get a promotion."

Mama turned to me. "What about you, Caleb? Your Aunt Melanie say nursing is booming in England, and it's for both men and women. Think about it, Caleb. Hospital workers always in demand. And another thing, the money be not bad."

"Oh, Mama," I said quickly, "you're forgetting that I didn't even finish high school. No school in England would take me without a Senior Cambridge or a GCE certificate. I'm better off holding on to my job here. And remember, Mama, Papa needs all the help he can get. And I'm willing to help."

Mama sighed knowingly. I was right. The family couldn't survive on just Papa's salary. Although I couldn't see Mama's hands after she let them fall into her lap, I knew she was clenching and unclenching her fingers the way she always did.

"So I guess is going to be Roberta," she said finally. "She the oldest girl. She going to be eighteen soon and she graduating high school next month. It has to be her. But don't say nothing. Let me talk to your father first."

During the next few days, I pushed the consequences of the letter into the back of my mind. I became absorbed in my watercolours and eagerly experimented with different techniques. However, my first attempts were tentative, hesitant, and raw, occasionally even unsuccessful. Sometimes I could be found pressed against our rattling windowpanes, privy to the commanding view of blue that would soon be reflected in my wild painted skies and horizons full of interacting oranges, blues, and greens and the sporadic splash of deep purple. I found it necessary to duplicate the exact shade of red of the wild hibiscuses that dotted the terrain. Blue-black John crows swooped and circled in the periphery of my paintings, and a viewer's eye would be unconsciously directed away from our humble cottage to the magnificence of the headland.

I longed to paint people, longed to capture the untamed beauty of my sister, Roberta; the serenity of my mother; and the gentleness of my father and brother. But unfortunately shyness held me back. In the end, it was only because Roberta was so enigmatic that she unknowingly invaded my creative expression. It happened when I was sent on an errand to Cornwall Beach to deliver packaged lunches for the cook.

No one was more surprised than I to see Roberta on the beach, looking comfortable and animated in the company of a group of tourists. I was grateful she didn't see me, because I saw a certain look on her face, a look of rapture that transcended the moment and seemed to crackle in the flash of her reddish hair and the glint of her green eyes. "Roberta, Roberta," I whispered under my breath. "Roberta, I love you." But I stopped myself from calling out, realizing she wouldn't welcome my intrusion. I respected her privacy by keeping out of her way, allowing her to be herself. But the memory of her sitting there so relaxed in the company of strangers etched itself indelibly in my subconscious and poured itself out from the tips of my paintbrushes into an unforgettable painting I timidly titled *Roberta on the Beach*.

Watercolours consumed me, and I was amazed at how quickly the pages of my sketch pads were filled.

One morning, arriving at work, I sensed excitement in the air and was informed by Alfred, the cook, that a white woman had come to see me the previous evening. When she couldn't find me, she left a note. I tore the message open the moment I got time to myself. A dim bulb hanging from the end of a long electrical cord was my only source of light as my eyes flew over the hastily written note.

Dear Caleb:

Just a note to let you know I'll be coming to MoBay with some students on June 25. It's a little sooner than we would normally be coming back, but I'm anxious to see your watercolours. Meet me at Pelican Beach on Friday at lunchtime, and don't forget the paintings.

Cordially, Valerie

How I wished I had had more time. What would Valerie think of the paintings I had done so far? Friday, as far as I was concerned, might as well have been the day of judgement.

On Friday afternoon I dragged my heels as I crossed the sand, heading for Pelican Beach, sketch pad in hand.

"Hi, Caleb!" Valerie shouted, seeing me approach. "Good. You brought the watercolours." She didn't waste a moment on small talk. Right there, out in the direct sunlight, she lifted the cover of one of my sketch pads.

"Some of those pieces are just tryouts," I said nervously, but she didn't respond. It was as though she were beyond hearing. Her eyes darted over the pages, and her index finger ran over the textures. "These are so good. You know, you could sell these in Kingston."

I didn't know what to say, then remembered the painting Roberta on the Beach. "Not the one with the girl on the beach, though."

"Why not? That's one of your better ones."

"Because," I said, lowering my voice, "it's my sister. I couldn't sell her."

"All right then, but what sort of prices should we be asking?"

"I have no idea. Why don't you decide? You know more about these things."

"Well, for starters, I'm going to buy this one of the cottage on the hill. I think it's worth about eight pounds."

That was how my business association with Valerie Ingram began, and thanks to it, our modest celebration on Roberta's birthday, combined with her high-school graduation, was a success.

Looking back now, I sometimes regret that neither Slim nor I had been as brave as Roberta and taken up the gauntlet. I can't help but feel that Roberta's chance at a future was our chance untaken. Even when she boarded the plane, looking so proud and confident, our timid hearts flew along with her. But mine was already broken when the final metallic scream of the engines filled my ears and struck me down.

A year later our beloved father died unexpectedly. His heart could no longer hold out. I wondered if he missed Roberta as much as I did. Slim and I managed to keep the family going, and kept the girls in school, including Roberta, since it was at our insistence that she didn't come home to say a final farewell to Papa. But Roberta left us stranded; her letters became few and far between.

XXX

How quickly the years raced by. Before long I was practically living off my art sales. Slim was now the headwaiter at the hotel, and Georgina was out of high school. Roberta had been away for a long time. Sometimes when I looked at my mother's face I shuddered. She had become too pale, too drawn, and streaks of grey had invaded her hair. I wondered if she was pining for Papa, and Roberta.

When Roberta finally did come home, it felt as if she had never left. Unfortunately she got on everyone's nerves. Lorraine felt she was a stranger. Sheila was tired of her disapproval. And Roberta's acquired English accent grated on everyone.

All of us felt Roberta suspected that Chester Daley, her Scottish boyfriend, wouldn't fit in with our poverty, so she worked hard at trying to force us to fit in with him. "It's a sign of nervousness," Slim said.

Why wasn't I more sensitive to Roberta's turmoil? Maybe then I could have prevented her disappearance. She wasn't in the house on the morning of Chester's arrival. A set of lone footprints leading from the house to the beach were the only clues. Where did she go during the night? Why weren't we more vigilant?

It was fortunate that Valerie was in Montego Bay. She was staying at the Coral Reef Hotel in room 403.1 knew that number well. It was where we transacted business, and where I was paid for my art sales, art that now hung in the Contemporary Artists Art Gallery in Kingston. On impulse I decided to ask Valerie for a favour.

Her hotel was more luxurious than the one where Slim and I worked. Crossing the large red-tiled lobby nervously, I made my way up the deep-piled stairs, breaking into a sweat. I barely knocked twice on her door before it opened. It was Valerie.

"Can I borrow your car?" I asked frantically.

"What's the matter, Caleb?" she asked, her forehead creased by a frown. "You look as if you've had a shock."

"You're right. Everything's going wrong. My sister disappeared, the one from England. And her boyfriend is coming from England today. We're supposed to pick him up at the airport."

"What do you mean your sister disappeared? People don't disappear in MoBay! You sure she's not visiting someone?"

"You don't know the half of it," I said. "She was only wearing her nightie. Mama is desperate, and my brother and sisters have organized a search party. But all I could think of is that the car might help."

"God, Caleb, this sounds serious. Only her nightgown, you say? I hope she's all right. She's the pretty one in that painting, isn't she? Caleb, take the car for the day. Don't worry. It has enough gas."

"God bless you," I said quickly, hugging her. "I'll take care of the car."

Valerie drew closer and put her arms around my shivering body, holding me so close that I let my head sink into the crook of her shoulder, where I breathed in the fragrance of fresh-cut flowers and sunlight. Tears crept stealthily down my cheeks, and she kissed them away with quiet reassurances. Then, growing more urgent, we melted gratefully into each other's eager caresses. With my face buried in the scent of her hair, I momentarily forgot my tribulation.

Hot as the flame of a candle, Valerie explored my shivering flesh, her hands as eager as my own in their groping. Quick as the blade of a cutlass, we tore at each other's clothes. I was amazed at how she matched my mounting ardour. She had the surety of a mare challenging a race against years, against the strict Jamaican class system, against the different colours of our skin, even against the unique danger of my immediate family concerns. Thinking all this, I gave in to my desire completely, and Valerie met my every thrust.

Long afterward we lay in each other's arms like survivors of a battle. How perfect the world felt at that moment. I loved this woman, I told myself, and the thought took me by surprise. Although I wanted to, I was too timid to voice my feelings. I was a weary traveller returning from a glorious, unexpected heaven, and I wondered if there was any possibility that sensible Valerie echoed my ecstasy. Then, suddenly, I remembered Roberta, and guilt crashed into my thoughts.

Valerie must have sensed my turmoil, for pale as a water lily, she placed a finger to lips so recently sweetened with our kisses. For the longest time she held me in a loving gaze, a look that spoke of laughter yet to come, gratification, and hope. "Caleb, I'm over forty. Forty-two to be exact."

I sighed. "It doesn't matter." Then, with great reluctance, I gave her a parting kiss that lingered on my lips for some time after. "I really must go. We mustn't forget my sister."

She squeezed my hand and, with downcast eyes, let me go. "Hurry! Take the car and God be with you."

Neither of us said another word about what had just happened, but as I walked away I knew her eyes were still on me. When I returned to our humble house, Slim asked suspiciously, "Where'd you get the car?"

"A friend from Kingston lent it to me for the day."

"Is it that white woman I've been hearing about?"

"Yes... We can use her station wagon to pick up Chester and look for Roberta, too."

"I don't think we're going to find her," he said.

I noticed a look in his eye, a sharp sadness, an expression as brittle as coal. Slim sensed I knew that neither of us believed Roberta would be found alive.

"There's been no word," he whispered.

I nodded. "I know. I can tell."

Later our excited sisters cleaned the station wagon so there was room among Valerie's art supplies for all of us. And when we all crammed excitedly into the vehicle, our only regret was that Mama would be left behind. But it was what she wanted. "Just in case she returns," she said hopefully.

Chester wasn't anything like I had imagined. Maybe it was because I had a tendency to think all Scottish men were like my Grandpa Trevor: dark-haired and ruddy. On the contrary, Chester was fair with pale blue eyes. And he had a trim, athletic build, unlike Grandpa, who had been stocky.

"Where's Roberta?" were the first words I heard him utter, and I liked the way he said her name. There was no hiding the affection, and I wanted to protect him from the hurt to come. When he wrinkled his brow, I saw his eyes dart to each of our faces. We all wanted to reassure him that everything was well, but we couldn't.

On the way home I noticed that his eyes had become unfocused and took no delight in the crashing of the waves against the rocks, or the funny little donkeys carrying produce, or even the boisterous higglers in bright prints selling fruit along the roadside. Mama liked Chester immediately, and I knew the feeling was mutual. I could tell by the wan smiles on both of their faces—expressions of hope, of joy, of sadness and sorrow. And when Chester fell into a sudden, fitful sleep, Mama called us together.

"Come, Sheila, Lorraine, Elaine, Maggie, Georgina, and you, too, Caleb and Slim. Let us join hands and ask God and the spirit of your father to protect your sister wherever she is. And another thing, this man Chester seem like a good man, and we ask the Lord to spare him from pain."

And there, pressed against our windowpanes, I glimpsed the wide expanse of sea and felt the presence of Roberta. Slowly I let my hands fall free of the loving circle and heard her say as if she were in the room, “Come, Caleb, come down to the beach.”

As I slipped out the door, I didn’t say a word to the others. No wind ruffled the heads of the wild hibiscuses or dry bracken. All was strangely quiet. My eyes wandered as far as the horizon, and then I saw it: a fishing boat as white as snow, just a little larger than a speck. I squinted into the sun and saw a flash of red, then a line of white spray and foam in the wake of the boat. It was then that I knew for certain. Roberta was truly gone. I raced with breakneck speed up the hillside to the cottage and burst into the kitchen like a wild, wounded animal whose cries could easily be heard for miles.

“Mama! Everybody! Come quick! Come down to the beach!” The wooden floors rattled menacingly under my feet as I ran out again under the clear, cloudless sky. My heart was heavy and black with rage that stung at my eyes with streaming tears.

Chester, Mama, and the others tore after me down the path to the sea where a piece of my heart was irrevocably wrenched from me. There, on the beach, we saw an old fisherman. He was crusty and black, with great sad eyes and a voice as soft as the foam that still clung to his boat. “Good day,” he said. At that exact moment we all knew Roberta’s fate.

XXX

Mama was our consolation, our confidante, our source of strength. When Chester decided to extend his stay, he took us by surprise, though we were more than grateful for his company. His presence was a comfort to us. I don’t know how often I would sit and watch him doing trivial or tedious tasks and think that he was the man Roberta had loved. He was like a brother to me, and whenever he wandered off along the treacherous cliffs, my heart stood still. Only Georgina had the courage to go after him. There wasn't a task that escaped his willing hands, and not a head among ours too heavy for his strong shoulders to support.

When Chester left us, it was an unnaturally cold day. The sea was wild and menacing as though a storm were brewing. Waves lashed the shore in a great show of strength, and the skies took on the deep purple hue of my paintings. Fittingly, all our hearts were grey with equal sorrow.

A month later we learned of our inheritance. Aunt Melanie left the bulk of her estate to Mama and Roberta, but now Roberta's share was to be divided among her brothers and sisters. We had been through so much together that I felt this was the perfect time to tell my family about the joy of my art, and about Valerie.

When I told her about my painting, Mama smiled. "Caleb, you don't think I suspect all along? Who you think do the dusting? Who you think clean the house? I just waiting for you to say something." She stared at me for a long time, then shook her head. "What about the white woman I been hearing about? You don't know news travel fast in small towns?"

I sighed. "Mama, that's Valerie Ingram. She's the one who's helped me all these years. She's the one who sells my work in Kingston and gets it into shows."

"Caleb, you in love with her?"

"She's a good woman...I don't know."

"I thought I hear she older than you. You lovers?"

"Yes, Mama, but only recently. She's in her forties, but it doesn't matter."

"Caleb, Caleb, who am I to judge? If you love her, what does it matter?"

"Maybe I do love her. I can't imagine life without her."

A day or so after our conversation a letter arrived from England for Mama. The sender was Dr. Suleika Ramsaroop, and Mama was just as curious as we were to find out what it was all about.

"Who is this doctor?" Georgina and Lorraine asked, each slipping an arm around Mama's waist.

"Is it bad news?" Elaine asked, sounding every inch like Papa.

"Is from a friend of Roberta's in England," Mama finally said. "They go to school together there. She only just learn your sister pass away. She extend condolences, say she fond of Roberta and want to come see us in Jamaica."

"When will she be coming?" Lorraine asked eagerly.

"Well, is up to us," Mama said. "I wonder what she think of us all."

"Oh, God," Lorraine gasped, "so we're going to have foreign company again!"

"Too bad it's not Chester coming back," Georgina added from behind the veil of her long black hair.

"Chester was like family," Sheila said. "This will be different."

"Well, the first thing different is we never hear of this Dr. Ramsaroop before," Mama said thoughtfully. "Of course, Roberta never write much to us about anything."

Even with this backdrop of excitement over Suleika's letter, I experienced a strange loneliness. The reason was obvious: I missed Valerie. It had been months since I had last seen her. Too consumed with grief over Roberta, it only now occurred to me that I hadn't laid eyes on Valerie since I returned her car on that fateful day. She had promised to come back soon, but she hadn't, and I had hardly noticed. Now I wondered if she had left a message for me at the hotel where she usually stayed.

When I checked, there was a letter and, according to the date scribbled in the corner, it had sat there for months. Out in the bright sunshine I eagerly ripped open the envelope, and a thin, pale note fluttered into my hand.

Dear Caleb:

I won't be in Montego Bay for quite some time. Don't be surprised. I've been asked to accompany a group of students over to Denmark. They'll be attending an art school there called Kuntz for six months. Sorry I didn't have a chance to tell you this in person, but since I still don't know your address, I took a chance and left this note here for you at the hotel. Your paintings are in high demand at the gallery in Kingston, so if you feel like sending a few more of your pieces, a friend of mine, a curator, is usually in Montego Bay on Fridays. He likes the privacy of Pelican Beach, so quite often he can be found there. His name is Purnell Barnes. Anyway, take care until I see you

—Valerie.

So she was in Europe, I thought. How I wished I had spoken to her before she had left. That Friday, on a sudden whim, I decided to go to Pelican Beach. The place was exactly the way I had last seen it, except for a group of gangly young men frolicking in the sea. I wandered over and asked, "Is one of you Purnell Barnes?"

"I'm Purnell," a tall, wide-eyed brown-skinned fellow replied, peering at me suspiciously before wading onto shore. "Who wants to know?"

"I'm Caleb Douglas, Valerie Ingram's friend."

"You are!" Purnell exclaimed. "I sort of expected you to look different."

"What do you mean?" I asked sharply. "Don't get me wrong, but from Valerie's description, I thought you'd be more destitute-looking."

"Why's that?"

"Don't take it personally, man, but the tumbledown cottage in most of your seascapes is rumoured to be your home."

"Is that so?" I snapped, disliking Barnes's attitude. "Well, I'll tell you something. I wouldn't go as far as saying we're destitute, but that little tumbledown cottage, as you call it, is home to me and my family, and a better home would be hard to find."

Purnell lowered his eyes self-consciously as I continued, and I noticed a tic in his jaw.

"When's Valerie coming back, anyway?" I demanded.

"What do you mean, 'coming back'?" he asked, puzzled. "You mean to MoBay?"

"No, I mean coming back to the island."

"Don't you know? She's here."

"What about Kuntz in Denmark and the students?"

"That was ages ago. Donkey's years, in fact." He stopped himself, as if he had already given me too much information. "It's just that she hasn't been too well lately," he added sheepishly.

"Not well?"

"Well, she's too sick to travel. Anyway, you know how it is."

"What the hell are you talking about?" I barked, sounding more aggressive than I ever thought I could.

"Look, man," he shouted back, "what's all this third degree? Don't you know the woman's pregnant? So there! Now you have it!"

"Oh, God!" I gasped. "How? When did this happen? When is she due?"

"For all I know she's probably had the baby already. I've been here on business for over a month. Call the people at the art school. They can give you more details."

Later that afternoon I asked permission to use the hotel phone and promised to cover the long-distance charges. I called the art school in Kingston and identified myself to the person who answered, and was surprised when he recognized my name.

"Caleb Douglas," he said, "what a pleasure this is. Your work is exquisite. What can I do for you?"

"I'm trying to locate Valerie Ingram."

"I have her number right here," the gentleman said. "She'll be glad to hear from you, especially since she's set aside a room at our gallery to display your work. I hope you have a pen handy. And if you come to Kingston, I'd love to meet you."

I copied the number quickly and almost immediately dialled it. The telephone rang six times before a woman's voice answered, speaking patois, and I knew it must be the household help.

"May I speak with Miss Ingram?" I asked. There was a brief silence before the woman spoke.

"Miss Ingram not 'ere, sar."

"Where can I reach her?"

"Di missis in hospital, sar," she said. "She not doing too well."

"What hospital is she in?"

"Is St. Joseph, but dem tell mi she not to 'ave no visitors or phone call ider. I'm di helper, name Esmie."

"Well, I'm her friend Caleb from Montego Bay. I'm an artist."

"Me know who you is. The missis left one letter 'ere for you, sar. She want to mail it, sar, to a 'otel in MoBay."

"Don't mail it!" I interrupted. "I'm coming to Kingston. Give me the address there."

As far as Mama and the others were concerned, I was going to Kingston to see an exhibition of my work. Elaine wanted to come, but because of exams couldn't take the time off from school. In the end it was Maggie, because she pleaded so pitifully, who was allowed to accompany me, since Mama insisted someone should represent the family. Mama made arrangements with an old school friend, Mrs. Edna Causewell of Constant Spring Road, for us to stay with her for a couple of days.

Neither Maggie nor myself had ever been on a train before, and at first the business of tickets and vigilant conductors was unnerving, but in the end we enjoyed it. The rattling train was mostly filled with higglers and other market-bound people who seemed to ignite the small carriage with their laughter and high voices amid the confusion of bulging crocus bags, live chickens, straw baskets of yams, cocoas, guineps, cucumbers, red peas, and star apples. Every jolt from the train scattered a quarter pint or so of red peas, and the live chickens squawked in protest as Maggie and I clung to our seats for dear life.

Among the other passengers, Maggie looked almost elegant and grown-up, although she was only fifteen. She was attractively dressed in a pale blue sundress. It set off her long brown hair and, with her dark complexion, made her look exotic. It struck me for the first time how much she reminded me of our proud sister, Roberta. She had the same tilt to her chin, the same half smile and merry eyes that looked as though they were enjoying a secret. I sat there in the close confines of the train, staring at her, teary-eyed. Then, without thinking, I confided to her my real reason for travelling to Kingston. It seemed as if Roberta herself were there, and I could almost hear my dead sister ask with her forced English accent, "What's troubling you, Caleb?"

Maggie listened, wide-eyed, then wrapped her thin arms around me affectionately. "Oh, Caleb" was all she said with a sigh.

As planned, Mrs. Causewell met us at the station. She was a heavyset, matronly woman with a yellowish complexion. Maggie recognized her instantly from Mama's description.

"So you're Hannah's children," she said. "Oh, my, you're both so tall and good-looking." Noticing our embarrassment, she quickly changed the subject. "Anyway, come, I have a car waiting."

Mrs. Causewell took an instant liking to Maggie. After a hotstew lunch, Maggie spent the afternoon looking around the plazas with our hostess, while I used the time to find out where the gallery, St. Joseph's Hospital, and Forest Gardens were. The last was where Valerie's house was located. I took a cab there first and found brightly painted, flat-roofed houses nestled under brooding purple hillsides. Pushing open the low metal gate of number 19, I walked up the long concrete walkway to the veranda. The moment I got there a dog next door began to bark furiously. I knocked on the door and heard a shuffle of feet. When the door opened, I saw that it was the household helper. She was small and muscular with very dark skin and wore a freshly starched white cap and apron.

She eyed me momentarily, then finally spoke. "Good day, sar."

"Hello, I'm Caleb Douglas."

"Oh, is you Mr. Douglas. Mi glad you cum. The missis didn't make it, sar. She pass along last night. Mi 'ave di letter 'ere."

"Didn't make it?"

"She dead, sar. Mi jus' straighten up the 'ouse. People going cum soon."

I don't know what kept me on my feet. I gripped the letter fiercely, finding it almost offensive as tears streamed down my cheeks. Sitting down heavily on the veranda ledge, I tore open the envelope and read through a sea of tears.

Dearest Caleb:

If you are reading this letter, then you'll know I'm gone. I have loved you for a long time. I know it will be hard for you to understand, but the moment I found out about my pregnancy I knew I couldn't risk losing you or the baby. So I had to tell you I was away in Europe just so you wouldn't try to see me. Forgive me if I was wrong, but I feel that a young, handsome man like yourself couldn't bear to be stuck with a woman of my age. My dearest, these few months have been very difficult in more ways than one, but especially with my not being able to see you. Please don't judge my actions harshly. I did go to Denmark, but only for three weeks. Caleb, I could almost tell that you loved me, too. I could tell by the way you looked at me. But there is no excuse for my not telling you that I am diabetic and knew the pregnancy would be difficult. My doctor is hopeful, but it has sapped my strength, and I truly feel I am slowly dying. But I must protect our child. Esmie, my servant, has been wonderful to me. I told her to give you this if something bad should happen to me. My doctor's name is Courtnay Adams at St. Joseph's Hospital. I have left instructions with her that our baby is to be released only to you, since I have no other family. I love you, my dearest. Take care of yourself and our baby.

Your ever-loving Valerie

"Valerie, Valerie," I sobbed, remembering the Job's tears. "You should have told me about the baby. Didn't I warn you about those bad-luck seeds?" Even as I spoke, I knew I was stupidly grasping at straws for something to blame.

Suddenly Esmie was at my elbow with a shot of whiskey. "Straighten yourself up, sar," she said briskly. "I jus' call cab for you. Go see your baby. We talk later."

The drive to St. Joseph's was a blur. When I arrived at the hospital, the kindly receptionist offered me a chair. "Take deep breaths, sir," she said. "It will help calm you."

"Thanks. I'd like to see Dr. Courtnay Adams," I said, managing to choke the words out. Dr. Adams, a thin, grey-haired woman dressed in a crisp white jacket, looked professional and assured. "How may I help?" she asked, extending her hand. "I'm Caleb Douglas, Valerie Ingram's friend," I said haltingly.

Dr. Adams leaned closer, smiling gently. "I'm so sorry about Valerie. But I'm glad to meet the baby's father."

I nodded and was grateful that she didn't register any surprise at my obvious youth.

"Your baby's fine. And in spite of a difficult delivery, she should be well enough to be released tomorrow. But because Valerie wasn't well throughout her pregnancy, we just want to be certain before the baby goes home that she's in excellent health. I'm sure you must be anxious to see your daughter. But try to be strong. No more tears. It's not what Valerie would have wanted." The room seemed to spin, and Dr. Adams steadied me with a firm hand. "Come, let's go to the nursery," she said soothingly.

All I could think was that I had a daughter, and I wondered if I would be able to distinguish her cry from those of all the other babies. I wanted nothing more than to love and protect her always.

As we approached the tiny cribs, Dr. Adams held back for a moment. "Wait here. I'll bring her to you." Almost immediately she returned with a squawking pink baby in her arms. "Here she is. She's so beautiful.

I stood in stunned silence, unable to take my eyes off the little pink bundle that was handed to me. The baby was unbelievably soft and beautiful, and her cheeks flushed with a healthy glow. Her thatch of reddish hair brought fresh tears to my eyes, and when she snuggled in my arms, I watched as her eyes fluttered open. They were large eyes, as green as Papa's and Roberta's.

XXX

Weakened by melancholia over the next long while, I wasn't able to pick up a pencil or a brush. I stagnated and allowed the ravages of hunger to devour me. Thin as a skeleton, I walked daily along the rocky shore near our home, battered by the wind, deprived of all feeling, as if I had no eyes or senses.

When Roberta's friend, Suleika Ramsaroop, stayed with us for a short visit, I was too traumatized to notice her. I crouched in the background like a broken piece of bracken and took no note of her leaving. I never even noticed when the cottage was renovated to modernize our existence.

My life might have continued in that vein were it not that one afternoon, sitting by the seashore, I suddenly became aware of the wind. I felt it sharp and salty as it slapped my face, spreading long, cool fingers in my hair. I felt it sting my eyes, seemingly for the first time. The wind brought a flood of fresh tears. It was an awakening. I wondered how many months had passed, how much I had missed. Looking toward the house, I saw Mama making her way down the path. She looked strong and strangely translucent in the hard sunlight.

Without saying a word she approached and handed me my sketch pad and a few coloured pencils. I fell upon her and wept joyfully in her nutmeg-scented hair. From the house I heard the first happy cries of my daughter. Running along the path to the house, I snatched her up and held her tightly in my arms. "A daughter! A daughter! Oh, God, I have a daughter!"

The first sketch I did was of a white dove, its wings outstretched in flight against an opaque sky. And far below was the cottage the way it had been. The more I looked at the sketch, the more I realized the bird represented me. At that precise moment I knew I had to leave home to be free, or my life would forever be spent memorializing the dead.

I had to make my life a fresh canvas. I still don't know why I chose Canada as a place to start over again, but I wasn't ready to tell anyone about my plans. Months passed like shooting stars as gradually my life took on a semblance of normalcy.

Then one day, returning home from a particularly tiring day of painting seascapes, I entered the house to find my sister, Sheila, staring out the window. She looked as serene as a statue of a mermaid. Her hair framed her face in beauty. Awestruck, I pulled back a step, aware of her gentleness and how delicately her hands, like flowers, moved through pockets of air as she clenched and unclenched her fingers. Beside her was a wicker cradle, and asleep in it was my child. There was such a glow between them, such an unseen loving connection, that it humbled me. I knew these two should not be parted. I decided right then that when I left the island with the baby, Sheila would have to come, too. I gazed at her for the longest time and felt inspired to somehow immortalize her. I wouldn't paint her, though. I had already done that with Roberta, and the unspeakable pain of her untimely death had affected me so deeply that I had promised never again to paint another human. Perhaps that drastic decision had stemmed from the fear of losing another person 1 loved, or perhaps it was my subconscious desire to allow Roberta, as she was in my painting of her, to stand alone as the pinnacle of my achievement in figure painting. To all of us, she would always be Roberta on the Beach.

XXX

The baby was given a strong name, one that would fortify her for the rest of her life. The name Maureen had a powerful ring to it when whispered in the cool Jamaican dawn.

Maureen, unlike her dark-skinned aunts, was fair, with a cascade of red-gold curls. "Maureen, Maureen, loveliest in all the world" were the words her father, Caleb Douglas, often whispered into the pink shell of the fifteen-month-old baby's ear as she slept in a rustic cot by the window of their house that looked out over the sea. If the baby had opened her green eyes, she would have seen the uncultivated headland in all its majesty, and the slate-grey rocks that jutted like pointing fingers toward the sky. Had she awakened she would have tasted sea salt on her lips from the warm Caribbean.

The baby was well loved. However, no relative was more devoted than her twenty-one-year-old Aunt Sheila. Even from the beginning, Sheila took her everywhere and made herself available to the baby's every coo and cry. Maureen gave her life purpose. For although she had graduated from high school, she hadn't yet decided about her future.

On a wall beside the baby's bed hung Roberta on the Beach, a watercolour done by Caleb. If one didn't know the true history of the painting, it would have been easy to assume it depicted an unknown adolescent girl. However, it was an extraordinary piece of art, for one could almost feel in that seascape the hot wind, the dry white sand, and the moisture in the sea spray. There was no escaping the overriding hopelessness expressed by the girl who sat surrounded by strangers, her hands in her lap, deep in contemplation as her hair took on the reddish tinge of the painted sunlight and her eyes glinted an extraordinary green.

There was a strong family resemblance between the baby and her Aunt Roberta. Whenever the baby was held up to it, she would reach out her small fingers and tenderly touch the solitary figure of the young woman, as if she instinctively knew her aunt.

"Robt'a" was the only word the baby would gurgle in the presence of the painting.

XXX

Slim Douglas, who was not yet twenty-nine, was employed in a much sought after public-relations position in one of the major Montego Bay hotels. It was sobering to see improvements, because hardworking Slim had entered the workforce at age fourteen.

When Lorraine graduated from high school, it was thanks to Slim's efforts that she was able to find work as an apprentice to a hotel beautician. Elaine and Maggie, the youngest of the sisters, barely out of their teens, were also gainfully employed in a Montego Bay gift-and-flower shop, thanks to Slim's connections. Mary Judson, the shop owner, knew Slim from years of business dealings with the Sea Horse Hotel, where Slim had started out.

Caleb's paintings were well-known and respected in Jamaican artistic circles. Maureen had become accustomed to her father's devotion to his work, accustomed to his jars and pots of colour, his brushes, canvases, papers, and oils. But she knew that if she could get him to stop whatever he was doing, he would let her nestle her bouncing curls against his smooth cheek and hold her in his arms. Then, together, they would gaze out the tall windows, letting their eyes follow the piercing blue line of the Caribbean. "Daddy, love you," the baby would murmur before struggling to be free.

Even on grey days Caleb painted outdoors—something in the gloom attracted him. He would cock his ear to the wind and listen. He was never sure what he listened for, but he did, anyway.

His eager fingers would grasp paint and brushes and, before long, he would be lost as the land and sea spoke to him gloriously in his artwork.

On one such afternoon Sheila decided to take Maureen into Montego Bay. She planned to pick up fruit, one or two household items, and perhaps something for the baby.

"Walk good, my girls," Hannah called after them as Sheila and the baby made the trek down the rocky hillside. Hannah's long black hair had become thick coils of silver. Life hadn't been easy for her, but she had faith that life for her children would turn out better, even for undecided Sheila. "Someone's watching over us all," she often said. "If only you were here to see them, George," she whispered into the emptiness that invaded the house whenever the rest of the family was away. "Ask Massa God to watch us all, the baby, too. And you know, George, sometimes I think you gone and get yourself dead just so somebody would be there to watch Roberta when she came. Did you know she was coming, George? You used to know things before their time." Then she shook her head and smiled. "Mustn't talk to myself so much. People will say I getting old."

XXX

Sheila knew Maureen would enjoy going into town, with all its bustling pushcarts, goats, donkeys, honking horns, beggars, and vendors. She thought of taking the baby to the gift shop where her younger sisters worked, but decided against it since there would be too many things there the baby might cry for. She bought a balloon from a vendor and an icicle that melted quickly down the baby's chubby hands. Then Sheila decided to make some household purchases while the baby was occupied. A crusty old black man eyed the baby's dripping icicle with disdain, and Sheila headed across the street to a narrow lane market cluttered with higglers selling fruit, vegetables, clay pots, calabashes, fifes, and whistles.

The market women called out to her, jostling for attention. "Come, darling, buy something for the baby."

"Sweetheart, a pretty girl like you should eat this nice pumpkin."

"My, my, your hair tall. Here's a blackie mango for the baby. Mi jus' wash it." Sheila accepted the small offering from this woman and, in thanks, bought bananas, oranges, and a star apple from her. While the woman was weighing the fruit, Sheila noticed a basket of small redcoat plums. Absentmindedly she popped one into her mouth. The market woman smiled. "That's a penny, ma'am."

From out of nowhere Sheila heard a deep Hispanic-sounding voice directly behind her. "Steal plums often?"

She turned around quickly and saw a stranger well over six feet tall. He appeared to be about twenty-nine or thirty, and as handsome as anyone Sheila had ever seen in movie magazines. She had certainly never seen anyone like him in Montego Bay before. His hair was straight and black and tied loosely back with a piece of cord. His eyes were dark and insinuating as a pleasant smile tickled his lips. Sheila felt faint. It was probably the crowds, she thought as she held tightly to the baby's wrist and moved into the shade of the market woman's ragged canopy.

"I'm Julio," the stranger said, joining her. "Is that your baby? What's your name?"

"No, it's not my baby," she replied quickly, paying for the fruit while the kindly market woman grinned and gave hearty thanks as though this was her first sale of the day.

"Anything for your husband?" the vendor asked hopefully.

"No thanks. Not today," Sheila said, flustered, as she tried to move casually on.

"You haven't told me your name," Julio said as he fell into step with her.

"Oh, I'm sorry. I'm Sheila."

"And do you steal plums often?" She laughed. "No. I paid for it, plus the woman even gave me a mango for the baby."

"So whose baby is it?"

"She's my niece Maureen."

"She's very pretty."

"Thanks. She's my brother's daughter."

"So what are you doing in Montego Bay? You Jamaican?"

"Yes, I was just getting this and that."

"You look Spanish. You're very pretty, you know. I'm from Peru. Do you know Peru?"

"Not really. All I know is it's in South America."

"I make films. I'm fascinated by the variety of people here. I'm making a documentary about it. Want to see my film? Please come."

Sheila wasn't sure what to do. The young man was persuasive, not just because of his good looks, but in the way he spoke. Sincerity seemed to wash over him.

"Come," he said, "bring the baby."

Julio reached down gallantly and hoisted the baby onto his shoulders. Sheila sneaked glances at his handsome profile, all the while keeping a careful eye on the baby. Maureen was delighted. Balloon in hand, she was as excited as a child on the way to a circus.

"I make good films," Julio said. "Sometimes I film in Haiti, sometimes in Canada. I have even worked with Gabriel Garcia Marquez in Cuba. He's a writer, and I hope to do something with the work of Mario Vargas Llosa from my country. Have you read his book *The Storyteller*?"

"No, I haven't."

"Look at this book," Julio said, reaching into a rucksack slung over his shoulder. "It's called One Hundred Years of Solitude. It's one of the greatest books ever written. I'll lend it to you. Read this book and tell me what you think. Here, put it in your bag."

Sheila squeezed the book into the shopping bag and shot another glance up at the baby in time to see the loose locks of Julio's healthy hair fall halfway over his face. She brushed her own thick mane back with her fingers and tried to imagine what it was like to touch Julio's hair. She hardly noticed the direction they were going as they wove in and out of streets, lanes, and alleyways until Julio stopped unexpectedly in front of a shabby store with a small hand-painted sign in the window that read: MADAME ROSARIO HERBAL HEALER.

"This is my sister's place," he said. "She can watch the baby. You live in town?" Sheila was taken aback. She would never leave the baby with a stranger. Then, as if reading her thoughts, Julio smiled. "Don't worry. I live upstairs. The baby will be safe. Come, meet my sister."

Julio pushed the swollen wooden door open to the soft tinkle of a bell. Somehow Sheila felt she could trust him.

"¡*Hola*!" he shouted. The room was as dim as the grey afternoon, and Sheila was surprised at how small it was. Then a female voice answered in Spanish, and a rapid-fire barrage of the language filled the room as Julio and a scrawny woman of about forty spoke. At one glance Sheila decided that Julio's sister definitely didn't resemble him.

"This is Alvarina," Julio finally said in English. "Alvarina, this is Sheila. Alvarina will watch the baby while we see the film."

For a brief moment Sheila noticed a nervous look in the woman's eyes and wondered again about leaving the baby.

But when Alvarina smiled, she handed Maureen over. The baby seemed docile, Sheila thought. The fresh air and the outing had probably tired her.

"I'll only stay a moment," Sheila insisted. "Be a good girl, Maureen. I'll be upstairs." She glanced back before leaving the room, noting the cluttered countertop of plastic bags containing various herbs, tiny bottles of healing oils, crucifixes, pictures of Our Lady, and an assortment of plastic skulls and stones. There was a lone window, but no light filtered in. A heavy piece of crocus sacking was placed over it to block the sunlight, and a red card table was set up with two chairs, as though Alvarina expected customers at any moment.

Sheila hesitated momentarily at the foot of a small wooden staircase, but when Julio took her hand and led her upstairs, she forgot her misgivings.

"Up here is my studio and bed-sitting room," he said. "It's best to stay in cheap places. That way I save money for the film."

Sheila nodded, wrinkling her nose at the dingy airlessness of the place.

"This is it," he said. "Come sit beside me."

Only then did Sheila notice the lopsided couch that perhaps opened up into a bed. In one corner of the room there was a projector and two or three film cans. "There's a screen behind the door. Let me shut it," Julio said, crossing the floor and raising clouds of dust. "Let me set up, then we can watch. You thirsty?"

Before Sheila could reply he took a swig from a half-full bottle of orange pop that had been sitting on the windowsill. Then he offered it to her. "No thanks. I'm not thirsty," she lied, examining the threadbare appearance of the room, which had practically no furnishings except a chest of drawers, the couch, and a stringy grey curtain as dark as the sky outside.

"Okay, everything's set up," he said. "This film will make me famous." The moment the projector started rolling, Julio slipped an arm around Sheila's shoulders. "Look," he said, "it's good, yes?"

Sheila couldn't concentrate on the images, couldn't decipher the Spanish. All she could think about was Julio's closeness.

"Kiss me," he suddenly said. "How long since you were last kissed?"

Sheila had no time to reply before his lips were on hers. At first she struggled against him, then she let herself relax under the fire of his passionate kisses as the projector whirred on. His hands were everywhere, clasping Sheila so tightly she couldn't have moved even if she wanted to.

"Stop!" she gasped weakly. "I have to take the baby home."

"Please stay. The film will be over soon."

"No, I can't. My brother will be worried."

An annoyed crease showed briefly on his forehead as he pulled away. "Okay, I'm sorry. But you must come again. How about Saturday morning at eleven? You'll want to see the end of the movie, yes?"

"Sure," Sheila replied quickly. All she could think about was escaping and taking the baby with her. She ran her hands through her thick hair and brushed off her dusty clothes.

"You're so lovely," Julio said, "and I love your ass."

Sheila blushed and raced down the staircase, afraid of going, afraid of staying. "Alvarina!" she called out sharply even before hitting the bottom step. "Is everything all right?"

"All's well," Alvarina replied, stepping in from an adjoining room where, in the dimness, Sheila glimpsed Maureen asleep in a quilted metal bed. "The baby all right. I just put her to sleep."

Sheila could hardly restrain herself from rushing into the room and collecting the baby when Julio came up softly behind her. "You like me, eh? I like you very much. I must see you soon again."

Sheila, flattered by his words, felt at odds with herself, for he was indeed charming, attractive, tempting. She had no idea where she got the strength to walk away with the baby so briskly, shopping bags swinging, her mind whirling with the memory of Julio's kisses. It wasn't until she got home that she realized she still had his book, *One Hundred Years of Solitude.*

"So the baby like the outing?" Hannah asked as Sheila set down her shopping bags on the living-room coffee table, then plopped into a wicker rocking chair, Julio's book in hand.

"She loved it," Sheila said, looking into Maureen's little face to see signs of agreement. But the baby had curled herself into a ball on the couch and her expression revealed nothing. "I got her a balloon, but it burst on the way back. That's why she's so sad."

Hannah smiled knowingly. "I never buy them. If I had a penny for every lost balloon... Some things don't last."

"Mama, did you cook dinner?" Sheila asked, hiding her eyes behind her hair, afraid that if her mother read her face, she might guess at the unusual circumstances of the afternoon.

"Tripe and beans ready in the kitchen. And I see your brother coming inside at last. So I glad it ready."

A weary Caleb flopped into a chair across from Sheila and their mother, then he leaned toward his daughter. "So how's the princess?"

"She's fine, just tired," Sheila said.

"Here, let me take her," Caleb said. "I like to feel her weight in my hands."

Hannah chuckled softly. "It was the same way with me and you children. And you going miss it when she grown."

"What are you painting, Caleb?" Sheila asked, trying to keep her voice level and act naturally.

Caleb mopped his brow, and his black hair fell forward, reminding Sheila of Julio's locks. Involuntarily she inhaled sharply, then sighed.

"You okay?" Caleb asked.

"Sure."

He looked at her thoughtfully, then answered her. "I'm doing a painting of the sea and the wild birds for a man in Kingston. He's putting up a housing scheme, and they want to put an original painting in the model house. I was lucky to get the commission."

"That's great! You'll probably get good money."

"I hope so. We have bills to pay."

"Ever read this book, Caleb?" Sheila asked, producing the volume she held tightly in her white-knuckled hand.

"What is it?"

"*One Hundred Years of Solitude*. I borrowed it today."

"No, I haven't read it, but I could use that solitude to do my painting."

"So you wouldn't eat?" Hannah chuckled. "Is a good thing I make sure you eat. Come into the kitchen. Dinner ready. Lorraine and Elaine resting in their room. Slim will soon come. Is only Maggie away. She gone visiting a friend in MoBay."

Caleb chuckled as Maureen, who was now fully alert, slobbered him with wet kisses. "So what's for dinner, Mama?"

XXX

Sheila had never had feelings like the ones Julio stirred in her. She had never even had a boyfriend, and she couldn't tell how often during the day her thoughts flew to the memory of Julio's kisses. A blissful smile played on her lips, and any observer would have thought it was because of the book she was reading. But One Hundred Years of Solitude was not an amusing story.

It was a story of family courage, determination, and passion. Sheila empathized with the characters and believed her own family was just as feisty. She finished reading the novel late Friday night and was still undecided about going back to see Julio. But though she might have denied it even to herself, she couldn't wait to see him. Hot blood raced in her veins at the thought of him. She could have sworn she had wings on her feet when, on Saturday morning, she headed into Montego Bay.

It didn't take her long to find the store where Julio lived. Only this time it looked even dingier. In fact, she noticed that a family of brown spiders had taken up residence behind the glass window out front. The paint on the wooden door was more cracked than she remembered, and the hinges looked as if they were about to burst. She had taken care to wear a watch. So, realizing it was only 10:30, she figured she would kill time elsewhere when the door flew open. It was Julio. He was shirtless. Sheila's hand flew to her mouth to stifle her gasp, but there was no mistaking the smile on Julio's face.

"Saw you from the window upstairs," he said. "I'm glad you came. Come inside. You tired?"

"I'm fine," she replied, the pounding of her heart practically drowning out the sound of her voice.

Julio reached out and tenderly took her hand. "Come, my sister isn't here today. And since you don't have the baby, that's good. We have the place to ourselves."

Sheila felt a rush of excitement, and wasn't sure if she should be wary. There was no doubt about Julio's intentions as he silently closed the door behind them and bolted it from the inside. "Good," he said. "Stand there. Let me look at you. You're so pretty." In a moment his lips were on hers, his hands groping for fastenings on her clothing. He didn't stop until she stood before him naked. Whistling with approval, he slipped out of his jeans.

Sheila stayed with him until well into the afternoon. She had no desire to eat or drink. She felt as though her whole body radiated pleasure as she and Julio lay on the musty fold-out couch. She told him that she loved him, and the film she had originally come to see was long forgotten.

XXX

Sheila didn't see Julio the next day or the one after that. He was busy filming, he told her. She expected that a man as attractive as he was had lots of women in his life. She agonized over imagined things he might be doing and grew increasingly depressed. Sheila didn't see Julio again until two months later, and only by chance.

She was in Montego Bay and he was riding down Market Street on a bicycle, looking like a god with his hair flying. He saw her and waved her over, then acted as though he had only recently seen her. He never explained his absence. Sheila wanted to grab him right there on the street, but restrained herself.

He was all set to leave when he kissed her lightly on the cheek. "See you soon."

She tried to think of something to say, anything that would detain him. "I finished the book."

"Good. Like it?"

"Very much."

"See you then. Got work to do."

Sheila felt weak. He had that effect on her, yet she also wanted to pound her fists into something. It was so frustrating dealing with him.

A month later he appeared on the beach, not far from where Sheila lived. He was filming wild birds, he said, and asked her if she wanted to come to his place. This time Alvarina was home with a client. She looked up sulkily as Sheila and Julio entered and climbed the stairs.

"Hello," Sheila called out, trying to be friendly. But Alvarina didn't reply, or else she was too busy reading tea leaves. She and the customer sat at the card table, teacups and a black potbellied teapot before them. The air was redolent with fragrant herbs.

There was something in that scent that was dense and biting, frightening and exciting. It conjured up memories of Julio and how his practised hands had pressed against her as she had stood before him that first time. Following her lover up the stairs, she thought her heart would explode with excitement, knowing she would have even more memories to savour.

XXX

It was another two months before Sheila saw Julio again. This time he told her he needed money to complete his film, otherwise he would have to leave Jamaica and return to Peru. She was devastated. She didn't even want to imagine what life would be like without him, because the times when she didn't see him were bad enough. How awful it would be if he wasn't here at all.

"How much money do you need?" she asked.

"Maybe a thousand dollars. Maybe more."

"What if I could help? Would you stay?"

"Of course I'd stay. I'd have to finish the film."

Sheila, who had never worked, wondered how she could get hold of a thousand dollars. She walked through several scenarios in her mind, then arrived at the answer. Didn't she inherit money in Roberta's will? Perhaps she could use some of it, and if that wasn't possible, maybe she could ask Caleb for help. But how would she explain Julio? For the moment, though, he was in her arms and his kisses were furious.

"When do you need the money?" she asked weakly.

"In three days at least, or my project will be shut down. Fuck those damn officials!"

Sheila didn't like it when he spoke like that. She liked to think of him as an innocent, even though the way he made love to her proved he wasn't.

"How much money did I really get from Roberta?" Sheila asked Hannah cagily, Julio's lovemaking still giving her a rosy glow. "Enough," Hannah replied. "Enough to start a career or put you through school. Thinking of going back?"

"No, Mama. I wanted to buy something." Hannah chuckled good-naturedly.

"So what you buying, sweetheart? A car?"

"It's sort of an investment."

"What you mean?"

"A friend of mine's making a film here and needs money to finish it."

"The film good? Who the friend?"

"You don't know him, Mama. His name's Julio, and from what I've seen of the film, it's bound to become famous."

"Tell me something, Sheila. Him ask you for money?"

"No...but I'd like to help him."

"You in love with him?"

"What do you mean, Mama?"

"Why you blushing? You sleeping with him?"

"Mama!"

"Tell me, Sheila."

"I love him very much."

"Well, I only hope he love you. You can't buy love. Remember that. Him nice? When I going to meet him?"

"Soon, Mama, soon."

"Hope is not too much you need."

"Only a thousand dollars."

"What?" Hannah was startled by the amount, but when she saw the pleading look on Sheila's face, she softened.

"Okay, I arrange it with bank. You happy now? I only glad is not the whole thing you want. And I hope to God this man love you."

XXX

When Sheila met Julio in his studio to deliver the money, she found him strangely formal. He kissed her on the cheek and said he would never forget her kindness. Still, she felt somewhat betrayed, since she had expected him to grab her and kiss her passionately, then ravish her with love. But he did none of those things. And although it was only six o'clock on a Saturday evening and the night was young, he told her it was getting late and he had work to do. He thanked her again for the money, then saw her to the door.

"I love you, Julio," she said, hoping to at least, in this way, arouse him.

"Me, too" was all he said before closing the door. A day or so later she was back at the shop. The Madame Rosario sign was still in the window. Sheila hesitated before pushing open the door, then gave into impulse. Alvarina was sitting at the card table, smoking a cigarette. She looked wretchedly gaunt as her red lips crooked into a smile.

"Is you, Sheila?" she said. "You come to see Julio?"

"Is your brother home?"

"Julio not my brother! What make you think him my brother?" She stubbed out the cigarette angrily. "He my lover. He have many lovers."

Sheila's stomach lurched. She grabbed hold of the card table for support, then sat down in the chair opposite Alvarina's. "Lovers? He said you're his sister."

"Julio joke," the woman said scornfully, lighting another cigarette. "He bring lots of ladies here. Spend lots of money, too. But he gone now to Hungary. Something about a film on Gypsies."

"No, Julio wouldn't go without telling me."

"See for yourself. His room empty. We make sweet love last night."

Sheila didn't want to hear any more. She felt nauseated and wanted to run away, but she had to see for herself if Alvarina was telling the truth. Felling weak in the knees, she climbed the stairs, then almost toppled over when she found the room empty except for the old couch. Even the chest of drawers was gone. "Julio," she whispered into the dimly lit room. "I love you so much." But nothing in the darkness replied.

Alvarina was waiting for her at the bottom of the stairs, cigarette in hand. "Want him back?" she challenged. "You have to try Obeah. No woman can hold him. I know as fact."

Sheila sat down heavily at the card table, head spinning. "Tell me what to do. I love him so much."

Alvarina grinned broadly. "I know you love him, but love never enough. You have to try Obeah. Is the only thing. Give me a few coins, okay, sweetie?"

Reluctantly Sheila handed over some loose change, and Alvarina's eyes glinted with satisfaction. "You have to get an empty box. Put piece of his hair or a picture of him inside. Put a magnet in with it, but put honey on the magnet first. It will pull hungry spirits. Close the box and light a beeswax candle. Tell the spirits to ask the Lady Ezili, who their queen, to bring your man back. Then snuff out the candle. Don't blow it out. Use your flesh, or else Obeah won't help. Go try it, okay?"

"I'll try, Alvarina. I'm so lost without him."

The fortune teller smirked. "So you not lost without the money you give him?"

Sheila turned her head away so Alvarina wouldn't see her tears. "I've got to go."

As she got up, the chair squealed mournfully along the wooden floor. "Bring more money next time you come," Alvarina called after her.

XXX

Sheila couldn't remember leaving the shop or how, through tears, she managed to get home, but that night she tried Alvarina's Obeah. All that came of it, however, was a sticky box with honey coating the only photo she had of Julio. She tried doing it again a few days later, just in case she hadn't done it right, but the results were the same.

One morning, after her sisters had gone to work, she found a book in Lorraine's room called Prayers of Petition in Time of Need. Sheila decided to employ all ten prayers. She prayed them for a week, but each time she returned to Montego Bay, Julio still wasn't there.

Alvarina sold her black candles, holy pictures of the black Virgin Mary, silver crucifixes, and small plastic key-chain skulls. Each item supplied became more expensive than the one offered before. Oil of Stay with Me, Oil of Love Me, and Oil of Never Leave Me were all on the list. It wasn't long before Sheila thought of soliciting the devil himself for help, since God seemed determined to ignore her prayers.

There were days when she asked Alvarina's permission to go upstairs and lie in the dusty room where she and Julio had lain. There, in the darkness, she fantasized he was with her again.

Then she had to choke back a fresh barrage of tears when she realized he wasn't.

At home the family was aware of the changes in Sheila. Gone was the happy, carefree young girl everyone knew. In her place was a hollow-eyed, withdrawn skeleton.

"Sheila, tell me what going on," her mother implored. "I hope is not that man with the movie giving you all this trouble. At least you don't look pregnant. Thank God!"

All the while, Sheila felt herself falling deeper into depression. "I want to die," she said out loud one day, shocking herself with the force of her conviction.

"You've got to get help," Slim said, overhearing her. "Caleb and I will take you to a doctor in Kingston. I'll take time off work. Don't worry."

"I don't need a doctor, Slim. I just want to die, and if you try to take me to any doctor, I'll run away. I swear!"

Slim and Caleb were forced to watch helplessly as each day their sister resorted to another magical formula. After a year passed, Julio still hadn't returned. Sheila had grown thinner and now wore her once-lush hair tied back with string in a ratty ponytail. And her shapeless dresses barely clung to her emaciated frame.

"Take me away, dear Roberta," she whispered repeatedly as she stared for hours at the much-loved painting of her dead sister in the living room. "I can't live in this world anymore."

Elaine and Lorraine, too, were unable to help their sister. Their fears increased when Sheila started wandering aimlessly over hillsides, picking wild buttercups and daisies and singing hymns she made up herself.

"I'll live one hundred years of solitude praising you, praising you. I'll live one hundred years of solitude to spend an hour with you, my beloved," she sang mournfully.

No one could reach Sheila. She burned nine black candles beside her bed, lit crucifixes aflame, made promises to each phase of the moon, and strategically placed jasper stones throughout the house to bring Julio back. None of her efforts paid off, though. Constantly she reprimanded herself for not having gotten pregnant by him. For, if she had, she believed that child would have been an eternal memento of their love. Thinking this, she would weep inconsolably.

"Julio, Julio, Julio," she moaned day and night. She prayed that everyone would leave her alone, and finally she got her wish.

Then, one foggy morning, she got up early. A distant voice was calling. It was a voice she could hardly remember, and yet it was so familiar. She threw open her bedroom window and looked out over the sea. Sunshine was a long way off. There was no purple dawn, no pink clouds in the sky, just a rage of dark gloom. Even the lovely rockery garden was almost invisible. Sheila stuck her head out the window and called to the slanting sky.

"Sky, come save me. Take me up to where I can fly like a bird." Her heart was heavier than ever as she strained to see. And there was the voice again, sweet and familiar. "Julio?" she said, pushing herself halfway out the window. With a hand sheltering her eyes, she made out a thin grey line where the sea brushed the sky. There, riding the crest of a black wave, was a fishing boat.

To Sheila, it was all too familiar: the white sail and the slow, dreamlike motion it made as it came toward her. She saw a crusty old fisherman sitting in the prow, saw birds wheeling behind the boat in the stark early-morning sky. But there was something else. Sheila could swear she saw something glint in the nonexistent sunlight. As the boat drew closer, she realized the unusual shimmering lived in the unruly hair of a proud young girl whose unearthly, motionless stance behind the fisherman made Sheila wonder if he was even aware of his lone passenger. The girl's eyes blazed like emeralds. Drawing closer to shore, she seemed to search Sheila out, her reddish-bronze hair streaming in the hot wind. Sheila had the fright of her life, for in a rare moment of perfect lucidity she knew the flame-haired young girl, luminous in the sweltering morning, was her dead sister Roberta!

She felt faint. Her heart stopped, and she shivered in spite of the morning humidity. Bracing herself against the windowsill for support, she really opened her eyes for the first time in months. She swore at the rising wind, not knowing whether to laugh or cry when, unexpectedly, the boat veered sharply and headed back out to the open sea. Mesmerized, Sheila had no idea where she got the strength to tear herself away from the window. Her feet seemed to grow wings, for with a sudden burst of energy, like a rage for life, she raced through the silent household.

In her haste she kicked over the old burnt-down black candles beside her bed and sent the honey box with the photo flying. She charged into the gloom, and though she searched, there was no boat, not even a speck on the horizon, only the lonely wind wailing among the rocks as waves lashed the jagged shore. And then Sheila saw her. Not Roberta, but Maureen, who had wandered out of the house while the rest of the family was still sleeping. The baby was at the very edge of the rocky overhang. Sheila's heart pounded. She was paralyzed, yet some inner strength propelled her up the awful precipice where she reached out for the fearless golden baby, enfolding her in loving arms. The sun broke through the haze, and a light breeze blew the cloud curtain aside. Maureen's bright curls picked up the golden glint from the sky. With the baby safe in her arms, Sheila leaned against the bitter rocks and cried.

"I love you, Aunt Sheila," the baby gurgled happily.

"Me, too," Sheila replied.

For the first time in a long while she felt as though she were truly awake and strong. Life would go on.

PRETTY PAUL

I have always watched stars. It started when I was quite small. My father used to sit with me on our porch steps pointing out shooting stars, falling stars, and extraordinary stars that seemed to be moving slowly.

"One day we might all go back to the stars." Father often said, but my father never had a chance to travel beyond our island. We could not afford it, and when in his fifties, he fell ill with pneumonia, he never recovered. I was eight years old, and my uneducated mother who had no interest in stars, chose instead to keep her feet firmly planted on the ground. So, I alone would watch stars, and imagine that some how my father had found a home up there amongst them.

Our small village Trejamby, was an outpost, not far from the Blue Mountains outside of Kingston. There were no schools or churches. We were taught randomly on porches at the whim of a retired school teacher. I was more accustomed to roaming with barefoot children, who waded streams and wandered the bushland like warriors. Pigs, goats, cows and chickens came upon us as we followed endless dirt tracks that dotted our landscape, and in our mind's eye, we thought of those animals as being our faithful subjects.

Behind our small houses were graves that were left over from the times when we had no burial ground, and beyond those graves was thick brooding bushland.

Just a stone's throw outside of Trejamby stood a tumbledown sugar factory. We all prided in the factory being a source of employment, and even the hum of its machinery reminded us of a living benevolent being, and we were contented. Strangely enough, my mother who was never employed at the factory, always had food on our table. It was extraordinary I thought, that after my father's passing there was always a basket of food left mysteriously on our porch at least once per week.

Though it wasn't much, the basket contained fruit, and vegetables, and sometimes rice, a little flour, cod fish, a can or two of corned beef, and on rare occasions a pint of kerosene oil.

"Where is all this coming from?" I'd ask, but my mother, in her naivety always said, "It must be from Pretty Paul. Thanks to him we'll never go hungry."

The whole village always spoke of Pretty Paul, though no one had ever seen him, since he was said to be a ghost. The people who worked in the factory spoke of him also, and claimed that at night Pretty Paul climbed out from one of the graves behind the houses, in order to find ways to help the living.

Sometimes, in the long evenings, I would fretfully watch the mounds where the graves were, fearing that I might perhaps glimpse Pretty Paul. Then I would watch the stars to see if he might be up there with my father. But I never saw him, and so the weekly baskets on the porch was my only proof of him.

When I was sixteen my mother passed away, and yet the food baskets still arrived. In my grief I mentioned how perplexed I was about the baskets, and my neighbours, would only respond with secretive mumbles, while dropping the name, Pretty Paul.

"What does Pretty Paul look like?" I'd ask the factory workers, and they too would speak in low tones, as though afraid.

"He is as dark as midnight." Said one man, "And his teeth are long and white as ivory. If he's good to you, don't question his generosity, things could change."

I soon resigned myself to keeping things internalized, especially things about Pretty Paul. How else would I have survived without his assistance? It was common knowledge that there was no local employment for young women such as myself, except perhaps menial work at the factory. But I avoided inquiring, since I noticed that the men there had began to eye me in such a way, that made me increasingly uncomfortable.

Then one day as I was going through the customary delivered basket, I found tucked amongst the food, a small slip of white paper with a note written on it.

"Come to the clearing in the bush behind the house at nine o'clock tonight, the stars are much closer there." What does this mean, I thought, as I read the note over and over.

"But this cant be from Pretty Paul!" I exclaimed aloud, "When since did a ghost write notes?"

Despite my rationale, I could not ignore the rush of excitement that ran through me. "Perhaps this is from someone who knew my father." I concluded, and the more I thought about that possibility, was the more my heart raced.

That night, I left the house, making sure not to bring my kerosene lamp, since it might attract unwanted attention as I made my way through the dense forestry. I felt no immediate fear, because the dense bush hid places that I was already accustomed to since childhood. However, as I got closer to the location where the clearing was, I was taken by surprised to see a lone figure bathed in moonlight ahead of me, and I involuntarily pulled back. The figure, which appeared to be male, turned in my direction as though sensitive to the sound of small twigs that cracked under my feet. My heart stopped as he approached, and I tried to smile.

"Who are you?" I stammered, "Are you Pretty Paul, or one of the factory men?"

He hesitated before answering, then slowly words poured out of him.

"I'm called Rayner." He said coming closer. I was surprised at his fair hair and skin.

"I am not Pretty Paul." He grinned, as though noticing my bewilderment.

"Mr. Rayner," I stammered, "I found a note in a basket, it mentioned the stars, so I thought someone who knew my father would be here. or perhaps even Pretty Paul. The men from the factory are afraid of Pretty Paul, he's a ghost. But Mr. Rayner they don't believe in a lot of things that I believe in."

Rayner's smile broadened. "And what do you believe in young Miss?" he asked"

"Mr. Rayner, I believe in strange things in the sky, and messages from stars. And Mr. Rayner, I also suspect that you might be from up there. It's your eyes, they remind me of stars."

Rayner's footsteps were soft, as he stepped aside, there was no crackle of twigs snapping, and no real disturbance to the thick undercover of bushes that he parted. I could not for a moment take my eyes off him as he stepped purposely towards the centre of the clearing.

"Should I follow you?" I called after him, sounding both anxious and hopeful.

Rayner neither replied nor lingered, though somehow my feet followed him.

"It's darker here." I murmured, "perhaps that is why the stars seem closer, the moon must have gone into hiding."

"Don't be afraid Celina. There will be light up ahead."

I was taken by surprise that he knew my name, though my curiosity was immediately distracted by the sound of birds fluttering, chirping, and making a general racket in the branches above, us. One would have thought that morning was approaching. But it was far too early for that. Within minutes a flock of birds swooped down to rest not only on Rayner's shoulders, but his arms, and even atop his head. The birds embraced him with their feathered closeness, as I hastened towards him full of the wonder of the moment.

I watched silently as Rayner welcomed each and every bird with a joyous smile and a chuckle, as though finding long lost friends. He ruffled their feathers, and spoke soothing words that reached me.

"Celina, there is a compassionate elderly man who lives near the village," he said, meeting my gaze, "That man, who might have been your grandfather, had always loved your family. His days have come to an end. He will be gone before daylight. He was your Pretty Paul. That old man spoke to the stars about his concern for you, and his fears for your future, and the stars heard his prayers, and that is why I am here."

There was a long silence between us. Many questions remained unanswered.

Then the birds that had settled on Rayner, immediately began to perch on me. It was as though they were intent on concealing every bit of my curiosity with their fluttering wings. I began to laugh out loud feeling strangely elated from their warmth and their closeness. It was no wonder that I did not notice when a mysterious humming filled the air around us, and a massive disk-shaped craft floated above the tree line, then slowly came level with the leaves and branches above us.

I doggedly followed behind Rayner feeling light headed, as laughter resonated between us. Being there with him felt as urgent as survival. I kept a steady gaze on him, before realizing that he was floating. He gently took hold of my hand, and together we ascended towards an opening in the air.

Then there was nothing but silence, and stars.

WORMING

It was a Wednesday morning that twenty four year old Kevin Taylor began to wonder if he had picked up an infestation of lice from the children at daycare. The day before, the public health nurse had come to inspect the heads of the children at the centre where he worked. Thank goodness he hadn't felt a thing, and as a result had passed up the inspection though one or two of the other teachers had taken the plunge and had come out clean and unscathed. But here it was six in the morning and he felt as though something was moving on his scalp and in and out of his chestnut coloured hair.

His first reaction was to brush at his hair with his hand, hoping that what ever it was would fall off. But after several tries the sensation had not gone away, and he swore that the something he felt was not in his hair, but probably under the skin of his scalp. It must be a nervous reaction brought on by the inspection he thought, and he tried to ignore the slow dragging motions he felt at the top of his head.

That night, he started having head aches. The pain was so severe that he grabbed an ice-pack from his refrigerator and used it on his head. It brought moments of relief but the pain did not subside. He proceeded to take some over-the –counter painkillers but found that they were practically useless against the pain. He plopped his head down on his pillow writhing in pain, and all of a sudden, he felt as though something was boring through the back of his head.

He could hardly believe it when what ever it was slowly moved and dragged itself to the very top of his head and stayed there. He lifted his hand slowly trying to feel what ever it was, but there was nothing there just the unrelenting pain. Now I'm starting to hallucinate, he thought, as he jumped up from the bed and decided to go to a hospital emergency.

The pain was still quite severe when he arrived at the hospital and he had to fill out forms and describe the pain. He was examined for lice and then given a CAT scan when he insisted that something was inside his head, but the scan did not reveal anything unusual.

The doctor he saw prescribed a strong pain killer and sent him off with the hope that finally the pain would dissipate. At first the painkiller seemed to do the trick, he could go to work and manage a day without sensations or pain. So, he didn't tell anyone about his pain or about his trip to the emergency. But that night like clockwork the pain returned, and it was back to ice packs on top of the pain killer. There was a snowstorm outside so he did not relish the thought of having to once again visit the hospital. But things got so bad with his throbbing head that he decided that there was no choice, and besides, perhaps the cold air outside might offer some relief.

This time at the hospital he saw a different doctor and a nurse who looked squeamish when he described his symptoms. The doctor informed him that he had just the thing that would help, and at that point gave him a pink liquid in a pill bottle.

"Slather this in your hair, then cover your scalp with a piece of aluminum foil, and keep it on for two hours before removing it. That should do the trick'"

Kevin hurried home and did as he was told, then watched two hours of TV with the foil on his head. At first, he felt intense activity in his scalp, as though he had stirred a sleeping beast, and then it all calmed down. He removed the foil and was alright for a couple of hours before his original sensation returned.

He returned to the emergency asking to see the same doctor, and then was told that one could not request to see specific doctors. He already could see that returning to see that same doctor was futile.

A day or so later he went in to see his family doctor. Doctor Peale smiled and assured him that there was nothing in his head, then assured him that she would request an MRI just to prove her point. It was a couple of weeks of torture before he took that test. He felt the thing crawl onto his scalp while he was in the mechanism and felt sure that the imaging would pick it up, but the results proved negative. Knowing the results did not stop his pain or the sensations. He pleaded with Dr. Peale to give him some relief and she smugly gave him a prescription for medicated shampoo, while telling him that the supposedly know-it-all doctor at the emergency had only given him hand washing liquid.

Dr. Peal then gave him a referral to a dermatologist. There was a four day wait before he could see her. He liked the fact that this new doctor seemed capable and he told her everything that had happened to him thus far. She did some blood tests and told him that his blood was fine, and that it was impossible for anything to live under his scalp. When he told Dr. Peale what had happened, she recommended that perhaps he could see an acupuncturist.

It was three more weeks of pain before he was able to see the acupuncturist. She seemed skeptical even as she put his fingers into some kind of machine, and then told him that she thought he might be lacking B vitamins. She backed out of using acupuncture on him, but before he left her office, she prescribed the said vitamins. “Let me know how it all turns out.” she said. But after a day or so on the pills, the pain was as raw as ever. Kevin stopped taking the vitamins and returned to Dr. Peale.

Every night was a night of torture, and even during the day time he had to resort to ice packs at work. “I’m having a bad headache” he’d say, without mentioning the fact that that something seemed to be crawling out of the back of his head or that the something seemed to be under the cap he had resorted to wearing

Around that time, Dr. Peale suggested that he should see a neurologist. It took a week before there was an opening for an appointment. The neurologist tested Kevin’s reflexes, and told him that there was nothing in his head. Kevin felt deflated; especially when once outside the office he put on his cap, and immediately felt the thing spring to the top of his head. He grabbed off his cap, and felt his head, but there was nothing there, Maybe I’m going mad he thought. But that night he was wearing a light weight toque, he felt movement and when he put his hand on his head, he could feel the outline of the thing under his fingers, and he knew for sure that he wasn’t going mad...

In the following days he noticed signs of hair loss not only in his comb, but at the spot on his head where the thing often settled. In desperation he returned to Doctor Peale. She seemed alarmed at the sudden hair loss and triumphantly told him about a case she had read about involving a person in the tropics who had an organism living under their skin. She had written down the name of the ointment used to release the organism. “We will eradicate this thing” she said, handing him a prescription.

He used the ointment for a week with no results then he received a call from Doctor Peale telling him that she had made an appointment for him to see a doctor of Tropical Diseases.

The doctor was a wise looking older man who nodded his head at Kevin's description of his symptoms... "I know what you're talking about" he said, as he closed the blinds and dimmed the lights in the room. But even in the dimness Kevin could make out the doctor's beady eyes and the thin line of sweat that appeared on his forehead.

"You know?" Kevin gasped, and for a moment he thought he saw the doctor's features fall away as though in slow motion. He blinked, and there was no mistaking the horror in the doctor's beady eyes.

"Your head, your head!" the doctor stammered as he backed away. "Heeelp!! He screamed. "It's alive!" Get me out of here!!"

Kevin was never to know what the doctor saw, because on hearing the scream two passing Orderlies full of questions, managed to restrain the flailing doctor, as they swiftly wheeled him away in a chair they had intended to deliver elsewhere.

Kevin was momentarily alone in the dim room when he felt something lunge from the top of his head, and he thought he saw something grayish move snake-like across the carpet, just as he made a run for it out through the door.

RETURN TO HELICONIA HALL

The house where Victoria Thompson resided was situated at the top of a broad slope that gradually lead up to a cliff face. It was a modern house, though its precarious location was only a few miles outside of Jamaica's capital Kingston. It was an ideal location, and even the sky above seemed to curve protectively over the property. All along the front of the house adjacent to the broad front steps was a lush flower garden. It blazed year round with the raucous colours of roses, begonias, ginger lilies and periwinkle. Large green leafy ferns proliferated, and the rich soil supported the growth of many sturdy flowering trees and shrubs.

The branches of the Poinciana, and Lignum Vitae trees were often filled with bird song. It was there in the cool shade of those trees that Victoria became accustomed to the various cries, coos and tweets of Cling Cling birds, Pitcharie and Canaries. It was no wonder that the garden reminded her of the home she lived in as a child, and inevitably she would be flooded with memories as she wandered amongst the foliage.

Victoria was a Jamaican of East Indian extract. Her grandparents had come to the island from India, though both her parents were Jamaican born as was she. Her parent's home where she had grownup was much larger than the one she now occupied. That house was old and rambling and it was called

Heliconia Hall. It was situated on a crumbling estate in a rural and rustic property half way across the island.

Dark dusky Victoria was the second wife of the well known journalist Harold Thompson. Harold Thompson, a Caucasian, had come to the island from England and established himself as a writer of travelogues, as well as six novels and innumerable newspaper articles. He was known and admired by all; though it had become common knowledge that in his private life he was unhappy. That was due to the fact that his then wife Laura Elizabeth who was also from England, was promiscuous and a heavy drinker. It was less than a year on the island, before Laura Elizabeth's reputation became fodder for local gossip. No one was surprised least of all Harold, when she ran off with a Scotsman and Harold finally filed for divorce.

At first it had been a surprise to his public to learn that fair haired blue-eyed Harold Thompson had remarried after two years of new found bachelorhood, and he had taken an East Indian Jamaican as his bride. However as soon as pictures of his new wife was released to the local papers, people began to see how attractive Victoria was. They also soon found her to be soft spoken and down to earth, when the couple was interviewed on a local television station. There was no denying the look in her and Harold's eyes that spoke of undying love for one another. Yet there were those, who swore that the marriage would not last, and sited Harold's preoccupation with his writing as possible grounds for a rift.

Victoria was more determined than ever to prove those critics wrong, and it was she herself that informed Harold that she too was into her second marriage, and that she had a daughter with her first husband. She also told him about the invaluable experience she gained from having had to run the household at Heliconia Hall, as well as supervise the plantation workers on its coconut and banana plantation. She also informed him of the once proud reputation that the house had had, when it used to be at the centre of social activities. She spoke with fondness about the imposing Colonial architecture, the balconies, the patios, and the classic columns. Then with sadness she informed him that the large house must be rattling with memories even though they both knew that her sister Caroline and her husband now occupied the residence. Both her parents had passed away, and her father Simon Bachan had left the house for both of his daughters.

Even after five years of marriage to Harold, Victoria could not bring herself to return to the property. That was so, even though she meticulously fashioned her present garden as though in a vain attempt to try to recapture the splendor she had left behind. But her efforts never quite lived up to her memories, and besides, her present yard space was much smaller and quite limited..

One morning while she was hard at work in the garden introducing alamander bushes, she was surprised when her household helper summoned her to come indoors. She was informed that there was a long distance call for her on the telephone. She approached the house with dread, knowing that Harold was away, and wondering if something had happened to him. Once inside the house, she found the rooms drenched with early morning sunlight, but even that was not enough to subside the involuntary chill that ran through her as she gripped the phone.

"Hello," she said cautiously, "Victoria Thompson here."

"Hello, its me Caroline, your sister." Came the reply.

"Is everything alright Caroline?"

"Oh yes, not to worry….but I had to call."

"What's happening?"

"Well, I know this will be difficult for you, but I wondered if you could come to Heliconia Hall."

"You can't be serious."

"I'm afraid I am."

"You know I haven't been back in years, I would need time to think about it."

"There's no time for that. I need you here this afternoon, something urgent has come up."

"What could be so urgent?"

"You'll be the judge when you come and see."

"You sound quite serious."

"Yes, I am."

"So why can't you tell me what it is?"

"It is something you have to see."

"Well I guess I have no choice then."

The long drive to Heliconia Hall was marred by showers. The drumming of the rain on the car, and the swish of the windshield wipers filled Victoria with nostalgia, for as a child she had driven through much the same kind off relentless rain with one or the other of her parents. She nosed the car through well remembered hamlets, where children and chickens scattered in the wake of the car. Then she took the twisted mountain road that meandered through the water sodden lush landscape of Mount Diablo. It was indeed a devil mountain, she thought, for every now and again the foliage would thin out to reveal sheer drops and menacing ledges where even in the rain, sure footed goats ambled. All along the mountain road, trucks, cars and vans jostled as they eased their way towards their various destinations. The close proximity made Victoria feel trapped, and bottled in and she longed to escape the confines, as she prayed that the rain would end,.

It was a relief to come down from the treacherous mountain. Banana and coconut trees swayed in the breeze as she drove by, and she caught glimpses of mango, orange and tangerine trees laden with fruit, and knew that in less in less than an hour she would be approaching the Heliconia property. Then there it was looming ahead and she was filled with dread..

The pillars of the house were a stark white against the gray stone of the house's exterior, and the broad windows looked out like eyes to observe her arrival. Then there across the wide expanse of the lawn, she saw Caroline her older sister running towards the car. She must have been watching for her, because there she was, as joyous as a colt with her long black hair flying. Caroline had outraced the line of hibiscus bushes, the roses and the alamanders, until finally she was at the car window.

"Home at last," she gasped, "My sister is home at last."

After a long embrace, Victoria finally spoke. "Who's here?" she said, as she looked towards the house expectantly.

"Calla's here, I wonder if you would remember her. She is the daughter of our old nurse maid Winsome."

"Calla! Of course I remember her; she used to play with Karleen."

"Yes, she was your daughter's best friend. But she is all grown up now. She is probably sixteen years old or so. Come, you'll have to see her."

"But why did I have to come all this way just to see her?"

"You'll see."

Arm in arm the sisters mounted the stone steps together, and on the broad verandah was Winsome the household helper who was waiting to bid Victoria welcome. The house had not changed. The furniture was still dark and brooding despite the bright sunlight that filtered in, and the wide staircase was as imposing as it ever was. "There are so many memories here,"

Victoria thought, "But I am no longer the child who laughed and cried here." She was lost in thought when Calla came and stood directly in front of her.

Calla was nothing like the child Victoria remembered, for that child had been wiry, with a knot of wild kinky hair that reminded Victoria of a tarantula. But here she was poised and attractive with skin as dark and smooth as ebony. Calla had come from the past to touch against the present, but the look of silent reproach in her eyes was not lost on Victoria, it was a look that Victoria remembered well. It was a look that seemed to remember things that were best left forgotten. It was no wonder that Victoria was jolted into remembering things that she had let slide to the back of her memory, and it all came to the surface like a pot on the verge of boiling over. She remembered her first husband Wilfred Wallace and how he disapproved of Calla's friendship with his child, and even now all these years later, she could still almost hear the echoing of his insults, reprimands and abuse.

The day that she had first seen Wilfred Wallace came back to her as clearly as though it had been that morning. She was fifteen years old, bored and with nothing else to do, she had left the safe confines of Heliconia and went exploring in the surrounding fields. It wasn't long before she happened upon a massive gnarled and wretched tamarind tree laden with fruit. She helped herself to some of the fruit and went to rest against the tree trunk where she became mesmerized by the delicate leaves in the towering branches as they shifted fern-like in the light wind.

It was an afternoon of deafening silence, for no birds sang, yet suddenly a high pitched hissing sound rippled in the air. Victoria recognized it as the very sound that the servants used to signal each other. She looked up sharply and witnessed the flight of dozens of small birds known as Grass Quits. Then she saw a young man coming across the field towards her, with a cutlass in his hand. He was bare-chested and built like an athlete, and his black complexion and chiseled features reminded her of an African carving. The hand he held out to her in greeting was neither coarse nor calloused, and she wondered how as a workman his hands were spared. But, she could hardly breathe; feeling a wave of sudden fear, as he took her hands and brought them to his lips. She stifled a scream.

and jerked her head aside as he lightly brushed her tear stained cheeks. But there was no stopping him, and there was no one to help her when he covered her mouth with his broad hand and took her forcefully in the surrounding under bush. She squeezed her eyes tightly shut against him, and against the pain, and the scent reeking from his body was that of the fields and wild tamarind.

She was barely sixteen when her daughter Karleen was born. Karleen's beauty paid homage to her mixed race heritage, and at her parent's insistence Victoria was married off to Wilfred Wallace a fieldhand. He was twenty years old and notorious for his many relationships which did not end after his marriage. He proved to be a strange young man who preferred to sleep in the fields, rather than in the big house, and he refused meals with the family, choosing to eat his portion outdoors in the wild. It was a weary time for Victoria's parents, who had offered him land only to see the land go unclaimed and fallow. And Victoria grew silent with hiding her shame as the man who was her husband showered her with abuse.

Life had turned out differently than the sisters had hoped, for there was a time that they had dreamed that one of them would become a lawyer and the other a dentist. But there was no chance for Victoria to study as she struggled hard to be a good mother and wife.

So it was Caroline alone who finally left the island for America, to follow her dreams. I'll come back." she said, "I wont be like those Jamaicans who leave and never come back home."

Victoria felt so alone and depressed after Caroline's departure, that under the recommendation of a doctor in Kingston, she was sent to get treatment at a hospital in London England. Her parents accompanied her on the journey, and in her absence, Wilfred who was fearful of being exposed for the tyrant that he was, slipped away from Heliconia; taking four year old Karleen with him. Bad news travels fast even across the Atlantic, and soon enough Victoria was to learn that her daughter was abducted. No amount of police investigation was able to locate either the child or her father, this additional trauma necessitated a longer stay in London, and it was a year before

Victoria was well enough to return home. And it was on her return home that tragedy struck.

Caroline too was home from university on a study leave, and had at the last moment turned down an invitation from her parents to join them for supper at the home of close friends who lived in the nearby small town of St. Marion. But she had instead planned to spend a quiet evening with Victoria discussing among other things, steps that could be taken to once again instigate an investigation to find the missing child.

The sisters thought nothing of it when after nine thirty their parents had not returned home. They were unaware that a large banana laden truck had veered into the path of their parent's car crushing the occupants . Distant relatives arrived, once the news went out, and they took over the reigns; by organized the funerals and the household schedules, before discreetly returning some weeks later to their own lives. It seemed that after a while it was only Winsome the household helper who was left to stand solidly by the sisters' side.

Caroline reluctantly returned to Howard University to finish her studies and Heliconia was left in Victoria's hands. It was sheer determination that pulled her through, and she gained the strong support of servants and laborers who came back to work on the property. Victoria grew strong in her new found role, and miraculously the plantation thrived.

Later that year, Caroline returned home as a bride, having married sensible Bertie Greaves a young lawyer whose parents owned the neighboring plantation. She and Bertie had grown up together and she had long ago promised to marry him even as a child when his glasses lenses were as thick as coke bottles. But despite her secret promise, she was never sure that her parents would have approved of a black husband, for something of their proud Indian heritage ran deep in their veins. As a child, Caroline would often refer to Bertie as her 'Black Prince' leading her mother to believe that the boy she admired was a dark complexion Indian.

Victoria and her present husband Harold had met as a result of Bertie being at Heliconia Hall.. Bertie was instrumental in finding her a divorce lawyer, and that lawyer just happened to be a friend of Harold Thompson. The lawyer a Mr. Shankid had liked the property so much after visiting there on business that he asked if his friend Harold, the travelogue writer could come to see the place. However, on the day that they had arranged to visit, Mr. Shankid found that he had an unexpected last minute appointment, so Harold went to Heliconia alone.

Harold and Bertie hit it off immediately and after a successful tour of the house, they had gone to sit on the wide front verandah and were sipping ice tea and discussing literature, when they saw a car approaching the house in the distance.

"That will be my wife and her sister." Bertie grinned. "They must have bought out the whole of Kingston. And by the way since you like the house so much, come again anytime. My wife would love to have you, and as you can see there are lots of rooms, and the servants will be glad to have somebody to fuss over."

"I'll take you up on that . Thanks." Harold replied his eyes fixed on the vehicle as it drew closer. "This would be an ideal place to write."

The car stopped at the end of the walkway, and Bertie sprang up from his sear. "I'll help her with her bags." he said, his eyes shining with pleasure.

"I'll give you a hand."

Both men bounded down the steps as the sisters emerged from the car. "Darling, meet Harold Thompson, we just toured the house and I've invited him to come visit us again.

Harold this is Caroline, and that's her sister Victoria."

When Harold saw the sisters he was taken aback by their beauty, but he couldn't help but notice that Victoria seemed to have been crying for her thick lashes were damp and her eyes swollen. He couldn't imagine what was making her sad, though he admired the bravery in her gaze as she met his eyes; and her sincerity seemed to come from her very core. Harold watched as Caroline and Bertie linked hands and exchanged light kisses on each others cheeks, and he felt a deep longing inside.

****

Face to face with Calla, under the dark brooding arches inside Heliconia Hall, Victoria was jolted back to the present, and only then did she notice the girl's red rimmed eyes, and how she toyed nervously with a air mail envelope in her hands. Victoria felt dizzy with fear, and she held on to the banister for support. But Caroline immediately steered both women into the adjoining living room where Victoria found some comfort in her father's soft easy chair. The very chair he used to sit in by the window to observe the arrival of the postman's bicycle.

Everything in the room was exactly as it had been when her parents were there. There were high back chairs, the mahogany coffee table with feet like an eagle's talons, the velvet sofa and the family photographs in silver frames: Even the roses and begonias in the tall vase on the mantle scented the air with the sweet odor of yesteryear.

The long low couch where Calla and Caroline sat was the very one that Victoria had nervously sat in when her wedding plans were being discussed by her parents. They had seemed unaware of their daughter's bulging stomach and rising shame. But all these years later she realized that they knew, and the plans was their way of sparing her embarrassment.

Dresden figures of a shepherd and shepherdess handed down from another generation still stood on the mantle next to the flowers, and Victoria felt somewhat comforted that things had not changed.

"This is the very room I used to play in." Calla said, and it reminded Victoria of the long afternoons when two little girls from very different social backgrounds used to play on the wooden floor like sisters. .But then, she could almost feel the long cold shadow of Wilfred 's disapproval; feeling that Calla was not good enough.

"I've always liked you Miss Victoria," Calla said, "I won't keep you in suspense any longer. This is a letter I received, and I'm going to share it with you."

As she spoke, the room fell silent as though an unseen hush had settled over it.

"Dear Calla," the letter began, "I hope that you are well and that you still remember me. I have lived in many places since I last saw you. First I was in Boston, and then Toronto, and now I am in New York.."

Victoria's heart leaped, could this be a letter from hr long lost daughter Karleen? Oh God please let it be her,." she thought, as she leaned forward to hear the rest of the letter.

"You wouldn't believe the life I have had to live," the letter continued. "Life has been very hard, and there were times that I felt that I couldn't stand another moment of it. Honestly if you had a father like mine, you'd feel the same way too. My grandmother Myrtle Wallace is convinced that daddy was mentally ill, and she should know because she was his mother. Daddy died a month ago. He was in a lot of debt and had used his good looks to inveigle money from his female companions. They eventually turned on him when he fell ill. He was the angriest man I ever knew, and I don't know how often he would end up beating me for no apparent reason. But enough about me, I would like to hear all about you. My grandmother suggested that I send this letter to your mother Winsome. Grandmother seems to think that Winsome might be able to help us locate the rest of my family. She and I will be coming to the island in the next week or so, so if I hear from you I will send our flight information. Big hugs from your childhood companion, Karleen."

Late that evening, Victoria returned to her home outside of Kingston. She was gripping ti the steering wheel tightly, as her eyes streamed with tears. Karleen had not sent a forwarding address or even a phone number; so there was no way that she could contact her. She would have to wait patiently for Calla's next letter. She paid no heed to the wonderful silhouettes of blue back palm trees that scratched against the night sky, and neither did she notice the lonely creaking of the bamboo trees that stood at the gates of the property. All she could think about was her daughter. How she longed to tell Harold about what had happened, but then she remembered that he was in London working on an article about West Indian immigration. But even that did not stay her hand, for as soon as she went into the house; she headed straight for the telephone and called him. Only then did it briefly cross her mind that there was a time difference of five or six hours,

Harold was up late into the early hours of the morning working on his article, and trying to meet a deadline, when the telephone rang. His first thought was that it might be a wrong number, but then he saw the call display, and he grabbed the phone. Hearing Victoria's voice, he broke into a smile. "Hello darling." he said. And hearing his voice Victoria hesitated momentarily. "Harold honey, I forgot about what time it is over there, I hope I'm not disturbing you."

"Never mind that Victoria, it is good to hear your voice. Is anything the matter?"

"Not really Harold, but are you ready for this, I found out today that my daughter Karleen will be coming home to Jamaica in a week or so. I don't know how you will feel about that, or even how she will feel about me. She probably hates me because of lies her father probably told her, and Harold, I am so afraid. What if she doesn't want to be with us, and what if she wants to live on the Heliconia property?"

Harold hadn't expected anything like this. Certainly he already knew about Victoria's daughter, but the reality of it had only just kicked in. But judging from the way he felt about her, he knew that if she had asked him for the moon he would probably try to get it for her.

"Make all the arrangements." he said, "I'm already your daughter's step father, and if she decides that she wants to live in Heliconia, then that's where we will live too, so stop being so afraid.."

A day and a half after that conversation, Harold put a halt to his research and returned to Jamaica. Victoria, unaware of his plans, was tending the garden, and oblivious to his soft footsteps on the grass. What a look of surprise was on her face when she looked up to see him walking across the lawn towards her.

"When is our daughter coming home?" he said, encircling Victoria in his arms.

A week went by before word arrived from Heliconia Hall. Karleen would be arriving at the Norman Manley airport on Saturday, and both Caroline and Calla would both be coming up from Heliconia to meet her. That Saturday was to find Victoria and Harold brim full of emotion at the airport terminal. Harold was pacing the floor like any expectant father, while Victoria, strangely silent, jingled her car keys nervously. Calla and Caroline had joined them briefly before heading to the viewing gallery from where they could see planes arriving and departing.. Then every now and again, they would come into the lounge to report on the arrivals.

"Why didn't she contact me?" Victoria sighed, addressing no one in particular, but it was Caroline who answered. "It is perfectly clear that that she couldn't contact you because of her father. Don't you see that he would never have allowed her to have anything to do with you? The man was a nut, isn't that what his own mother said?""

Harold drew Victoria to his side reassuringly, "Our daughter will be here in a few minutes, let's forget the past. We have to face the future together as a family."

Calla who had remained watchful up in the gallery was the first to see when the plane arrived from New York. She watched as the passengers disembarked and burst into the lounge to join the others. "She's here!" Calla shouted, and she thrust her clenched fist defiantly into the air.

Harold was the first one to see Karleen. He knew her immediately for there was no disguising her resemblance to Victoria. "Our daughter is here." He smiled.

Seventeen year old Karleen was tall with long black hair, and an easy dimpled grin on her face. She was wearing jeans and a T shirt like most of the other teenagers, but the way she held herself was reminiscent of her mother. After she checked through customs Karleen came grinning into the terminal recognizing everyone except for Harold, in the small party that awaited her. Then she broke step with her grandmother and the other passengers and ran forward with her slim arms held wide. “Mummy” she cried.

NIGHT RIDE

Waiting for a Streetcar on a cold winter night, has to be among one of the worst things I have to do. The wind and cold seeps into my boots and coat, and it is unbearable, even though I trample snow and pace around at the streetcar stop attempting to keep warm. I don't know how often I've wondered if I would ever thaw out. Quite often, my fingers are too numb to even grip my bus pass properly. All I can think about on nights like that, is, "Where is that darn streetcar? Why isn't it coming? Was there an accident? "Not likely, though, or else there would have had to be an accident every Monday night.

What a relief it is when the car finally arrives, and I manage to find a seat, though it is beside a frost encrusted window. I have no choice but to vigorously rub my frozen hands together to return them to normalcy.

It was on such a night, that as I was sitting stock still aboard the car, observing other half frozen passengers. Everyone else seemed as desperate for warmth as I. But I imagined that none of them wove tales in their minds as I did. I became aware of a group of young people engaged in lively conversation which included the weather, and I imagined that they were interplanetary visitors from an unusually warm planet. I smiled to myself, and craned my neck to listen more closely to their conversation, perhaps hoping to stumble upon clues about their alien origins. But, without warning, my nose began to twitch, it was almost as if I were trying to stifle a sneeze. Then I noticed a strange stench in the air.it reminded me of rotting meat! Was it one of those aliens trying to divert my attention? None of the young people mentioned the odor, and their conversation expanded into current topics, music, politics and social media. I couldn't help but feel that perhaps I was wrong about them, but was I the only person on the streetcar that noticed that horrible smell.

I was sitting near to the front of the vehicle, and it was useless trying to track down the source of the odor. The car was crowded, and besides I was jammed into my seat, and there wasn't much room for movement. I tried to turn my head away from the stench, but it continued to linger, as though it were following me. "Did I step in something?" I wondered, "That would be totally embarrassing." I glanced down and checked my boots, but they looked fine. It was not until I came to my stop, half way across the city, that I realized that the horrible scent had finally worn off.

Night after night I was confronted by that smell on the streetcar. It didn't matter which car I was on. I knew, because I began to take note of the numbers on the outside of the cars. It wasn't the driver either. There were so many different ones. There was one who seemed cheerful despite the weather, who would occasionally burst into song. Then there were more somber ones who never responded even when I'd say "Thanks for the ride."

I even began to really take notice as people boarded and left the car. "Could he be the one, could she be the one? I made notes in my mind as to when the smell became noticeable, and when it petered out. But I was somehow always distracted by the stories I continued to imagine regarding fellow passengers. I imagined that the old gentleman across from me was just returning from a frosty visit to his wife's grave. The small girl at the rear of the car must be fussing because she found herself in the company of kidnappers. She might even be an heiress and a vulnerable target, and so on. It seemed I could never keep tabs on everyone, since something or another would divert my attention.

Then one night, I was taken aback when an elegant woman, past middle-age boarded the streetcar. She was so well dressed, I assumed that she must be going to the theatre to meet her lover, and confront him about his neglecting her, and in my mind, I could even see her long black expensive coat, with its mink collar, swirling dramatically around her, as she reprimanded him. However, she seemed entirely out of place, on the streetcar, since the rest of us passengers were practically scruffy in comparison. The woman took a seat near the front of the car, and a man who looked like a laborer, nodded in her direction. But she barely acknowledged him, but in my mind, he became a knight eager to joust for her favor. She kept her back as straight as a ram rod, as her fingers curled protectively around her purse. Perhaps it is filled with diamonds, I chuckled.

No smile escaped her painted lips. Her lowered lashes were thick with care, and her impossibly darkened hair was impeccable. With a sweep of my eye, I glanced at the lone ring on her left hand, and saw that it was plain. Then the most unlikely thing that even I could not have imagined, occurred. I was completely taken aback, realizing that the offensive elusive odor that I had been trying to track for so long was coming from her!!!

I had a hard time accepting that fact. She looked so well put together, and posh. But the scent was definitely coming from her, and it was uncommonly overpowering. It was no wonder that I found myself heading to the back of the car to escape it.

When we came to a stop near Ossington, the woman disembarked, and the air cleared, and I like a whale came up for air. Several nights passed, the scenario was repeated., with her sitting near the front of the car, and I retreating to the rear. Then one night when I hopped on to the car, there wasn't an empty seat in sight. I grabbed hold of a pole, prepared to bump and lurch with each of the stops and starts of the car's jerky progress. But just then, a well-mannered young black man politely got up and offered me his seat.

I was grateful for it, and thanked him. My goodness, he was tall. A few stops later, the person beside me got off and the young black man, who in my mind had become a world renown basketball player sat down beside me. We did not exchange a single word, just a quick nod and a smile.

As fate would have it, when the streetcar eased up to the next stop, the elegant woman came aboard. She looked exhausted, as she furtively glanced around for a seat. "She must be getting tired of going to the theatre." I thought, and I was shocked, when at that precise moment the young black man beside me, stood up and offered her his seat. I was noticeably in a panic, imagining sitting next to some kind of rot. I sprang to my feet and made it to the back of the car, though there were no available seats there.

Days passed, then weeks and there she was as usual, and I, trying my best to keep out of her range. Then one night, when I boarded the car, I saw that t here was a homeless man occupying the seats at the front of the car .He sat in one seat ,while his bags occupied the seat immediately beside him. He shivered and shook, and even snored as the streetcar charged through the night. Finally, when he must have heard the announcement that we were at Ossington, he with great effort, gathered his few belongings, rang the bell, and lumbered towards the door. The back of his trousers was soaking wet. It was clear that he had not, or had refused to make it to a washroom. Whiffs of urine engulfed his countenance even as he exited the car. I wasn't sure if I should be sympathetic, ashamed or repulsed by it all. It was a minute or two when we arrived at the next stop, and the elegant lady in black came aboard. Before I could even say a word of warning, she plopped herself down on to the one vacant seat where the homeless man had been sitting!!

Almost immediately, she let out a piercing scream, and shot up from the seat, shouting hysterically.

"My coat, my coat, my beautiful coat is ruined. It's soaking in pee, and it smells. I can never wear it again. It's disgusting, just plain disgusting!! It's even worse than the abattoir where I work." With this, she seemed to fold herself over in utter despair as she sobbed and tore at her immaculate hair, all the way to her stop.

I never saw the woman again after that night.

FOR SHE IS PART OF US

Rhiannon, you are only a year old, so you might never really get to know your great grandmother. She is already ninety years old. You are too young now, but there will come a time when you will slowly remember all these legends that I will tell you about her. You will probably think that your great grandmother always looked the way that she does now, like a pile of bones held haphazardly together, by loose slack beige coloured skin. You will see her knees as swollen and wobbly. You will remember her arms as thin sticks holding you lovingly against her sunken breast. And you will cry. She cried too, to feel you so new and gushing with life: struggling to be let loose and free. Did you know that your great grandmother 's hands are the very hands that once held my world in sway? I have watched you, with your pale face and greenish eyes all lit up with joy in that certain way that Hispanic eyes can show, as you watched her struggling like a wounded warrior going off to battle in her aluminium walker. I was never quite sure if it was the walker you admired, or if it was her bravery. She barely makes it to the bathroom and back, but it is an act of courage for her, even to try.

You might remember her thinning gray hair, that barely covered her scalp, reminiscent of the fibers that covers dry coconuts. The face you might remember might not be a beautiful one, for she is old now. But there was a time when she was young with a blaze of long dark hair. She being black, and part East Indian, as a child was often called 'Coolie gal', but she never minded, for that is how she was.

She was not the first of our family to pull up roots and relocate to another city or country. Most of our varied ancestors did that, but she is the oldest of our living pioneers. Try to imagine her Rhiannon, in the nineteen thirties, she was a young woman, and there was a war on.

Times were hard in the West Indies, even in tourist towns like Montego Bay where great grandmother lived with her parents. Remember too Rhiannon, that back then there were no TVs no stereos or DVDs. Radio was the only luxury, yet your great grandmother left her comfortable home to relocate to a rural hamlet in a Parish at the other extreme end of the island. By today's standards, it is a short journey since it was not thousands of miles away. But back then, considering the transportation, a mere hundred and forty mile journey; was punctuated by many fuel stops, visits to washrooms, and pauses for refreshment, that added the time up to at least four hours.

You might wonder Rhiannon why she made the journey to what was to be such an isolated place. I will tell you, and I will try to keep as close to the very words she told me.

She told me that when she was just a child of ten, she chanced to meet a young man who was perhaps seventeen years old. He was tall and lithe with startling green eyes. His ancestors included Jews from Portugal, and blacks from Jamaica mixed with Scots. The boy's name was Edmund, and no doubt, with his good looks, was a favorite with the girls. But when he met the child who was to become your great grandmother, he felt compelled, or perhaps fated to speak to her.

"Wait for me." He said, touching his heart, "One day I will marry you."

Great grandmother took his words seriously. You would have too Rhiannon. She waited for him, but learned that he had left the town, and gone off to marry someone else in the capital city. Great grandmother's heart splintered like a broken dish. She was not to see him again until many years had passed, and she was in her twenties and brim full of dreams. Edmund, now a young widower, came and sought her out and proposed marriage. He told her about his home, and its isolation many miles away. He told her about the sugar plantation, and the factory there with machinery that incessantly pressed sugar from the cane, and he told her about the office in an old plantation house called The Great House where he worked as the estate's accountant. And she agreed to go with him and be his wife. She felt that she would not be lonely, since they had each other.

Back then, great grandmother was ripe and ready for adventure, much in the way that you are now Rhiannon. Would you believe that she married her Edmund, not once, but twice before she left home? At first, they eloped and married in a civil ceremony, and then to appease her religious family, she married him again in the church.

But the place that Edmund took her to seemed to breath loneliness. It was cut off from everything your great grandmother was accustomed to. It was far inland, and she was used to being near the sea. Even the people she met there were quite unlike any she had ever met before. There were mystics, strange religions, Obeah and even witchcraft, interlaced with Christianity. And there were others who strongly believed in ghosts, mermaids, and mythological monsters. Strange as it was, great grandmother felt that she would have followed Edmund anywhere.

All of your great grandmother's children were born there, except for me, I was born in the city, and received hospital care. I and my siblings remember that place as magical, it abounded with adventure for us, and we were exposed to wonderful natural storytellers, who were our servants, gardeners, cabinet makers and even our grocer. How close to each other we children became, we were interwound like vines. There was no one else there, to play with. The class system prevented us from associating with lower class children, who were perhaps our age. The children we infrequently were allowed to associate with, were either British born or Canadian. We were familiar with their given names, Danny, Peter, Tizzy and Jilly. We were not obliged to add the words Master or Miss before their names, since we were in the same social strata. But there were times, when we must have felt as wayward as the hosts of wild flowers that bloomed along rude paths, river banks and hillsides that called out to us.

Rhiannon, if I told you that your great grandmother loved that isolated place as much as we did, I would not be honest with you. Because she always longed to leave it. Then one day, her dream came true. I was seven years old when we all moved to the capital city. It was a strange new world for us. There were buses, telephones, wide streets and neighbors close by and the best schools the island had to offer. After awhile the magic that had settled on us, in the isolated place of our childhood, slowly evaporated. We became city children, accustomed to facts, figures and scientific explanations.

Your great grandmother even found work outside of the home. There was a time when she worked as a bookkeeper in the Command Pay Office of the British army that was stationed in the city. Rhiannon, I know it might be difficult for you to imagine your great grandmother working, but she did more than that. She even went to England, on doctor's orders, having suffered from sinusitis, and was assured the cool damp weather in England, would be the best convalescent place for her, and she lived there for months until her recovery.

I saw her leave on a ship called the Irpinia, and on that journey, she made unforgettable stops in Portugal, Spain, and Madeira. And on her return great grandmother filled us with wondrous tales about her journey, none of us ever dreamed that one day, we too would travel.

When your great grandfather Edmund died in the sixties, we feared that great grandmother would fall apart, or even worse, die too, for her heart was broken. But thank goodness, she rallied, and took the reigns as head of our family. But as time passed, enormous changes came to our island. Even the British soldiers, who we had always felt protected us, were called back home. Our island declared independence from Britain. And as a result, great grandmother lost her job, and it was with great determination and assistance from faithful old friends, she found a position as a clerk in one of our larger department stores.

It was during that time that the eldest of my brothers married, and had children, then later decided to immigrate to Canada. Our homeland had become gripped in violence and struggles beyond our control, and our thoughts too, turned to leaving. It was not long before great grandmother joined my brother in Canada, and Pioneer that she was, great grandmother not only found work, but studied to be a nurse's assistant, and even found time to teach English to Spanish speakers.

Can you imagine it Rhiannon, great grandmother growing old, and all her days still full? When she turned eighty, she had not slowed down. She made a trip to Germany to visit a friend, and your mother who was twelve years old at the time, went along with her. Maybe someday, you too might watch your son, or daughter leave home to go travelling, just as I watched your mother and mine. But no matter how far we all have travelled, none of us are able to forget that splendid isolated place of our youth that rooted us. Great grandmother was like a rock that held fast, her memory sharp as a tack, even in her last years at ninety. She had wanted to meet the millennium head on.

The family has taken on many shades, from the different races we intermarried, and have established many new ancestral lines, but there is not one of us, who does not burst with pride as we remember that black woman, that was your great grandmother. I hope my ramblings will bring her more sharply into focus, now that she has passed away, and she will inspire you, because, where ever she is now, she still is part of us.

ONCE AT CHRISTMAS

There are some grand old houses in Parkdale, that might have been mansions in the old days. Today they stand proud, though not as distinguished as they once were. Tall leafy trees with broad trunks and branches that withstood all kinds of weather stand guard in their lush gardens, and along the side walk. But there are no such houses or trees on a small street nearby. The houses there, though built around the same era as those affluent homes, are much smaller, and unassuming. These houses were built with ordinary folk in mind, who were desperate for places to call home.

All these years later, in the 1970's one of those small houses went up for sale. There was nothing outstanding about the small brick house, it like all the others, was painted gray, two stories high and boasted a tiny front porch. A medium sized window on both floors overlooked the street protectively, as though purposely keeping privacy in.

Prospective buyers trampled through the house daily, there were college students, bachelors, a retired old couple, and many others. In the end, it was a young family whose offer was accepted. Alan Edmunds and his wife June were the lucky ones. June had recently found that she was pregnant, and was more than pleased that with summer coming to an end, the small three bedroomed home, would shelter herself, her husband and her widowed mother Viola.

June worked in a bookstore not far from their new home. She could even walk home for lunch, though by December, she decided against all that walking. The wintry sidewalks could become quite treacherous she thought, and Alan agreed. Alan worked as an electrical apprentice downtown, and took public transportation, and knew full well the hazards of winter. It was his habit to head straight home after work, since nothing delighted him more than being with June, and he also enjoyed her mother's conversation.

That summer, their weekends had been spent sprucing up the postage stamp sized front garden, as well as the dilapidated grape vine out in the back. It was mainly because the house's interior was already so extensively renovated by previous owners, that the couple did not personalize the space with anything else except their furniture

When December came, Alan bought a Christmas tree. It was suitable for their tiny living room, since it did not block the chink of light from the window. Everyone pitched in to decorate, and soon the tree sparkled with fairy lights and silver ornaments. "What a splendid tree." Viola murmured, as she stepped back to admire it. "Aluisius should see it."

"Who's Aluisius?" June asked, raising her brow.

"Just a friend." Viola sighed, and the young couple exchanged glances and smiled.

The next day, when Viola mentioned Aluisius again, June became curious.

"So where did you ever meet someone with such a distinguished name, is he an old friend?"

"Oh no," Viola said, turning sharply towards the front door, and gesturing. "He came here one day, when I was alone. He's just a child. Maybe nine years old."

"Was he selling chocolates?"

"No dear, he was looking for his sister?"

"Really?" Alan piped in, "Why'd he think his sister was here. We don't even have kids."

Feeling somewhat under pressure, Viola breathed in sharply, "He said that a neighbor told him that they saw his sister, who by the way is called Primrose, come up our walkway. And they didn't see her come back down."

"Are you sure he said that?"

"As sure as anything Alan."

"So, what does this kid look like?" Alan inquired sounding like a lawyer.

"Oh, he's black, with lots of curly hair and large brown eyes."

"Maybe he's a neighbor Alan," June laughed, "Lots of kids play on this street, he's probably one of them."

A day or two later, Viola heard a sharp knocking at the front door. She hurried to see who it was through the glass in the door, and saw Aluisius, and she opened the door a crack. There was a tear on the boy's cheek, and he looked quite distraught, standing there in his yellow sneakers. "What's wrong?" Viola said wearily, "Are you alright?"

"I can't find Primrose. Is she here?"

"No, I have been alone all morning."

"Please let me come in. I just want to make sure."

"Come in if you must, but I can assure you she isn't here."

Aliusius squeezed past Viola, and immediately headed for the stairs. Viola watched his yellow sneakers as he bounded up the steps, two at a times. She stood at the bottom patiently waiting, and when he didn't return, she climbed up the stairs herself and found the boy sitting on the floor in the middle bedroom, sobbing softly. His eyes were swimming with tears. "Every thing here is changed. Nothing's the same, Primrose would not like it here at all." He bleated.

"What do you mean? Was primrose ever up here?"

Aliusius didn't answer, he stood up slowly, wiped his tears with the back of his hand, then stamped his foot defiantly. "I'm never going to find her!" he shouted in exasperation.

Before Viola could say a word, he dashed past her, and ran out of the room, then down the staircase. She heard when the front door closed with a bang, and knew without a doubt that he was gone. She didn't mention a word about the visit to either June or Alan, knowing full well they would be reminding her not to let strangers into the house, and besides, there was something about the boy that somehow made her want to protect him. "I should have offered him some juice and cookies." She thought to herself. It's the Christmas season."

A couple days went by, before Aliusius returned to the house. This time he didn't knock. Viola who had been watching television, suddenly became aware of him at the window adjacent to the porch, peering in at the Christmas tree. Viola who had planned to do some laundry after her show was over, felt neglectful of her task, so she dragged the bag to the hallway, before opening the door. "So, what do you think of the tree?" She smiled.

"It's alright." The boy replied.

"So you're back, did you ever find your sister?"

"Yes, she was sleeping under the grape harbor in the backyard."

How did she get there?" Viola wondered, "Wouldn't she have had to go through the house to get to the backyard."

But she chose not to ask any questions, and lifted up her laundry bag intending to head to the laundry machines in the basement.

"Primrose knows how to sneak around, just like me."

Viola stood momentarily at the closed basement door, as though weighing the possibilities of taking her bag down or just tossing it down the stairs. Her hesitation was not lost on Aliusius.

"The steps are sure steep. I'll help with that." He said taking a corner of the bag, as Viola held the other and opened the door. "So how did you know that the steps were so steep?"

"Me and Primrose been down those steps dozens of times."

"Really! Did you have friends that lived here?"

"No, not exactly."

The two of them successfully managed to maneuver the bag to the bottom of the steps, though Viola couldn't help smiling at their struggle.

"Thanks so much. You've been a big help."'

"Hey look Miss," Aluisious hissed, stopping in his tracks, "Isn't that the cold storage room? It usually has apples, carrots, cabbages and potatoes. Primrose liked hiding in there and eating the apples. Know what? I'll have to check to see if she is there, before we go back upstairs."

Viola began to feel a bit uneasy, as she and the boy sat side by side in silence watching the machines do their job.

After a long spell, the boy finally spoke, his voice was hushed and confidential.

"Did you know there was a fire here a long time ago?" He whispered.

Viola couldn't help but be alarmed, and it dawned on her as to why the house was so thoroughly renovated. Her skin prickled with fear, yet she remained rooted to the spot. The cold storage room was the only unrenovated room, she concluded.

"Everyone upstairs died, we couldn't find Primrose."

That evening when Alan came home, he seemed more animated than usual, he called June over and spoke softly in her ear.

"Viola can't hear this, we are going to have to move soon." he said, "I don't want to alarm her, but a guy at work named Eddy offered me a ride home this evening. When he saw our house, he looked stunned. I thought he was admiring our decorations, but he told me that this house burnt down about thirty years ago, French fries caught fire in the oven, and the whole family was wiped out, except for a little girl who was hiding in the basement. My friend Googled the story and told me that the little girl was in long term care for several years, but died recently, after telling the staff that her brother who was looking for her, had finally found her."

Previously Published

Segovia Stories, Published 2000 Villa Fair Collection Dundurn Press. ***Close the Blue Door***, Published 2000 Villa Fair Collection Dundurn Press. ***Ackee Night in Canada***, Published 2000 Villa Fair Collection Dundurn Press. ***Roberta On the Beach***, Published 2000 Villa Fair Collection Dundurn Press. ***Framing***, Published 2017 in Commuter Lit On Line Fiction To Go. ***Soup Morning***, Published 1997 in Wasafiri Magazine, St Mary's University London, England. ***Long Night Until Morning***, Published 2014 in Kola Magazine (Montreal). ***Just a Single Word***, Published 2019 in Polar Borealis online magazine. ***Return to Heliconia Hall***, Published 2011 in the Anthology, Beyond Sangre Grande, Mawenzi House Press